Dreaming Together
Till Morning

Dreaming Together
Till Morning

Joann Radford Ware

Copyright © 2011 by Joann Radford Ware.

Library of Congress Control Number: 2011902218
ISBN: Hardcover   978-1-4568-6775-1
         Softcover   978-1-4568-6774-4
         Ebook   978-1-4568-6776-8

All rights reserved. No part of this book may be reproduced or transmitted in any form or by any means, electronic or mechanical, including photocopying, recording, or by any information storage and retrieval system, without permission in writing from the copyright owner.

This is a work of fiction. Names, characters, places and incidents either are the product of the author's imagination or are used fictitiously, and any resemblance to any actual persons, living or dead, events, or locales is entirely coincidental.

This book was printed in the United States of America.

To order additional copies of this book, contact:
Xlibris Corporation
1-888-795-4274
www.Xlibris.com
Orders@Xlibris.com
94227

CHAPTER ONE

I had been taking classes at Pocohontas Community College for four years, two years longer than anyone really should. The semester following my twenty-first birthday had to be my last. I had always said that I would not waste any more than four years of my adult life at any school, community or otherwise and also, I had applied and had been accepted for fall enrollment at Old Dominion University in Norfolk. This was a good thing. By my last year at PCC, I had completely exhausted my choices of classes to take in the college catalog. I realized this when I went to sign up for the spring semester and there was nothing offered that I hadn't taken before or in some cases had retaken. I really had to dredge the bottom of the course catalog to put together a full, twelve-credit course load and what bobbed to the surface wasn't very pretty: Irish Folklore, Post-Colonial Literature, Music Therapy, and History of the United States, Part II: Reconstruction to Present Day.

I had actually been pretty excited about taking the U.S. History course, being a history buff or at least a loyal viewer of the History Channel. Little did I know that the instructor, Dr. Presbyn Schindler, would be the human equivalent of Phenobarbital. I really liked Dr. Schindler. It was hard not to like him. Physically, he reminded me of the pictures I had seen of Norman Rockwell—tall, gangly, gray-haired, with an endearing grandfather-like look to his long, weathered face. He had a calm, easy-going manner and acted as though he were as comfortable standing in front of the class as he was sitting at home in front of a roaring fire with a cat on his lap.

It was a warm Monday morning in April and the church bell a block away chimed ten times, signaling the beginning of another deadly dull session of Dr. Schindler's United States History Part II. Right as the bell sounded for the tenth time, Dr. Schindler strolled across the threshold as he had every morning, dressed in the same brown corduroy pants, plaid shirt and dark green cardigan that I believed was the only outfit he owned, or else

7

everything he wore just looked the same on him. No matter the season, Dr. Schindler was always dressed for crisp New England weather.

"Now, folks," Dr. Schindler began as he took his place behind the podium, "for those of you who have been keeping up with the syllabus, you know that we were to begin studying World War I today. But I have decided to postpone that unit until next week."

This worried me. Here we were, less than six weeks away from the end of the semester and we had barely even gotten into the twentieth century. I had chosen this history course specifically because it covered the latter part of American History which I had never managed to get to in my past history classes. In sixth grade, my American History teacher, Hildegard Mumford, (terrible name—even worse teacher), spent so much time on the Colonial and Revolutionary eras that everything which occurred Stateside after the mid-twentieth century mark was condensed into a series of very abridged lectures, each more baffling than the next. For instance, on one particular day we started on the New Deal and by the end of class, FDR was dead, black students were being integrated into previously all white schools and American soldiers were fleeing Vietnam from rooftop helicopter pads. My high school teacher, Carol O'Donnell, (better name and somewhat more interesting lecturer) had such a grudge against Richard Nixon that for one entire six-week's grading period we lived and breathed Watergate, culminating in a field trip to the famous Washington hotel where Nixon's burglars not only bungled their jobs, but also, according to our teacher, struck the death knell of America's faith in its leaders.

Usually at this point a certain panic ensues in the U.S. History teacher when faced with the dilemma of covering nearly a century of history in six short weeks, but Dr. Schindler wasn't sweating yet, not even in his green wool cardigan on such a warm April morning.

"The other night I began re-reading Walter Lord's great book, *A Night to Remember*, and I enjoyed it so much that I have decided to begin a week-long unit on the book's subject, the sinking of the legendary *Titanic*."

Oh, and he would have to stall the remainder of the syllabus on a subject almost everyone knew, I thought. I was sure that even the purposeful dullards who were taking the class with me knew the fundamentals of the story: Big ship sets sail on its maiden voyage for New York only to meet with catastrophe in the shape of a huge ass iceberg in the North Atlantic resulting in the deaths of many men, women and children.

I myself had been acquainted with the rhyme of the ancient maritime wreck when I was little and my Dad, an avid antiques collector, had purchased a deck chair that had supposedly floated off the ship and into the hands of a local dealer. As far as I knew it was still in his garage somewhere among the myriad *ojets de rien* he kept in storage there. This seemingly benign purchase had far-reaching consequences for me. Reportedly, Dad had used money earmarked for my future college education to buy the chair and never bothered to put the money back. Had this not happened, I might have been on my way to graduating from a better school.

"I have often said that *Titanic* aficionados aren't made; they're born," Dr. Schindler continued, "And it takes just the right impetus to unleash the beast, so to speak. For me, that impetus was Mr. Lord's book, which I read cover to cover when it first came out. I remember I was visiting my parents' old summerhouse in the Outer Banks of North Carolina. My wife and I had just had our second child . . ."

That was another thing about Dr. Schindler. He apparently thought that the title of the class was "The History of the United States, Part II, Through the Personal Experiences and Observations of Presbyn Schindler, Ph.D." I was convinced that was the course's official title. The other words just got lopped off due to space limitations in the college catalog. I knew all about Presbyn Schindler's treasured boyhood growing up in Western Ohio and then in Scarsdale, New York, in the 1930s. That was when his father moved his veterinary clinic to be closer to his ailing parents. Though it grieved him to be so far away from all of his school chums, if they had not moved, young Presbyn would have never met his wife of thirty years, Velma, who was his rod, his staff, his salvation, and apparently one hell of a listener. Sometimes I would be mindlessly jotting down notes for nearly half a class before realizing that what I was transcribing was a lengthy anecdote. Most of my notes had been worthless for tests and exams, but I knew too that if Dr. Schindler ever sat down to write his memoirs, I, and the rest of the rapt scribblers in the class, would have him covered.

"I have express ordered copies of Mr. Lord's book and they should have arrived in the bookstore this morning," Dr. Schindler said, returning from his brief sojourn into his past and back to the present time. "I would like for you to begin reading the book today, which just happens to be the anniversary of the *Titanic's* launch at Southampton on April 10, 1912. I would like for you to continue reading in twenty-page increments each day so that you will be finished by Friday, April 14, the anniversary of the ship's last night at sea. I would also like for you to keep a reader's journal in which you will record all your thoughts and observations while reading the book. Once you have finished the book, you will turn in your journal and it will be graded. That grade, when combined with the score from a test you will take on the material next Monday, will determine your final grade for the assignment."

A hand went up in the back of the class and I heard a female voice ask, "What kinds of things do you want for us to write in our journals?"

"Anything that comes to mind," Dr. Schindler said. "It's up to you. Any feelings, any questions, any criticisms that you have about the book should go into your journal entries. Just use your imagination."

"What if all we can think to write is, 'This book blows'?" asked one of the boys in the back row.

"You're entitled to your opinion," Dr. Schindler said diplomatically, "But I'm sure that once you get into it you will not think that the book, as you said, 'blows.'"

Dr. Schindler let us use the remainder of the class to go buy the book. I was one of the very few who did actually go to the bookstore. Dr. Schindler's class was my last class of the day and I didn't know if I would have a chance to get back to campus that afternoon. I had a lunch date with my best friend, Janet, that afternoon at one and then the two of us had planned on doing a little shopping at the mall.

I arrived home that day at about twenty after eleven. Home then was a small, gray, Cape Cod style house off of Warwick Boulevard, just about a hundred feet from the shipyards along the James River. My parents and I had moved here when I was four years old. Before that, the three of us lived on a commune in southwest Virginia where I had been born in a barn one cold February morning while Mom milked a cow. I was dangerously premature and nearly died. All the frailties of my early life were often recounted to me whenever my mother wanted to stress how important I was to her. But it was always as though she were talking about someone else. None of the events of that early time were real to me until I found my baby book one rainy nothing-to-do afternoon when I was ten. All the evidence was there, pasted with yellowing scotch tape. When I held my tiny pink bracelet that was no bigger than a bottle cap and saw the index card with the starkly typed block letters reading, "Baby Girl Cranston," I knew how close I had come to not existing at all. But somehow that baby had survived and I, grown and healthy, could hold the remnants of my struggle to exist between fingers that could easily wear that bracelet as a ring.

The house had been a dump when we first found it. It had been left to my mother by an uncle who had just let the place rot while he himself festered in an old folk's home in Norfolk. But over time, the house was resurrected from a near-condemned status and brought back to the good graces of the health department thanks to my father's carpentry skills. The green shutters didn't always stay in place and the tiles on the roof sometimes blew off during hurricane season, but it was charming and attractive in its own unassuming way.

More often than not, my father wasn't there. He made his living as a contractor and was always away on sites out of town. At this particular time he was at Ohio State putting the finishing touches on a new dormitory and was due to come home at any time. Those of us remaining were all eagerly awaiting his arrival, not only because we missed him, but also because the whole house had been in a state of disrepair since he had been gone. Just recently, during a six-week hiatus between construction jobs, my father had decided that the entire kitchen needed to be renovated. So, like a termite on cocaine, he began destroying it from the floor up. He had just begun the task of replacing all our old, worn appliances with shiny, stainless steel new ones when he was called away. Since that time, the kitchen had looked like the inner workings of a cyborg, all exposed wires and steel casings. While the new appliances waited for installation in their new homes, all of our old appliances were in the laundry room on the backside of the house. While still usable, they were practically inaccessible since Dad had left the new dishwasher wedged in the doorway between the kitchen and laundry room.

The one saving grace was that he had taken the time to install the new microwave oven and my mother was finally forced to come to terms with this modern-day marvel. She also relied heavily on her aged slow-cooker, which she routinely loaded up with vegetables and meat in the morning and then forgot to turn on. She worked only part-time as a real estate agent and saw clients and showed properties in the late afternoons and early evenings. During the morning and early afternoon she was free to go to the store, call friends and do whatever a mother does while unsupervised. This is only conjecture, but I believed that most of her downtime was absorbed by talk shows. Whenever I came home from school, she would always ask me things like, "Do you know anyone who smokes this . . . crack cocaine?" or, "Tell me, Lucy. If I were to get my breasts enlarged and become a stripper, would you still talk to me?" or, my favorite, "You haven't been in touch with any of these dirt-eating cults, have you?"

As I was getting out my key to open the front door, the fourth member of our little family unit greeted me in pink curlers and a quilted robe.

"I've been waitin' for you's," my father's aunt, Teese, said in a low rasp.

I knew what she wanted right away. She had that look on her face like in five minutes she was going to self-destruct.

"Oh," I said, brushing past her into the entryway. "Why is that?"

"I'm dyin' for a cigarette. Ya got any?"

"I don't know," I said, completely aware of my cigarette inventory.

"Can I borrow a couple, just until I can get to the store?"

Aunt Teese was not supposed to smoke. She knew this, Mom and Dad and I knew this, but after nearly six decades of nicotine devotion, she was a permanent slave to tobacco. Two heart attacks, time under the surgeon's knife and repeated warnings from her doctor had not convinced her that it was due time for her to stop. I had heard that quitting smoking could add up to ten years to a person's life, but honestly, I didn't know what Aunt Teese would have done with those ten extra years. At eighty-two, she was a confirmed couch potato, living for re-runs of *Perry Mason* and *Gomer Pyle* and downing cola by the liter while eating her weight in cheese curls every day. At night she became "Bingo Woman," donning her best polyester duds and going from one end of the Peninsula to the other, searching for the VFW or Moose Lodge with the biggest pot. Sometimes she would win and whenever she did, she would spend all of the loot paying the overdraft fees and medical bills she couldn't pay while she was on her losing streak. This week she vowed that she wasn't going to play bingo anymore, but Thursday night was coming, a big night for bingoists in Hampton Roads. She would be among them.

I wasn't going to argue with her and took two cigarettes out of my purse. Usually when we had these little illicit dealings, I would say things like, "This is the last time," or, "You're going to have to start stocking up because I can't support both our habits," but on this day I just gave her what she wanted and hoped she would go away before she thought to ask me something else. That didn't happen, unfortunately.

"I've got an appointment with the podiatrist on Thursday morning. He's gotta dig out my ingrown toenail. It's gotten full of pus again," she said.

"Lovely," I replied.

"I asked your Mom if she was available to take me, but she said no. Can you give me a ride?"

"I think I have class."

"Your Mom said you don't have class until 2:30 and I'd be done by then."

Good one, Mom, I thought.

I sighed. "What time do you have to be there?"

"Eleven thirty," she said.

"I guess I could."

As I walked away from her I heard her say, "I'm sorry I have to impose, but if your father would let me drive, I wouldn't have to ask you's for rides, would I?"

"And he would be glad to let you drive, if you hadn't mistaken a MERGE LEFT sign for an excuse to plow into oncoming traffic." I said, referring to the traffic accident Teese had been in two years before that had ended her time behind the wheel and had made me the proud owner of her 1985 white, four-door Buick Century.

No one in the family was really sure how or when Aunt Teese and I became adversaries, least of all myself. I have been told that Teese and I once got along beautifully and I had seen pictures of me as a young child sitting on her lap and looking rather happy to be there. As a matter of fact, I was the one who nicknamed her Teese when my young mouth could not pronounce her real name, Theresa. Having taken a few psychology courses, I could only speculate that because Aunt Teese came to live with us when I was four years old, an age when most children acquire or have acquired siblings, subconsciously I identified Aunt Teese as a new rival for my parents' affection. It was the family joke that Aunt Teese was bequeathed to us. When Grandma Cranston died, we got her living room furniture and her good silverware. When Uncle Ernest passed away, we got his antique humidor and golf equipment. When great aunt Nellie died, we got one good Renoir reproduction and a fair Rembrandt knock off. And when Uncle Bert died, we got Aunt Teese.

I found Mom drinking coffee in the kitchen sitting at the unfinished counter, her eyes focused on a stack of papers in front of her, which she was sifting through very slowly between thoughtful sips from her mug. My mother was the most amazing looking forty-something I had ever seen. Slender but not scrawny, clear complected and nearly wrinkle-free, she looked just as she did when she was in her twenties, only with a few exceptions. She now kept her blond hair trimmed to a chin-length bob instead of down her back and parted in the middle and her real estate agency issued gold blazer now replaced the zigzag striped ponchos of her hippie heyday.

I have always thought myself a perfect synthesis of my parents' genes. At the age of 15, I had topped off at 5'8"—a happy medium between my mother's heel-influenced 5'6" and my father's six-foot height. I have what has been called a sturdy frame which either means I'm well padded or the type of thing people should hold onto when tornadoes strike. My hair is and always has been blond, my eyes a deep azure blue, and my face is sprinkled with a light dusting of freckles as is my mother's. My height is in my legs and so, unfortunately, is about three-fourths of my weight. I would dwell on this, but I don't think there's ever been a woman alive who has liked her thighs.

"Thanks for covering for me, Mom," I said.

Her blue eyes opened wide. "How's that?"

I bent near her ear and whispered in my best Aunt Teesese, "'I got a toe full of pus again.'"

This didn't register with Mom at first, but then she said, "Oh. That. I hope you don't mind. Thursday's a big day for me. I'm closing the deal on the old Marple place."

"That's great, Mom," I said, silently marveling over the fact that my mother, erstwhile Haight-Ashbury devotee, was now using phrases like "closing the deal." I opened the fridge—the one appliance that had not been relegated to the back porch—and got out a diet cola.

"Lunch is what you make it today," she said. "But for dinner, I think I might get something from that new place that opened up on Jefferson. Montoni's, I think."

"I heard they have bugs," I told her.

"Really? Who told you that?"

"Some guys at school were talking about it. They went there one night and a big cockroach crawled out of one of their salads."

Mom's mouth flew open. "You have got to be kidding!"

"Anyway, don't go to any trouble. I'm meeting Janet for lunch."

"Janet..." Mom said as though I had just tossed out an obscure reference from ancient Norse mythology. I think her mind was still on the roach salad. "Oh, Lucy, she just called not two minutes ago. She says that she's sorry, but she couldn't find a sitter for the kids this afternoon, so she has to stay home, but she'd like to go out for drinks on Wednesday."

I was almost glad about this. Janet had been my best friend since we met at day camp when we were twelve and she was one of my last friends left in the area from that time in my life. She had married a local man and now had two children, Joshua, twenty-six months, and Christina, fourteen months. Every time I had gone to lunch with Janet since the kids came into her life, the kids had always accompanied her. The last time Janet had taken me to lunch, her children left behind a path of destruction seldom seen outside Florida during hurricane season. After we left the restaurant, our section had to be cordoned off and disinfected, I'm sure. The "fun map" the waitress had given the children became confetti which they threw back and forth at each other while Janet begged and pleaded for them to finish their meals, which, except for a few cold french fries and parsley garnishes, were either chopped into fine bits on the table or mashed into saliva-soaked morsels on the floor.

"At least if we have dinner," I said to Mom, "the kids will probably stay at home with their father. I mean, I love Janet's kids. They're sweet. But sometimes I just miss how things were before Janet got married and started having kids. I feel as though we don't have that much in common anymore. It's like she's in suburbia taking Polaroids and I'm in a cavern making cave paintings."

"Now, why do you say that?"

"I don't know. It just seems that we don't have that much to talk about. She's all into her kids and her home and her husband and I'm still in school. It just kills me that she had to get married so young."

Mom shook her head. "I don't have room to talk. I married your father a month after we graduated from high school."

Even though I had heard this countless times before, it still astounded me. When I was a senior in high school, I could not even fathom being married, even though I had a steady boyfriend whom, at the time, I was considering marrying, but in the distant future. The way, *way* distant future. Then, at eighteen, I thought twenty-one was a good age to be married. At twenty-one, I began to think that twenty-four or twenty-five would be better ages for lifetime commitment. I had a feeling that when I was twenty-five, I'd be targeting thirty.

"It's still hard for me to think of Janet as being a mother," I said. "I mean, when Janet used to baby-sit, she'd always call me if the kids needed their diapers changed because she couldn't handle the stench."

"It's different when they're your own," Mom assured me.

"I'd like to know what kind of hormone is released in the female body that makes baby poop smell like gardenias."

"I didn't say motherhood improves the smell. It's just . . . different, that's all."

Mom took a final swig of her coffee and then pushed off from the counter. As she did this, she suddenly cried out and pulled her curled hand up in front of her face for observation. "Look at that! A splinter! God, I can't wait until your father comes back and does something about this kitchen," she said as she gingerly plucked the tiny shard of wood from the bottom of her palm.

"Yeah. And then he'll be onto something else. Like your bathroom."

A flicker of fear flared in my mother's blue eyes as she imagined the potential for mess there. She was probably envisioning the toilet sitting in the middle of the living room right beside the Duncan Phyfe settee.

"What are your plans for this afternoon now, Lucy?" Mom said as she gathered up her papers from the counter.

"I don't know. Maybe I'll do something wild like . . . oh, I don't know. Get a jump on the reading that Dr. Schindler assigned today."

"Schindler . . . isn't he the—"

"—boring guy with all the cardigan sweaters? Yeah, that's the one. He just suddenly decided to assign us another book to read after I nearly got a hernia carting home all those paperbacks I had to buy at the beginning of the semester."

"Well," Mom said, slinging the strap of her purse over her shoulder. "Whatever you do today, make sure you get something to eat. Woman cannot live on diet drinks alone, despite what some of those fashion magazines say."

After Mom left, I fixed myself a sandwich with the remainder of the deli turkey and sat at the counter and thought about what I was really going to do with the rest of my afternoon. In previous years I would be driving to work about this time. I had always worked since my junior year in high school and had alternated work with school during my years at PCC. For the past five years I had been working at a clothing store at the mall, folding jeans, stocking T-shirts and listening to way too much Harry Connick Jr. on store's sound system. But after last Christmas, in an effort to get me off to ODU as soon as possible, my parents agreed that they would support me until I finally earned enough credits to transfer. By the end of this semester I would have all the credits I needed, plus some.

After I finished my sandwich, I tried to find a quiet place in the house where I might be able to read and maybe take a nap. But with morning game shows being what they are and Aunt Teese's hearing being what it was, there wasn't a single space in the house where I couldn't hear breathless contestants on TV screaming out the prices of bathroom cleaners and rice side dishes. I decided this might be the perfect day to use that backyard of ours.

The garage in our backyard housed two of Dad's lifelong ambitions. In one part, the carport, he kept his 1965 custom painted electric blue Ford Mustang, which my father used to drive on our weekend antique hunts. My mother's allergies could never stand the dust that is par for the course at most antique and second hand shops, so as soon as I could walk, I became my father's accomplice in the crime known in our household as Operation Clutter. We used to putter around Hampton Roads and sometimes go all the way to Williamsburg, going from one dilapidated old junk shop to another. I never really minded accompanying him because most of the time my willingness to participate was rewarded with a used toy or a piece of costume jewelry that I could play dress up with. These trips were tutorials, intended to school me with a love for anything decaying, mildewed and in desperate need of repair.

Just a few summers before, all four of us had packed off for Texas on a road trip in Mom's station wagon. Somewhere outside Corpus Christi, Dad's notoriously weak bladder failed him and he bailed out of the driver's seat to relieve himself in a roadside ravine, leaving the car to idle on the shoulder. After letting us roast like game hens for nearly fifteen minutes, Dad emerged from the underbrush, covered in mud and brandishing and old Grape Ne-hi sign like a shield. "Look what I found!" he exclaimed in delight.

I was never able to put my prejudices aside and see junk as being anything other than junk. Dad finally realized this when I was twelve and ready to begin the sixth grade and he tried to force an old Monkees lunchbox in my hand to take back to school with me. When I declined in favor of a grocery bag, I think he realized that all hope of my ever being a true antique aficionado was lost and from then on he pursued his treasures alone, still sometimes bringing me a piece of jewelry or a musty book.

The Mustang had ceased being roadworthy around the time I stopped going with him on his weekend antique hunts. On his way home one Saturday the engine blew up and turned all the metal under the hood into a Salvador Daliesque landscape of melted muck. The mechanic who towed the car for Dad that sad Saturday told him that there was very little that could be done for the old '65 except put it out of its misery, sell it for usable parts and squash in into a cube. But like a grieving man who refuses to have the life support terminated on a vegetative loved one, Dad never gave up hope that one day he and only he would have the time, the skill, and, judging by the far-gone condition of the car, the magic to bring the Mustang back to roaring life again.

Next to the carport was Dad's shed, there was a slim sliver of a place where he kept the overfill of his collections and all of his woodworking tools. I rarely went in there. I always felt that I was intruding when I did visit there, that I was seeing a side of my Dad that he didn't want me to see. This was where he had his place to dream, where he could be the man in his mind and not the man of the household who had all of the responsibilities of keeping the bills paid, making repairs on the house, and being counted on for whatever judgment or decision Mom was incapable of making on her own.

As I sat and read, curled up on a blanket under the spreading oak tree in our back yard, I was finding it hard to concentrate on what I was reading. A single question kept going through my mind, distracting me every few sentences or so.

I wonder if that deck chair is still in there?

By the time I had finally decided to quit reading, this thought had become a regular obsession. I knew if the deck chair did exist, it had to be in Dad's shed, awaiting refurbishment just like everything else around the house.

Suddenly I was seized with curiosity. The more I thought about it, the more excited I became. I remembered when I was ten and had found some blue stones in Mom's flower garden. Though I was old enough to know better, I imagined that I had found a fortune in sapphires. Just the thought of holding a cache of precious stones in my hand was enough to make me believe that what I had found could pay the mortgage on my parents' home, allow Mom to quit work and let Dad play permanent Geppetto in his shed. Even after Mom explained to me that what I had found were actually shards of glass from an old candy dish she had broken years before, I somehow wasn't disappointed. It was just the thought, just the *thought*. There was enough of Dad in me to make me believe that sometimes the most ordinary things could be extraordinary with a little imagination.

And there I was wondering about that deck chair. True, in Dad's nearly three decades of hunting and gathering antiques he had never brought home anything good. But what if that time, he had struck gold?

I knew I had to investigate. I knew I had to go in that shed.

When I cracked open the door of the shed that afternoon, I half expected to see Dad sitting there at his carpenter's desk. But when I walked in, I was enveloped in the chill of his absence. Dad's winter work boots were there at the door, encrusted with red earth and grass. A snow shovel was nearby and I remembered the last week he was home there had been a light snowfall. A calendar from a local pharmacy hung lop-sided by the window over his workbench with half the days of February crossed out in red ink. The seventeenth was circled, the day he left for Ohio. On the desk was a stack of drafting papers, the top one showing the layout of the kitchen. I ran my finger across it, creating a trail of white through the thickening dust and almost laughed when I looked in the corner of the drawing and saw that Dad had signed his name like a school boy.

There was precious little workspace now. Dad's collections had long clogged all the closets and crawl spaces in the house and had burst like an aneurysm into the back shelves of this tiny refuge from Dad's reality. Here Dad kept all the things deemed too dirty, too rusted, or too broken to be displayed or stored in the house. There was a Schwinn bicycle he had scored at an auction about fifteen years ago and hoped to restore for me so that I could learn to ride on a "real bike" like the one he had been trained on. Dad quickly learned that for the price of restoring the bike he could have outfitted me and the rest of the family with new bikes and the project was soon abandoned.

While looking through the items, I spied the Grape Ne-Hi sign that had stalled our Texas vacation by the side of the road all those summers ago. This too he had hoped to refurbish, but for now it was resting comfortably between a balding Topo Gigio doll and a soft drink can commemorating the 1982 NCAA championship basketball tournament.

After more peeking about the shelves and uncovering more and more about Dad's obsessive-compulsive buying urges (*The Best of Bread* on 8-Track *and* LP?), I looked on the bottom shelf. Between a monocled Mr. Peanut and a laughing ceramic Buddha, I found what had sent me searching there in the first place.

First I saw the arm, extending its woodeness to me from under a white sheet. I pulled on it, dragging the body of it along the bottom of the shelf and pushing still more stuff to the front. I grasped what I presumed to be the back of the chair and pulled hard, knocking over a stack of Life magazines so black with mildew their color covers looked like photo negatives. The chair was large and quite heavy, requiring me to use both arms and a lot of creative maneuvering to keep a set of nearby Fiestaware dishes from clattering to the floor. Once I got it out, I set it down in a cloud of dust and stray cobwebs and removed the sheet.

The chair could very well have come from the *Titanic*. It certainly looked as though it had weathered some stormy seas. Time had turned it a brownish gray and there were fine splinters running down the length of the chair like spokes in a music box. The wood was very sturdy, something like oak or pine. Having never taken a class in wood shop or been employed as a tree surgeon, I couldn't make an educated guess. There were no ornaments or decorative carvings anywhere except for a tiny white star etched into the center of the headrest. The style was very simple, almost Shaker-like. The seat itself was very low to the ground and I imagined that any lady wearing the costumes of the day would have had a hard time getting in and out of the thing without a boost.

I wiped my hand down the back of the chair and my palm came up black. It hadn't been in the water, presumably, for many decades and it was due time for a wash.

I took the chair outside and gave it a good blast with the garden hose. After the first dousing, it became obvious to me that the wood wasn't going to come clean with just plain water, so I went inside to get a bucket, a brush and some dish washing detergent. When I got to the kitchen, I found Aunt Teese standing at the sink running the garbage disposal, a halo of smoke encircling her head.

"Aw, shit," she said, "I thought you was your mother. Now I only got one cigarette left."

I clicked my tongue. "Too bad."

On my way to the broom closet under the stairs, I heard her cursing me. When she got really angry, she could never think of precisely what she had wanted to call me, so often times she just said whatever came to her mind first. That day I was a "stupid turnip."

Back outside with my pail and cleaning supplies in tow, the sun was hotter than before and right over the shade tree. I pulled the deck chair over to the other chairs in the yard and I almost felt sad for the old thing, looking so shabby compared to its newer, plastic and canvas comrades.

As I sat cross-legged on the cool grass, I thought to myself that I hadn't worked so hard at anything outside for years. This poor object had been neglected for so long. If my father had really paid such an exorbitant amount for this piece of history, it seemed to me that it would have been pretty high on his "things to restore" list. I had seen him spend more time on things that were worth practically nothing. One Saturday he came home with a box full of utensils that he swore were real silver. And after spending an entire afternoon scrubbing the "silverware" with tarnish remover until his fingers turned black, he realized all he had were a dozen or so mis-matched tin knives, spoons and forks, two of which had come from an old Army issued mess kit.

With a pail full of coffee-colored suds and a brush full of bent bristles, my work on the chair was finally done. It looked pretty much as it did before. What it really needed was a good sanding and a coat of varnish, I thought. But I wasn't going to get into that.

I still had some reading to do.

I grabbed the blanket I had been sitting on and draped it over the chair, since it was still wet and rough to the touch. I caught the open pages at the spine of the book with my thumb and sat down. The novelty of the situation was making me practically giddy as I thought, *"I'll bet there were many people who read books in this chair on the* Titanic, *but I'll bet I'd be the first to sit in it and read a book on the* Titanic.*"*

I eased myself into the chair very carefully, listening for any groan or crack in the wood that would mean the end of Dad's investment in the past. I thought to myself that this was the dream of any kid who's ever been to a museum and has seen the red velvet ropes around priceless Queen Anne and Louis XVI chairs and the signs around them saying, "Please do not sit." Here was my opportunity to thumb my nose at all those museum officials who made those rules. Here I could sit with no one to tell me not to. As I scooted my bottom along the seat, I thought to myself that I had never sat in a more uncomfortable chair. I lived in an age where man had perfected lounging. This was no Lazyboy recliner. It wasn't even a bean bag. Even though I was lying down in the warmth of the sun, I felt like I was sitting Shiva in a cold parlor.

Soon after I began reading, I found myself nodding off, which is not a comment on Walter Lord's story telling. I read the book with a great deal of interest, even going beyond the twenty-page limit that Dr. Schindler had set. After a certain point, my thoughts began to go in a slow spiral and as I was looking at the words on the page, they too began to swirl as though being sucked down a drain. My head kept falling against the back of the chair and the more I attempted to pull it forward, the less control I had. It was as though I were slowly being lulled into paralysis, with each part of my body shutting down and slowly easing into atrophy. My mind was aware of what was happening at first and then suddenly I had no thoughts at all, except *"This is very strange . . . this is very strange . . ."* as though I had become the observer commenting on the side about the inner workings of my own mind.

And then, I sensed involuntary movement in all my limbs as if I were being carried on a cloud jetting fast across the sky. I tried to press against whatever it was that was holding me, but I couldn't feel anything, not the hardness of the chair, not the warmth of the sun, not even my own skin.

Through the shield of my closed eyelids, a light was beginning to glow from the darkness and slow thoughts were now forming in my head. I was conscious of thinking, "Where am I? What's happening? Where am I going?" But I wasn't at all scared or tense; I just felt slow and soft like a clutch of feathers falling. The light grew more intense and the skin around my eyes tightened into a squint, but the light would not dim; it anything, it grew more intense as though supernovas were forming in each of my retina.

I have died, I thought. *I have died in my own backyard and Mom is going to come home in a few minutes and find me dead in this chair. The chair must have broken while I was in it and impaled me with a loosened support on the back. This is how I've always heard it would be. You go towards the light. You just go towards the light . . .*

But this light was menacing, almost like fire, red and coming in licks of flame against my face. I tried to cover my face, but I couldn't find my hands.

It's so bright, I can't stand it! It's so bright! Why won't it stop? Oh, God . . . am I going to hell? Is that where you're sending me? To hell?

Just when I thought I couldn't stand the light anymore, I felt myself moving very slowly to a shady place. All at once, I was cold, as though suddenly submerged into a mass of refrigerated air. Then darkness enveloped me, an opaqueness just as intense as the light had been. I began to get a sense that I was being reformed, starting at the middle of my chest and radiating all over my body, the atoms of my being realigning and making me complete again. When all the pieces came together I felt solid and whole again, but very cold as though the molecules charged with bringing me together were made of ice.

A support emerged against my back. *The chair! I'm back in the chair!* But I was still under a heavy drape of darkness. And I was cold . . . why was it suddenly so chilly? Had I been asleep so long that evening had come? Had Mom forgotten about me and left me in the yard? Mom was forgetful, God bless her, but not so scatter-brained that she would have left her only child to starve and freeze in her own backyard.

"Miss?" a strange, masculine voice was saying. "Miss?"

My eyes tried to probe the blackness. But although I felt my eyes moving, I could not open them. The lids were sealed shut.

"Miss, are you all right?"

I recognized a British lilt in the voice, which was presently being spoken right over me. I was trying to answer, but nothing was coming out. I was locked in a state of drowse where speech and movement were not allowed.

"Miss, are you hurt?"

YES! I must be because I'm in a coma or something!

I felt a hand against my cheek and heard a whispered swear word. Then I was being lifted, my body going totally slack in the arms of this person I couldn't identify. My head snapped back and dangled over his arm as he carried me swiftly away. I struggled to regain control over my movement as the stranger grunted and cursed with every step. I heard what he was saying, vaguely, but his words were being filtered through layers of dense confusion.

"Sweet Jesus . . . Christ . . . sweet, holy Jesus Christ!"

There was complete darkness for most of the way and silence, intermittently peppered with the stranger's exclamations and pants. And then, after I sensed we turned a corner, I heard loud pounding as though the stranger were attempting to kick in a door. For a few seconds, I was still in the stranger's arms as his breath became more labored. In another minute, the pounding was repeated.

"Bride, open the door!" the man carrying me shouted.

He stood there holding me for the longest time and then suddenly, where there had been darkness, there was now a whitish glow and I was being drawn into it.

"Good God!" another voice boomed in a British accent. "What the bloody hell?"

I had the sensation that I was being taken into a warm place, a closed in space, like a closet. The voices seemed very near, but I still could not respond to them. I couldn't even open my eyes yet. It was as though I had become a newborn baby again.

I was being set down now, very gently, into a hard, wooden, straight back chair with arms. I felt the chair collect me and I desperately wanted to conform to the chair's shape, but again I felt my body going slack, the backs of my heels dragging across the floor as my bottom slid clear off the seat.

"Oh, God, what's wrong with her? Is she dead? Should we fetch the surgeon?" the second stranger was saying.

The first stranger's presence moved in on me like a phantom. He pressed his head against my breast, right under my chin. "She's got a heart beat," came his muffled, authoritative voice. He moved away and spoke over me now. "At least we know she's alive."

"At least there's that. Where did you find her?" the second stranger was asking.

"In one of the deck chairs. She's very cold. Been out there for hours and hours, I suppose. She's certainly not dressed for this weather, though." A hand was running up and down my arm. "Oh, she *is* freezing. Quick! Get the blanket from the bed. And turn the heater up a bit."

The stranger's voice continued to soothe me as the things he had asked for were sought after and done. In seconds I felt the warmth of a woolen wrap around me, all the way down to my knees. My rescuer was now tucking the blanket behind my back, underneath me, surrounding me in a cocoon of warmth. When finished, his hands went to my cheeks, gently rubbing my skin. "Miss? Can you hear me at all?"

Yes, I can hear you, but my words are trapped!

"Perhaps she had too much to drink," the second stranger theorized.

"No, no. I can't smell it on her. She smells like," and he made a pronounced sniff, "Coconut, I think."

"Do you suppose someone lost her?"

"Good heavens, Bride! She's a woman, not a set of cufflinks!"

"I'm only saying that someone might be looking about for her, wondering where she is. It is quite late, you know."

"If only she had some sort of identification with her—a purse or something. But I didn't see one on her."

"Do you suppose that someone could have robbed her and caused her to faint?"

There was a pause and I felt the first stranger's hand against my cheek again. "That's possible."

"Well, if that's the case, shouldn't one of us go fetch the surgeon? She could have hit her head or something."

Yes! Get the doctor! If I keep on like this I don't think I'll be able to breathe much longer!

"That would probably be a step in the right direction."

"Do you want me to go?"

"Yes. You go and I'll stay with her and keep trying to bring her about," the first stranger said, vigorously rubbing the length of my arms again.

Even though I had not seen his face yet, I somehow trusted this stranger. There was something about his voice that made me feel safe.

Just then I heard a door open and with it a gust of cold air, followed by the sound of an older gentleman's voice greeting the pair who were tending to me as "Bride" and "Phillips." I heard the heavy trod of footsteps against the floorboards, but then they stopped almost as soon as they began.

"What have we here?" this new gentleman said in a deep, British baritone.

The two men called this new stranger "captain" and they both began speaking in unison, talking so rapidly I couldn't understand them. They were talking about me, though. Found this girl . . . she must have been attacked and her purse and jewelry stolen . . . don't know who she is . . .

I became aware of a new presence right in front of me. My nose caught the scent of cigar smoke. A cold hand fell against my cheek. Once I felt this caress, my brain seemed to click back on. In the grip of sudden wakefulness, I sat bolt upright in the chair.

In that hot cold flash of consciousness, I could only give everything a blank stare. My thoughts were moving in slow waves, struggling through currents of confusion as my mind grappled with the challenge of putting my surroundings in perspective. A trio of gawking strangers stood over me. To my left was the one whom I was sure had been found me, a brown-haired, very pale young man in an ill-fitting navy vest with brass buttons over an untucked white shirt. The man in the middle, whom had been identified as the captain, was a white-bearded, elderly man, probably in his mid-sixties, dressed in a heavy black overcoat. The third man, the one who had been in the room when I arrived, was dressed like the first stranger and was decidedly boyish with a head of sandy-colored waves

"Calm yourself, Miss," the captain was saying to me in whispers and sibilant S sounds. "You're safe. Safe and sound."

I looked up at him. I had seen that face before, long ago and his name occurred to me and then instantly vanished as I looked into his eyes. His eyes . . . they were trained so keenly on me I felt as though I were being examined through and through. My perceptions of things suddenly turned to jelly, all runny and sticky and jammed up at the base of my brain. I sat there staring blankly. When I tried to speak, the words could not even be formed in my head because there was nothing there to form them, nothing but space and an overpowering lightness that made me feel glad I was sitting down.

"Do you know where you are?" the old gentleman was asking me.

I shook my head slowly, still finding even slight movement a great challenge.

"You're in the Marconi Station on board the RMS *Titanic*," he told me.

There was a vague familiarity about the name, but I didn't know how I knew it or where I had heard it before. I looked around and found that I was in a small, windowless room, a little larger than a walk-in closet. It appeared to be some kind of electrical room. On a table not far from where I was sitting there was an array of different knobs and gadgets, a few tesla coils short from being the lair of a mad scientist. I looked up and overhead was a skylight and through it I could see the night sky streaking by.

"Have you been drinking from that cup over by the in-box, Mr. Phillips?"

"No, sir," Phillips replied.

"How's the tea?"

"Probably very cold, sir."

"It won't matter. Pour a little for her."

I still wasn't steady enough to hold the cup on my own, so the captain positioned the cup under my bottom lip as I sat and tried to muster the strength to swallow the tepid, tasteless brew without strangling.

"Can you tell me who you are?" he asked me.

For a moment my mind was seized with fear. *I didn't know my own name!*

I shook my head. Another sip of tea was forced into my mouth, administered by the captain, who crouched down in front of me. After the last sip, the captain handed the cup over to Phillips and took me by the chin, making it so that I could not look away. His line of vision was now drilling its way into my eyes like a tractor beam. The congestion in my head began to abate and the gatherings of clotted thought became to disperse. A little trickle of sense made its way from my brain to my tongue and what emerged came out gravely and coarse, but still audible.

"Lucy Cranston," I said. "My name is Lucy Cranston."

The old gentleman smiled. "Well, hello, Miss Cranston. I am Captain Smith. The other gentlemen are the Marconi operators on board my ship. To your left is Jack Phillips, the senior operator, and to your right is his junior, Harold Bride."

There was a mumbled "How do you do" from the two other men and I acknowledged them with a head bob. That was all I could manage.

"Do you know what happened to you out on the deck?" Phillips asked me.

I shook my head, still lacking the mental agility to put more than two words together.

"Do you remember being out on the deck with anyone or encountering anyone?" Bride asked.

Again I shook my head.

"Perhaps I should fetch the surgeon. If someone robbed her, she could have been struck on the head," Bride was saying. "Does your head hurt at all?"

It didn't hurt, exactly. My mind was churning, the way a stomach does when it's upset. I was having a hard time trying to stay focused. A thought would form and then quickly dissipate. When a clear thought did emerge, it was as though it were being hand-selected by some inner, invisible force that had the ability to override anything I was thinking or feeling.

"Miss Cranston?" Bride was saying again.

My head did an involuntary sway in his direction.

"Your head, Miss Cranston? How's your head?"

My tongue uncurled and unleashed a response. "It's all right. I'm a little . . . a little . . ." *What was I trying to say?*

"Confused?" Phillips asked.

I looked over at him, thinking him a genius at intuition. I nodded.

"Perhaps a good night's rest is all you need, Miss Cranston. With the day's excitement and the late hour, you're probably exhausted. Do you know where your cabin is?"

"Cabin?" I asked. *Cabin . . . cabin . . . like a house made of logs set back in the woods . . . woods with trees, large trees, huge trees spreading all over forming a ceiling of leaves. Leaves swaying on the trees in the wind. No, there was only one tree, but a big one, right over me, I thought. It had been there. But there was no cabin, there was only a shed . . .*

I sat up, allowing the blanket that was covering me to fall to my lap. "I wasn't here before," I said.

"No, you were not. You were out on the deck." the captain said.

"In a deck chair," I said.

"Yes. Mr. Phillips found you unconscious in one of the deck chairs."

"But I wasn't on the deck. I was somewhere else . . . somewhere . . ."

And then what I had been thinking went right out of me in a burst of brightness.

"Phillips, you're at the end of your shift, are you not?"

"Yes, sir."

"Would you please escort Miss Cranston to her cabin? I'll arrange to have the doctor meet you there." The captain was smiling at me as he got to his feet. "Are we feeling better now?"

"I'm all right," I said, though I wasn't sure. I was feeling strange, but not ill. Just out of sorts, out of place.

"I'm certain that all you need is a good night's rest in your own, cozy cabin."

Once the captain left, there was some gradual clearing in my head that allowed me to at least form a few consistent thoughts about my surroundings again. Phillips went behind a green curtain hanging over a door across from the desk where the equipment was set up and I was left alone with the other man, Bride, for a few minutes. I watched him, over by the desk, as he flipped through some bound pages in his hands.

"Let's see . . . Cranston . . . Cranston . . . Oh, here you are. Miss Lucy Cranston. B93."

"B93?" I said slowly.

"That's your cabin."

"Are you sure? I mean, I don't remember . . ."

"See for yourself."

He handed me the bundle of papers and my eyes followed the long list of alphabetized names to the C's. Cornell, Cotterill, Coutts, Coxon, Crafton . . .

And there I was, Miss Lucy Cranston of Newport News, Virginia.

A wave of dizziness engulfed my head as I stared at my own name printed there. It was such a strange sight to me, as though I were finding my name already carved on a tombstone.

Phillips emerged from behind the green curtain. He was now wearing an overcoat and he was presently sliding on a pair of brown gloves. He had put on a cap with a shiny black bill. He looked over at me, as though trying to gauge my fitness for the walk to my cabin.

"Are you all right now, Miss Cranston?"

"Yes, I'm fine," I said, wondering if I looked as peculiar as I felt.

Phillips helped me to my feet as I tried to steady my head enough to stand. Once I was out of the chair, he offered his arm and I took it, gratefully, if not gracefully. He asked Bride if he had located my cabin on the list and Bride told him where he could find it.

"That's simple enough. The entrance to first class is right 'round the bend."

"First class?"

"Yes, Miss Cranston. Did you not know you were traveling first class?"

"No, I didn't."

"How could you not—?" he started. And then he just shrugged.

He led me out the door and back out onto the deck. Once outside, I was reminded again that I was ill-dressed for the weather. In fact, until I was out in the night air again, I didn't even realize what I was wearing and couldn't remember putting it on. I was dressed in a floor-length yellow evening gown. I felt down the bodice and found it was beaded with sharp crystals. The neckline was low, just shy of plunging. *Where did I get this thing? Have I been in a wedding?*

I shivered a little in the ocean breeze, since there was nothing covering my arms. Phillips saw my discomfort and slipped out of his overcoat. He put his hand in an interior pocket and removed something—a small, silver case that shined in the moonlight.

"Oh, no, I couldn't," I said.

"Take it," he insisted as he draped the coat across my shoulders. "Just so long as I get it back."

We were walking very slowly, since my legs weren't fully cooperating with the rest of me yet. Phillips did not try to start a conversation and I was glad of this. My answers would have been so idiotic he would have thought that he had been charged with escorting a zombie or someone suffering from the after effects of experimental brain surgery.

We took a turn and were presently walking down a stairwell. When we got to the bottom we found ourselves in a place filled with white light. I looked up and overhead was a glass dome, which appeared as a giant white eye, observing us as we descended. There was a slight tinkling coming from it, like the sound of a filament inside a shaken light bulb after it has burned out. All around me was the most extraordinary wood paneling I had ever seen, gleaming with new varnish, appearing slick as seal skin. *This must be the grand staircase*, I heard myself say inside my head. But how did I know that?

The dual staircase merged in the middle and we glided past an object on the wall that made me catch my breath when I saw it. Just to my right and just above my head was a clock, fixed into the wall, surrounded on either side by two bas relief classical figures, each gently adorning the timepiece with ivy. I stood there, looking at the clock, half in admiration, half in total mystification.

I heard my own voice say, "Honor and Glory crowning Time."

Where had I heard that before? If I knew what this was in front of me, why couldn't I recall the number and location of my own cabin?

I heard Phillips asking me a question—something about the lifts. We were walking again down the staircase to a wide-open area with palms and plump, wicker chairs. As we got to the bottom, I noticed a statue of a little cupid holding aloft an elaborate light fixture like a bouquet. Just ahead was a shiny white parquet floor. In the air was an odiferous cocktail of smoldering cigars, woody oak and fresh paint.

Right in front of us was a pair of iron-gated elevators. As the red-coated attendant saw our approach, he smiled.

"Are they lettin' you blokes from the radio room out to hobnob with the passengers now?" the attendant asked.

"No, no. I'm just doing a special favor for the captain," Phillips said.

Well, gee, I hope I'm not putting you out, I thought. I could have found the cabin myself, if not that night, by the morning at least.

The attendant closed the gate and pulled a brass lever down one notch. The elevator slowly crept down a level. Once stopped, the attendant folded back the gate and we stepped off into an all-white corridor. As we walked down the narrow hallway lined on either side by silent, closed doors, Phillips kept quiet. His arm was very rigid and when I looked over at him I saw that he held a very serious expression on his face as though he were the sole participant in a military dress parade. As we continued to walk, I began to feel as though lead weights were being applied to my eyelids. I had felt tired before, but now I was becoming so exhausted I could barely hold my head up. My steps were dragging and I began to sense that the rigidity in Phillips' arm was more a reaction to my slumping stature than any innate shyness.

"Are we almost there?" I asked.

"It's not much further now," he replied.

"Good. I don't feel well."

He immediately picked up the pace.

Suddenly we were racing down the hall. As the doors on either side whizzed by in that silent hall I heard a familiar voice ringing though the air, faint at first but steadily growing louder with each step. "Lucy... Lucy..." the ethereal voice called, high and sweet as an angel's. I was fighting off a creeping blackness in my mind that was dissolving the whiteness around me into darkness.

I stopped walking, tugging Phillips to a halt as well.

"What is it?" he asked.

"I think I hear my mother calling me," I said.

And just as soon as I said that, I felt my knees buckle underneath me. The last things I saw was Phillips' face reeling from the shock of seeing me spiraling to the floor. The next thing that came to me was the sound of my mother's voice right over me. When I opened my eyes, she was there, standing beside me, staring at me quizzically.

"What are you doing?" Mom was asking.

I was still trying to adjust my thoughts to this abrupt consciousness. Again I felt the hardness of the wooden deck chair under me. Overhead was the spreading shade tree rocking its infant buds in the breeze. The wind blew, seeding little chill bumps on my arms and legs.

Mom tapped me on the shoulder. "Hey, did you hear me? What are you doing?"

I had heard her. It was just that I wasn't expecting that question. I thought she would have asked me something more along the lines of, "Where have you been?"

I stretched and looked at the position of the sun, thinking it should have been much lower. It seemed I had been out for hours. "What time is it?"

"A little after one," she replied. "Why on earth did you get out this old thing?"

"I don't know. Just curious about it, I guess."

"Your father would flip if he knew you were playing with it."

Playing with it? What was I, seven? I let that comment slide and asked, "What are you doing home?"

"I was on my way to this new property and I left the address in the kitchen, so I came back to get it. You know, I don't see how you could even sleep in that thing. It doesn't look very conducive to sleeping. But you were really out of it. Like you were in another world."

My fingers were still curled around the book, my thumb marking the place where I left off.

I could have been.

Mom, Aunt Teese and I were in the living room watching *Fatal Attraction* when the phone rang a little after eight and, with all of our nerves on edge, we all jumped at the sound. In *Fatal Attraction*, whenever the phone rings, it's never good news on the other end. We all stared at each other with mutual dread. When no one volunteered by the fourth ring, I got up and grabbed the phone in the kitchen.

"Hey, Lucy," my friend Janet said on the other end. She sounded very old, I thought. I could hear the fussy whimpers of two nap-deprived children in the background. "Just wanted to touch base with you about Wednesday. Are we still on for drinks?"

"Yeah. I'm looking forward to it," I said.

"I'm thinking Danny's. Would that be OK?"

"Sure, whatever."

There was a pause on the other end of the line. "Is this a bad time?"

"No, Mom and Aunt Teese and I were just watching a movie. But it's one I've seen, so it's OK."

"Hey, guess who I saw today?" Her speech was infused with a sudden zest now.

I wasn't going to try to guess. I never understood why people prefaced revelations with this question when they knew an outright guess would probably be wrong. "I don't know. Who?"

"Doug Hanssen!"

"Doug Hanssen? What's that loser still doing hanging around Hampton Roads? I thought he moved to Pittsburgh."

"He did, but apparently he's back."

"Where did you see him?"

"At the grocery store. Buying Pampers."

"I hope he was doing a friend a favor because it he's been allowed to procreate, there's no hope for mankind."

"Lucy, you did date him for a half a year."

"Yeah, and I really liked him. In high school. But after a while he got on my nerves. For one thing, he was more into comic books than anyone over the age of twelve really should be. He had piles and piles of them all over his house, stashed in drawers, under tables, in benches, in cabinets."

"So you dumped him because he liked comic books."

"No, that wasn't the reason. I dumped him because I started seeing Eric Strassman."

"Oh, yeah. The baseball player. What was wrong with him?"

"He had selective memory. He could tell you the name of every major leaguer who ever hit a ball out of Yankee stadium, but he couldn't remember my phone number, or the fact that I hate action-adventure movies. Every time we went to see a movie, he'd always pick something like *Maximum Testosterone Level* or *Extreme Violence III*."

"Who did you dump him for?"

"Actually, he dumped me. Then I went through a dry spell until I met Jerry."

"Jerry?"

"Jerry Malone. And he cheated on me like a dog. He told me he couldn't take me to a dance at the student union because he had to go out of town, so I went by myself. And he showed up with another girl who I think still had some of her baby teeth."

"Wasn't there another Jerry you dated who always wore camouflage?"

"Jerry Dickerson. When I was dating him, I could never sit through dinner without thinking he was going to have to exit early and go storm a desert or something."

She laughed. "You're so picky, Lucy."

"So you think if I lowered my standards, I could be a victor in the dating game?"

"No, but I do think you look for reasons why you should dump a guy."

"Well, usually I don't have to look very hard."

Just then I heard her son, Joshua, saying something through gulping sobs. He must have been standing beside her.

"Oh," Janet said, "Joshua wants to tell you something." There was a long pause followed by Janet saying sweetly, "Go ahead, Joshua. Tell Aunt Lucy what you saw today."

A child's high volume enthusiasm came blaring through the receiver. All I could catch was something about a monkey and two giraffes and everybody went ha, ha, ha.

Janet was back on the other end. "Did you hear that?"

"I'm not sure. Can you translate?"

"He saw a movie at the sitter's about the zoo today and it was really funny, apparently. He's been talking about it all day. Does the movie you're watching have a monkey and giraffe in it?"

"Nope. Just one very dead rabbit in a stew pot."

"God, Lucy, how can you watch that movie? I had nightmares about it for weeks when I first saw it!"

I laughed. "It's a good one." And then I decided to change the subject to a slightly more current issue. "Speaking of nightmares, I had one hell of a dream this afternoon when I was taking a nap."

"Oh?" she said. "Was it one of your erotic dreams about David Cassidy?"

"No."

"Shaun Cassidy?"

"No," I said, wondering if she was going to name every crush I had ever had before she ever let me just tell her what the dream was about.

She took in a mock breath. "Sean Connery?"

"No. And those 007 bondage dreams were your kinky fantasies, not mine, Janet."

"Everybody should have those dreams once in a while just to keep life interesting. Believe me, when I've been home with the kids all day, mopping up grape juice and using ice to get chewing gum out of their hair, sometimes the image of a young, buff Sean Connery strapped to a table is all I have to make me smile."

Sean Connery had been Janet's dream man ever since she saw a late night screening of *Dr. No* on cable during a sixth grade slumber party. Though she knew there was no one in real life that could compare to the suave, tuxedoed, martini-swilling Scot, she had none the less always found men to date who were somewhat in that vein: tall, older, sophisticated. In high school she never dated anyone her own age and held true to that conduct in her adult life, though some of the sought-after traits fell by the wayside when she found herself submerged in the Hampton Roads dating pool. Her husband was ten years her senior, he was short, slightly balding, and a former New Yorker who suffered from a chronic sinus condition and astigmatism. She may have been aiming for a 007 double with a license to kill, but instead she ended up with a Woody Allen clone with a license to whine.

Just then Janet let out an exaggerated gasp. "No, no, Christina! Bad girl!" Then she returned to me. "Listen, I've got to go. Christina just pulled off her diaper and decided to mop the floor with it. Which means, I now have to mop the floor. Christina!"

I understood the abrupt click too well and didn't think too hard on it. I had no idea why Janet always seemed to call when her kids were at their worst. Each of our conversations lately had convinced me that the extra poundage I was putting on with my new birth control prescription was well worth the anguish.

Before leaving the kitchen, I grabbed a handful of tortilla chips from the bag on the counter and went back into the living room. The TV was off and the lights were back on and my mother was now sitting alone. She was bowed over her appointment book and she didn't look up when I entered the room, though I was munching on my chips quite loudly.

"Where's Teese?" I asked.

"Oh," Mom said, stretching, "She went up to bed. Glenn Close scared her off, I think."

"Remind me to write Ms. Close a fan letter tomorrow," I said.

"Lucy, don't be mean." Mom noticed that I was eating and said, "You should have gotten some yogurt instead. We need to use that up before it spoils."

"I think it's already expired. Besides, it's the fruit at the bottom kind. I hate that."

"There are bananas, too."

"Mom, have you seen them lately? They're all spotted like a leopard."

"They are? Well, that's funny. They were as green as limes when I got them at the store the other day."

"Now the bread's green."

Mom sighed. "We've just got to stop eating so much take-out. If only I had my kitchen. God, I miss my kitchen. I just can't do anything with that microwave."

"I don't know, Mom. Your meatloaf the other night was good."

"Really? I thought it was a little dry."

"The ketchup helped," I offered.

"If only I could get your father back here for one weekend. Just for one weekend so that he could put all the appliances where they should be."

"The only problem with that is, he'd finish working on that and then he'd notice something else that needed attention, like the upstairs bathroom. Or Aunt Teese would want the shelves lowered in her closet so she can reach them without standing on tiptoe. Pretty soon we'd all drive him off again. At least when he's working with the company, he's getting paid."

"I didn't ask him to redo the kitchen," Mom reminded me. "I just asked him to fix the dishwasher and then he decided all the appliances had to go. Silly me for asking." Mom yawned and closed her appointment book. "Anyway, when I close the deal on the Marple place and my commission comes through, I might just pay someone to come in and finish the job."

"You do realize that Dad would probably never speak to you again if you did that."

"I've still got you and Aunt Teese." She got up from the sofa then, stretched once more and said, "Well, I've about had it for tonight. I'm off to bed." She came over to me and kissed my forehead. When she was almost halfway down the hall to her room, she called back over her shoulder. "Lucy, you will shut off all the lights and lock all the doors before you go to bed, won't you?"

"Yes, ma'am," I said between partially gritted teeth. What I wanted to say was, "No, I'm going to leave all the lights burning, the doors wide open, and put a sign out front that says, 'Burglars welcome! We've got a house full of antiques and not a brain among us! Come in while we're still stupid!'"

I stretched out on the empty sofa, snuggling against the pillows, warmed from where Mom had been sitting. I was thinking about Janet and the baby poop smeared on her polished wood floor courtesy of Christina's diaper swabbing. I imagined Janet gagging as she wiped the mess up with a damp and soapy paper towel.

I wondered if Janet ever thought she was missing out on her youth, or that she had given up her best and most vital years to fuss and struggle with two little beings whose noses perpetually ran with green snot, who tore up her otherwise immaculate house and who most likely drove her a little more, day by day, to the brink. Twenty-one seemed too young an age to be saddled with all the responsibility of keeping kids from killing themselves and keeping floors doody-free.

I tuned the TV on. *I Love Lucy* was on. It was the episode in which a largely pregnant Lucy thinks that everyone has forgotten her birthday, so she joins up with a band of Salvation Army types who call themselves the Friends of the Friendless. At the end of the episode, Lucy learns that she has been mistaken and all along Ricky has been planning a huge party for her at the Tropicana. On the TV, Ricky was serenading his birthday girl with her theme song, looking at her with his loving, melty chocolate eyes. She looked so happy, I wondered if it really had been her birthday and that she had truly been surprised. People all around her were inundating her with wrapped gifts as they sang the chorus of the song in unison. After the last of the four trumpet blasts signaled the end of the song, I snapped off the TV and headed upstairs, shutting off the lights as I went.

Since my attempt at relating my afternoon dream to Janet had been aborted, I decided instead to confide the dream in my journal, which I was supposed to be keeping after every reading. I realized it would sound more than a little strange to Dr. Schindler, but it would at least be interesting reading for him. I could only imagine what the other brain-dead drones in the class were writing. "These people were on a boat. It was big. The big boat hit an iceberg. I think this is sad."

Once I had the dream down in words, it seemed even stranger to me than it had when I was in it. As I tried to go to sleep, I couldn't shake the feeling of that dream—the wonderment, the sense of awe, the silence of that evening back in time. A little whisper of curiosity still sounded in my head. My lucid thoughts turned perverse and I began to think that I really had been there and would be there again tonight when I slept. I was so anxious for the return, I had a hard time getting to sleep, but once I was in that state, I remembered nothing until the next morning when I awoke.

CHAPTER TWO

The next day was Tuesday, which, like Thursday, was a sleeping day for me. I had just two classes on Tuesdays and Thursdays and they were both late in the afternoon. I woke up around ten, craving my morning dose of Cocoa Crispies, coffee and a cigarette.

When I came downstairs, the den was filled with cigarette smoke. Aunt Teese was parked in front of the TV watching her hero, Perry Mason, badgering a nervous defendant to the point of suffocation. I took it that Mom wasn't home and I hoped that those weren't my cigarettes Aunt Teese was smoking.

I went into the kitchen and took down the cereal box from the top of the fridge. As I was getting the milk, I noticed Mom had left a note for me, telling me that she was at a meeting and that I should spend my time before class straightening up the house.

Since I had let half the morning get away from me as usual, I had to quickly itemize which chores were more important. It seemed that cleaning my room was the top priority of the day. Otherwise, when Mom came home, see would see that it hadn't been touched and she would start throwing out anything she deemed trash, which meant anything lying on the floor. I had lost bras, panties, homework papers and my entire collection of David Cassidy albums this way. As I sat munching on my cereal, I tried to think of what might be lost if I slacked off and worked on the kitchen instead. There was a green sweater lying over by the bedside table, my brown moccasins, a couple copies of *Vogue*, some shorts, a few pairs of socks, some jeans, an REM poster that had come unstuck from the wall . . . I knew that if I wasted much more time I wouldn't have a single item left to call my own. I quickly finished up my cereal and gulped down the rest of my coffee.

When we first moved into the house, my bedroom had been a small room adjacent to my parents' room. As I got older, my need for more privacy fortunately coincided with a time that my Dad was seeing great opportunities for renovation in the storage space upstairs. Back then what I wanted most in the world was a pink bedroom with frilly lace curtains, a canopied bed and a pink shag rug. I actually drew up the plans myself on a sheet of Hello Kitty stationery so that when my Dad found time between contracting jobs he would have all my specifications down on paper. In the spring before my thirteenth birthday that downtime came and by summer, I had the bedroom of my dreams. This was one of the very few household jobs my father ever saw to completion and it was still a source of great pride for him. At first I too was impressed with how well his craftsmanship matched the vision in my head.

As I stood at the threshold of my room this morning, I tried to remember that first day when I moved my things in and made that room mine. I had thought then that I was seeing the wonderland of all my little girl dreams brought to bright pink reality. Everything was pink, every inch of wall space, every yard of wainscoting, every plush fiber of the wall-to-wall shag carpeting. Even the furniture was pink, if just a shade lighter than the walls to save the room from total Pepto Bismol abomination. The only thing that fell short of my dream was the bed. Not canopied because of the short and slanty ceilings, it was just a plain double bed without a headboard, but it did have a gingham pink and white comforter and matching dust ruffle my mother had custom sewn in the sewing room my downstairs room had become when I moved up in the world.

My fascination with all things pink quickly faded. Soon I was a teenager, a typically sullen teen who would have preferred to see the walls coated in black rather than the pale rose color of my idealistic preteen years. I had actually approached Dad once about changing the color, not too drastically, but maybe just a hue so that it wouldn't be so damn . . . pink. But as with antiques, we would never see eye to eye on this issue. He compromised by allowing me to put up whatever posters I wanted, something that had been previously forbidden because the mounting tape would have ruined the paint job. Over the years I had amassed quite a collection of faces and places on my four walls—a virtual gallery of all my passing fancies. There were so many posters that the only evidence that the walls were ever pink showed through just above the nightstand where my poster of James Dean did not quite meet the top of my pink-shaded reading lamp.

As I bent down and began picking up some of the clothes just inside the door, I noticed that the carpeting had gotten coarse and matted like a sheep's wool. Shag carpeting, of course, had been the ubiquitous floor covering of the seventies. I thought of mine as being sort of a wall-to-wall time capsule. It was the hardest kind of carpeting to keep clean and nearly impossible to shampoo and dry when it did get dirty. Over the years it had begun to yellow, fuzz up and flatten. It was screaming to be replaced, but like so many things around the house, it would have to hold its tongue and be patient until Dad came home. The John Henry in Dad would not allow the steam engine of other commercial contractors to touch one splinter of the house while he was away.

After scooping all the dirty clothes into the hamper, the room was beginning to look halfway decent. It wasn't the picture of tidiness Mom had hoped I would maintain from the day I moved up there, but a little straighter anyway. Mom had often said that she could tolerate clutter but not outright mess. I think she acquired this mania for cleanliness through her work and had become so accustomed to cavernous, empty houses that she began to think that was how all houses should look. Sometimes I thought she would be happy if we all chucked our belongings out the window and ate and slept on the floors. This probably wouldn't have mattered much to my Dad, who always had his garage, or to Aunt Teese, who would be content with an outfit to change into for bingo games and an ashtray. As for me, I needed my things and in that way I was very much my father's child. My room, though awfully pink and immature, was the curator's storage space of my life. Most of my toys were still in my closet. Some of the clothes I had worn as a child were hanging in that same closet, clothes that I had worn for class pictures, for weddings, for holidays. Here I had a permanent connection to the person I had been. Here was a direct link to my inner child that people in this day and age are paying large amounts of money to connect with in psychiatry sessions.

Even in the simple exercise of picking up my clothes, there were already beads of sweat gathering on my forehead. It was going to be another unseasonably warm April day. Since I had seen Aunt Teese garbed in her quilted robe, I knew there wasn't a chance that the air conditioner would whirl that day. I flicked on the oscillating fan on my desk and went over to the window to let some air in. My room overlooked the backyard and from that window I had a perfect view of the garage, the shade tree and the deck chair.

The deck chair.

I began to think about the dream and what it possibly could have meant. Now, awake, I was still just as baffled as I had been when I walked past that clock on the staircase.

Right before I went to sleep in the chair, I had been reading about the Marconi shack. The captain had just ordered Phillips to send a distress call—a CQD. Bride tried to make light of the situation by suggesting Phillips use the new call—SOS, seeing as it might be his last chance to use it.

It made sense that I would have dreamed about the telegraphists since they were the last people I was thinking about before I went to sleep. But what about the prelude to the dream? That brief instance in which I seemed to have been hurtling towards the sun?

I tried to clear my head and concentrate on the other matters in my life. My room was finished and there were some other tasks I needed to check off before I went to class, including some homework I had left for the last minute. I would have to find some time to finish my assignments for Irish Folklore and Music Therapy. There wasn't a lot to do—just a chapter for the former and a quick listen to an audiotape for the latter. But it was such a pretty day. The newly minted spring grass was undulating in a breeze of warm air. The tall oak groaned a little as its boughs swayed heavily in the air against a bright blue sky. Another pretty day that I would miss, I thought dismally. But then, out of the gloom, came sudden brightness. I thought that if I combined both assignments I could be done in thirty minutes and still have time for a shower, some lunch and maybe a glance at the afternoon soaps before class. Even better, I could go outside and read, maybe get a head start on my summer tan. If Dad's erstwhile *Titanic* deck chair had transferred my thoughts to that great ship, maybe today I would be transported to Ireland where I would magically heal people's souls with the balm of music.

I quickly changed into a tank top and a pair of shorts. I came down the stairs with a hamper full of my dirty clothes, the towels from the upstairs bathroom and a week's worth of plates from midnight noshings. That made three things I could write off. The rest would have to wait. When I made it to the landing in the front hall I noticed that it was almost noon.

Aunt Teese was still in front of the TV with a cigarette in hand. As I walked past the living room, I heard her shout, "Bid a dollar! Bid a dollar! The other son of a bitch overbid on his showcase, you moron!"

I carried my hamper to the laundry room, which, in the days before my father's mad genius, used to be an easy task. Not anymore. After jettisoning the dirty plates into the sink, I dropped the hamper over the dishwasher into the laundry room and then hoisted myself up and over the appliance and hopped down onto the floor. I heard Mom musing lately that the three of us could possibly move the dishwasher if we all pushed at once, but move it where? Placed anywhere else it would just be blocking other things.

From the top shelf over the washer, I found the family sunscreen, still peppered with sand from our last beach trip back in September, and then I checked the dryer. That chair had not been very kind to my backside the day before and could have used some extra padding in addition to the blanket. Luckily, there were some dry towels in there and I grabbed the first one on top. Back in the kitchen, I found my Irish Folklore textbook and got out my cigarettes from my purse hanging on the back of one of the chairs there. I counted them carefully, having noted that Aunt Teese seemed to be smoking an inordinate number of cigarettes, even for her. All ten were there. She must have contacted one of her other sources. Then it was back over the dishwasher and out the back door.

I decided to pull the chair out a little more towards the center of the yard so I wouldn't be so much in the shade. With the breeze coming through I would need the sun to keep me warm. As I dragged the chair into the sunlight, I saw that a bird had left its brand on the headrest right over the star. *Oh, shit*, I thought. *Dad's going to rage if he sees that.* I scraped my thumbnail against the milky white excrement, scattering powdered residue down the slats on the back. It came right off, leaving just a hint of a dark stain where it had been. But there were so many other stains it was nearly indistinguishable when viewed as a whole. I fluffed out the beach towel and proceeded to sit down. Once my book was open, I flipped on my Walkman and cued to the tape to the day's assignment.

A calming, female voice came over the headphones and then the treacly sounds of the cassette series' bad synthesizer theme music. "Music Therapy. Music for therapeutic use, Volume 1, Number 1: Listening with our ears to keep our bodies in tune. Listen to the following musical selections and note your responses. In a minute, you will be asked to turn the tape off and record your thoughts in your listening journal."

As I began to smooth the lotion on my arm, I stared down at the text of the day's reading assignment. Today's folklore lesson was on the origin of the banshee, a mythical creature whose ghostly wail is said to be a portent of death in the family.

Irish Folklore had been a huge disappointment. For one thing, it was taught by the irascible Johnny Mumphrey, who, on the first day of class, actually greeted us with a hearty "Top of the mornin' to ya'!" Four weeks into the semester, he admitted that he had never been anywhere near Ireland and before he moved to Newport News, he had spent most of his time between

British Columbia, and Milwaukee, Wisconsin. Sometimes his [obli]que phrasing actually did hit the mark, but most of the time he [sou]nded as though he had seen *The Quiet Man* one too many times.

[I]rish Folklore would have won the semester sweepstakes for least [wo]rthwhile class if it weren't for the other bane of my existence, Music Therapy, which I had assumed would have something to do with helping people seek awareness through music, as the catalog stated. The assignments often touched on this facet, but the class lectures never even came close. For one thing the class was taught by a recent Bosnian émigré who had been in the United States two, maybe three minutes before he signed on to teach the class. Still bitter about the war that was tearing his country apart, he never dwelled much on the course curriculum because the soldiers took away all the music in his life. His only hope was to teach us "children of freedom" about what it's like to live in a country drained of it.

The reading that day went along perfectly with the music coming into my head: The mountain-bred tone of a dulcimer strumming out the strains of the old hymn, *Simple Gifts*. This was a song I remembered from childhood when my Mom and Dad were trying out different good influences on my life. During one of these misguided attempts at making me a well-rounded child, the three of us joined a Presbyterian congregation and I was immediately installed in the church's junior choir. I was just about seven and could barely read words, let alone music. But for most of my first grade year in elementary school, each Thursday after school was spent in the church basement under the tutelage of Maxwell Soames, a small-town director with Vienna Boys Choir aspirations. *Simple Gifts* was his favorite hymn and it didn't take us long to completely ruin it for him. Some of the older boys in the choir outfitted the song with the alternate lyrics "'Tis the gift to be simple/'Tis the gift to be free/'Tis the gift to live in a hollow tree." Unfortunately, those were the words that sort of stuck in our heads and they were the words that made it to the final performance, soliciting gales of laughter from even the staunchest blue hairs in the congregation.

As it turns out, Maxwell Soames' contempt for us little rascals cloaked a dark desire. He liked little boys a bit too much and was eventually brought up on charges of child molestation after one of the boys in the choir told his parents that Mr. Soames had followed him into the bathroom to watch him urinate. Barring legal action, he was forced to resign and then moved on. Unfortunately he didn't get to hear the choir scribes' next go at the song, a musical tribute to him that went, "'Tis the gift to be simple/'Tis the gift to be free/'Tis the gift to watch little boys go pee."

The woman's voice cheerfully bounced back into my head. "Now that you've gotten the basic tune down, see if you can pick it out of the following selection from Aaron Copland's *Appalachian Spring*."

I finished up the reading and dropped the book to the ground. The sun was beating down on me and I could feel my skin starting to tint. As the epic swirls of strings enclosed *Simple Gifts*, I closed my eyes, squeezing out the sunlight. Like a dummy, I had forgotten my sunglasses, so I would have to make do with an impromptu visor. I picked up the book and opened it onto my face. The pages smelled like my own pink room. Copland's piece was building to its conclusion. I saw nothing but darkness.

The music had drained away and was now replaced by the repetitive rapping of someone knocking insistently at a door. Now instead of being on my back, I was on my stomach, face down on a soft layer of quilted down. I lifted my head and stared around. A little light was coming through a window, illuminating a mirror and, in the dim light, what looked to be a vanity table. But it wasn't my mirror or my vanity. This wasn't even my room.

My head felt heavy as though full of stones. My eyes struggled to focus but were tired and reluctant to do anything but stay closed. Then the knocking came again, louder this time. And then there was a voice behind the door, slightly familiar, with a little anxiousness spiking its plaintive pitch.

"Miss Cranston? Miss Cranston?"

I was fully awake now, or at least conscious enough to realize I was on a bed. I pushed myself up and swung my feet over the side. Groping for a light switch, my hand slapped a lamp beside the bed. I switched it on and then padded across the floor, going towards the sound of the knocks.

When I opened the door, I squinted out into a white hallway. In front of me was a young man in a dark blue uniform. As my eyes adjusted to the new light, I began to recognize him.

"Good evening, Miss Cranston. I'm sorry to be calling on you so late, but I am just getting off my shift and I wasn't able to get in contact with you earlier today." He looked at me with a look of sheer puzzlement and when I took a look at myself, I was amazed as well. I was wearing a long, yellow evening gown with a studded bodice and deep neckline, not something people commonly wear to bed. "Miss Cranston, I'm sorry. Were you sleeping?"

I rubbed my eyes. "I must have been."

"The captain told me you were still awake."

"Who?"

"The captain, Miss Cranston. Captain Smith. You met him last night. Remember? In the Marconi station?"

I did remember that. But it seemed ages ago. "Oh, right."

He looked embarrassed. "Then this really is a terrible imposition."

"No, really. It's all right. You're fine, I'm fine. Everyone's fine," I said, trying to re-establish myself in these surroundings.

"I just wanted to come down and see if you were all right after what happened last night."

I had no idea what he was talking about at first. But then I started remembering something from the day before, something about walking down a hall with this man and hearing my mother's voice. I couldn't recall much after that.

"Can I ask you something?" I said.

"Of course."

"What did happen last night?"

"Well, I was escorting you to your room when you fainted. We were right near your door, you see, and you turned to me and told me that you thought you heard your mother calling you. And then you sort of tumbled to the ground. I tried to catch you, but you just went. Luckily the doctor was rounding the corner and the two of us were able to get you into your room. The doctor examined you, but he said there was nothing physically wrong with you and that you had just fallen into a deep sleep."

"How did you know that?"

There was a hint of a smile on his face. "Let's just say that you were making noises that people usually make when they're asleep."

I felt myself blushing. "Oh, God! Was I snoring?"

"Yes," he said.

"That is so embarrassing. I am so sorry you had to deal with that."

"No, no. Not at all."

I was astounded by the fact that there were two strange men in my room and I wasn't even aware of that. A doctor had examined me while I slept? I felt I needed some clarification on some points.

"You said that there was a doctor with you last night?"

"Yes, there was."

"Were you in here with him while he did the examination?"

"No. I stayed outside your cabin until he finished."

"How long was that?"

"About half an hour, I'd say."

"You mean you waited out here all that time?"

"I was concerned about you, is all. I've two sisters at home and if either one of them was alone on a ship at sea, I would hope that someone would see to it that they were taken care of properly."

"That's very considerate of you."

There was an awkward silence as though we were both trying to determine if we were finished with what we had to say. Finally, he said, "I'm sorry to have bothered you, Miss Cranston. I hope you have a good night." He put his thumb to the brim of his hat and turned away.

I watched him walk a great length down the hallway and as my eyes followed his steps, I was thinking to myself, "I can't let him go. Not just yet." It was as though he were the only person I knew in the whole world—or at least in this one—and I felt a need to keep him with me.

I wanted to call him back, but what was his name? Something ordinary, something there would be dozens of in a phone book. Jones, Johnson, Simpson, Wilson . . .

"Phillips!" I said.

He stopped in his tracks and slowly turned in my direction.

I met him halfway. "Look, I was thinking. Since you were nice enough to see me to my room last night, I'd like to return the favor if I could."

He nodded. "That would be lovely. Only I would make a suggestion for you, if I may."

"All right."

"Since we'll have to be out on the deck for a portion of the walk, perhaps you should put some shoes on."

I looked down at my stocking feet. "I guess I should."

"If you want to wear the ones from last evening, I put them next to your bed after I took them off your feet."

There was a touch of naughtiness in the way he said that. The thought of this strange man holding one of my bare feet sent an erotic charge all the way through me, though I had never considered myself to be a foot fetishist before. I didn't even like shoes very much.

Back in my cabin, I found a pair of yellow, low-heeled slippers right where he said they would be. They were not tossed haphazardly, but neatly arranged side by side with the toes pointing away from the bed. I went over to the vanity mirror and had a look at myself. My hair, which had been molded into a chignon, was falling down in little parachuting fly-aways. I knew I wouldn't have time, or know how to put it back the way it had been, so I felt around the back and untangled the pins from the mass of hair gathered there. I looked at the things that had been laid out for me: a mother of pearl hand mirror and matching hair brush, a perfume atomizer, an ornate brass pot of deep red rouge, two jeweled hair combs and a pair of white, opera-length gloves lying side by side. I picked up the brush and a little chill ran through me when I saw strands of my own blond hair intertwined with the bristles.

I was looking a little pale, so I ran my index finger across the top of the rouge and smoothed some across my lips. I remembered how unforgiving the night air had been to my exposed skin the night before. I looked around. There had to be a closet. There was a door that I assumed led to a bathroom. But when I opened the door, I immediately caught the scent of new fabrics. I felt for a light switch, flipped it on and stood back as the light revealed the contents within.

Inside were clothes, all carefully aligned, swaying just a little with the motion of the ship. There were dresses in all colors from sky blue to deep purple to ruby red. As I ran my hand across them, I felt the richness of their textures—all slippery satin, smooth taffeta and rough shantung. My fingers ran upon something soft and furry—a fox stole. I couldn't bear the look of the jeweled eyes on the poor, dead thing or its teeth clamped eternally on its own tail. Skipping past the carcass, I found a nice, sturdy blue coat that almost went to my feet and I quickly put it on.

I emerged from the cabin to find Phillips standing by the door. When he saw me, he took an audible breath. *God, I didn't think I looked that bad.*

"I had to take my hair down," I said. "It was bothering me."

"That's quite all right," he said. "You were taking such a long time in there, I was just worried that you had fallen asleep."

"Sorry. I have so many clothes. I don't know what I was thinking when I was packing." *Or if I packed them at all.* "Which way are we going?"

"We need to take the stairwell aft and go up to the open promenade on A deck and then onto the forward stairwell to the boat deck."

"Well, you lead the way, because I have no idea what you just said."

The stairwell was just slightly down the hall and when I first saw it I thought it was the same one we had descended the night before. But Phillips informed me that one had been the forward first class staircase. This was its nearly identical twin. It too was bilateral and the wood appeared freshly stained as though the painters were literally blowing it dry as the first passengers embarked. I ran my hands along the railing as we ascended and felt the smooth, unblemished craftsmanship glide beneath my fingers. At the top of the stairs there was a smaller, less elaborate clock, which read 11:35.

We emerged from a door off the stairwell into the night air. We were walking out onto a wide deck, open to the night air and I heard the rush of the waves far down below. We strolled to edge of the deck and I put my head out to let the wind whip my hair around. A little twinge of excitement burst in me like a firecracker when I looked down the side and saw the sheen of the ship's iron hull, nearly black in the moonlight. Further down, the ocean was churning. The air brimmed with sea salt and accomplishment.

Phillips got out a small, silver case from his pocket. I remembered that case from the night before. He had extracted it from his coat before he put it on my shoulders. From the case now he selected a cigarette.

"Do you mind?" he asked.

"Not at all. As a matter of fact, if you've got an extra one on you, I'll take it."

He suggested that we go have a seat on one of the benches. From the bench he had chosen for us, we had a perfect view of one of the giant funnels that topped the ship. The stack stood tall as a high-rise against the star-filled sky, miring the heavens with puffs of thick, black smoke from down below. Looking at it made me shocked all over again that I was really there. I tilted my head to view the very top of the stack and thought it looked a lot like a fat cigar going to waste in someone's inattentive hand. We sat in silence for a few minutes as we smoked and looked up at the stars.

"Since you put me to bed last night," I said, taking a long pull on my cigarette, "why don't you call me Lucy instead of Miss Cranston."

"All right, Lucy."

"And since I feel like I'm calling a dog when I say Phillips, is there something else I can call you?"

"You can call me Jack, as everyone who knows me does, or you can call me Sparks as the officers of the ship do."

"Sparks. Is that short for anything?"

"No. It's just a general name used to identify a telegraphist. It applies to either me or Bride, my assistant. Most of the officers can't tell us apart, anyway. But that's what I've come to expect from these larger liners."

There was just the slightest hint of disappointment in his voice as though he took the officers' inability to tell the difference between him and his assistant to be a personal affront. There was loneliness in his voice, as though the behemoth that was this ship often made him feel a stranger to everyone he met and more than a little lost.

"Bride, who you met last night, is good company, though," he continued. "Awfully young and a bit of a chatterbox. He can say the most amusing things sometimes. Reminds me of me when I first started out. We've both served on the *Lusitania*, though not at the same time . . ."

I was thinking when he said that, "Oh, the poor *Lusitania*" and then my mind was engulfed in blackness as though someone had kicked over a bottle of ink onto my brain. A minute later he was still talking and I was trying desperately to recall my former train of thought.

"Have you been on any of those ships, Lucy?" He was asking me.

"I'm sorry, what?"

"I was telling you about the other ships I've served on. Have you traveled on any of them?"

"No. I don't think I've ever sailed before." I was noticing how beautiful the sky was, pitch black and ablaze with a billion stars.

"Never?"

"I don't think so."

"I find it hard to believe that a girl who lives by such a busy seaport as Norfolk, Virginia, has never sailed."

"How did you know I lived near Norfolk?"

"I read the manifest. It said Miss Lucy Cranston, Newport News, Virginia. And I know Newport News is near Norfolk. But that's really all I know about you. That and you're a rather deep sleeper."

I wondered if that really *was* all he knew about me.

"I suppose you have family there," he continued.

"Yes, I do," I said, automatically and without thinking.

"Does your father work in the shipyards there?"

"My father?" I asked. For a moment, my heart was stilled in my chest as the realization hit me: I couldn't remember my father. Not a single detail about him came to mind. I knew I had a father and a mother too. But who were they?

I closed my eyes and let my mind go blank. A picture began developing in my head.

I saw a kitchen, all done up in avocado green wallpaper and burnt orange cabinetry. Right before me was a sun-freckled face, broad and large, with blue eyes that looked the size of dinner plates. It was my mother's face. The air was hot—summertime on the coast. I felt my legs sticking to the vinyl of the chair I was sitting in as I swung them in protest over the peas and carrots being forced into my mouth. There was a loud noise, the thwack of a door coming open and slamming shut. The plate jumped in my mother's hands. Peas fell to the floor like unstrung pearls. A booming voice came into the room before the person entered.

"Eve!" the voice shouted, "We've got to change Lucy's name!"

"What on earth for?" my mother said as she bent over to pick up the peas, one by one. I watched her from my high chair as she rescued each pea between her thumb and forefinger.

"That Johnson bastard who started all this mess has a daughter named Luci, spelled with an I at the end, and I don't want anything in common with that asshole!"

Mom put a finger to her lips. "Dan! The baby!" she whispered sharply.

"I'm sorry, Eve. You know how that lying son of a bitch ticked me off. If elected, he would not serve. First we sent advisers, then soldiers, and then people we went to high school with. You remember Roger McPease?"

"The captain of the football team?"

"He stepped into a booby trap in one of the jungles over there and got blown to bits. His body's being shipped home tomorrow. His mother called me at the jobsite. She was looking for someone to speak at his funeral. It seems all his buddies are either serving in Vietnam or dead too."

There were hands underneath my arms, strong hands that lifted me from my seat. I smelled him first—sweat, aftershave, his lunch of tuna salad, heavy on the onions. And then I saw him. Yes, there he was. The sandy hair, the sun-baked complexion, the blue eyes rimmed in red, the slight scar on his chin, a remnant of a childhood with too little parental supervision and too many sharp corners in the house.

"You don't want to share a name with someone whose father would send good people to die young, do you Lucy? Do you? Lucy? Lucy?"

"Lucy?" someone was saying. This was my companion, probably wondering why he had suddenly been shut out. "Is something the matter?"

"I was just thinking about my father," I said. "I live with my father. And my mother." I was electrified with this sudden clarity I was experiencing. "Yes! I live with my father and my mother!"

"I suppose most young girls do."

"And there's a third one. Teese! Yes, my Aunt Teese!"

"Any brothers or sisters?"

"No, there's just me. Only me." I didn't know what had happened, but I suddenly had memories, I had a past. I knew who I was. This was exciting to me and I wanted to share who I was with this man and I wanted to know about him too. "What about you, Jack? You have anyone to go home to?"

"My parents and my sisters. My father manages a drapery shop in Godalming. That's in Surrey. I think I mentioned I have two sisters, Ethel and Elsie. They're twins. They were practically grown by the time I came along."

"When's the last time you saw them?"

"During Christmas furlough. It was great fun seeing everyone again. Not too much fun that I would ever want to stay there till old age, but just enough."

"Is that why you became a wireless operator? To get away from home?"

"No, I love my home and my family. But from an early age I can remember having a longing to see other places. And I was sort of interested in gadgets as well. Something with a bit of noise, my Mum would say. I was never much for schooling. Went about as far as grammar school in Godlaming." He gave a little laugh as he considered the lit end of his cigarette. "I think my father worried that I was setting out to be a dullard. He got a private tutor for me while I was in training at the post office as a telegraphist. Mr. Madeville. Saw him at Christmas too. I think my parents had envisioned something apart from what I'm doing now. Early on my Mum sort of hoped I would be a singer, I think. I was a chorister at the church back home."

"Chorister. Like a singer? In a choir?"

"That's what I mean."

I was charmed by the image of him, years younger, all decked out in a red choir robe and white smock, wrapping his rounded mouth around choruses of alleluias and glory be's.

"I used to do that too. For a little while," I said.

"I think every child has to be subjected to that humiliation at some point in their lives. Mine was mercifully short-lived. My voice changed at age twelve and sort of put an end to my mother's hopes of my being the next Caruso."

"But you like what you're doing now?"

"Absolutely. After all this time, it still amazes me that I can sit all alone in a room while in my ear and at my finger there's the entire world. Voices from hundreds of miles away, some people I've met, some people I've never seen or will see, but we're all somehow coming together. I'll admit it does get a bit repetitive after a bit. Sometimes it's the same old thing over and over again, a lot of 'wish you were here's' and 'best of luck's.'"

"And what do you do when you're not on duty? Socialize with the other officers?"

"No. I may be the senior wireless operator, but that means little to any of the men on the bridge. I'm not an officer on the ship. I've been hired out by the Marconi Company to work here for the duration."

"So you don't even eat with them?"

"No. There's a saloon down on C Deck where I take my meals with the men in the mail room."

"Saloon?" The name conjured up images of rough men in cowboy hats drinking mugs of foamy beer and women in fishnet stockings and tight corsets laughing loudly while wild piano music played.

"Perhaps not the sort of saloon you've heard tell of," he said, no doubt after witnessing my confusion.

"Oh, so I guess you try and refrain from smacking each other over the head with bar stools and random gun fighting."

"Whenever possible," he said with a smile. "Have you ever been out to the wild West?"

"Texas. Which I guess is kind of Southwest."

"And what's Texas like?"

"Big, hot, flat. We didn't see a whole lot of it. My family was there to visit some cousins of mine in Corpus Christi. I was very young. I couldn't have been more than five or six. All I really remember is being trapped in a car with my parents and Aunt Teese smoking cigarette after cigarette. And I found out that I was related to someone named Dwayne."

This made him laugh for some reason. "Dwayne," he said.

We sat in silence for a while. I noticed that he was sitting closer to me than before. I noticed too that when we were talking, he seemed to be taking in every word as though trying to assemble the pieces of a jigsaw puzzle of a busy Seurat painting. Every time he thought that I wasn't looking at him, his eyes were on me, emitting a sort of soft, growing glow of affection. But when my eyes met his, that look would go away, as though inwardly he were thinking, "Can't let her see that just yet. It's too early." I wondered too if he saw that same look in my eyes. I was beginning to like this man who whiled away his hours on this ship in a tiny room talking to the entire world.

"It seems that what you do would be very lonely work."

"It can be," he said. "But you get over that soon enough. If you didn't, you couldn't manage it. Mostly, I'm far too busy to be lonely. When you've been an operator as long as I have, you begin to recognize other operators just by the way they send their signals. So a lot of times I find myself speaking to operators I know. Sometimes it's almost as though they're in the room with me, even though they may be hundreds of miles away."

"But you're really not in the same room with them."

"No. But it does *seem* that way."

"But there's really no substitute for human contact, is there?"

"No, there's not. Man has perfected sending messages from great distances, but you can't send the touch of a human hand across the miles."

He uses International Morse. I know International Morse. Somehow.

"Give me your hand," I said.

"Why?" He was giving me a sheepish look as he tapped out the remains of his cigarette on the armrest of the bench.

"Just do it," I said, tossing my own cigarette over the railing of the deck.

Warily, he put his hand on mine. I began tapping out a series of dots and dashes on his palm. His features pulled together in concentration and then finally he smiled when he realized what I was attempting.

"Hello yourself," he said.

"Let me try this."

- .... --.-.--. -----..-..---.....--...--..-...
-...-....--...-.

Which I hoped translated as "Thank for you helping me last night."

It must have been a fair attempt because he tapped back, "My pleasure."

"Was that all right?" I asked.

"Yes. You're quite good. Where did you learn International Morse?"

"I don't know. It just came to me." I looked down and saw that he was still holding my hand. "You can let go now if you like. Demonstration's over."

He looked a little embarrassed. "Oh, right. Sorry."

I knew that I really shouldn't have said anything about the lingering handholding. It was cold and his hand actually felt nice wrapped around mine.

"You find out a lot about human nature through the messages people send, or at least about the sort of passengers traveling on the ship," he said. "There's one couple on board who've arranged to have their private train meet them in New York when they arrive."

"New York? We're going to New York? As in, New York City?" I asked.

"Yes, of course. Where did you think we were going?"

"I didn't know. I've never been to New York before. Are you're sure we're going to New York?"

"That's the plan."

"Holy shit!" I said, leaping up from the bench, infused with such energy I didn't know what to do except jump up and down like a mad woman. "New York City!"

"You didn't know the ship was going to New York?"

"Not until now. I'm so excited! I am so excited!" I said, clapping my hands. I sat back down breathlessly on the bench next to Jack, still giggly about seeing the Statue of Liberty in person—her strong face, her sandled feet, her lamp lifted beside the golden door.

"So you just hopped on a ship, having no idea where it was going?" he asked.

"I think that's what I did," I said. Still, all I could think of was New York, all sprawl and traffic, all noise and frenzy.

"Well, I think that's brilliant," he said.

"Yeah? Why is that so brilliant?"

"Just shows that you are a very brave girl," he said. "May I ask what you were doing abroad?"

Of course he had every right to ask me *this* question in the interest of making conversation. I had absolutely no idea how to answer. As I sat there, wondering what I could possibly tell him aside from the idiot's reply of "I don't know," I thought, why not just make something up? I could tell him I was on vacation from school, which was probably the truth anyway.

"I was on . . ." And it occurred to me that I should use a different word for vacation so that he could understand. "I was on holiday."

"Oh, really? Where did you go?"

Another tough one. "All over."

"Well, you must have been in England at some point, since you embarked at Southampton."

I did?

"Where else, then? Scotland? Wales? Ireland?"

"Yes! The last one!"

"Ireland?"

"Yes, that's it! Ireland!" I seemed to recall something about Ireland.

"I was in Ireland for two years, working at the Marconi station in Clifden. Did you make it up there?"

There was a name coming to me, Murphy or Mummy. "Mumphrey!" I said.

He looked confused. "Mumphrey? Where's that?"

I tried again. "Banshee?"

"Never heard of that, either. There's the wail of the banshee, the banshee being a creature whose call is supposed to—"

"Portend death! I learned that . . . somewhere." The wheels of my mind were spinning. I could hear the turn of each cog. "In Irish Folklore. That's a class I'm taking with . . ." and then the name I had been trying to think of materialized, "Johnny Mumphrey!"

"Oh, so you're a student, then. At university?"

"Not really. It's a community college."

"Community college," he said carefully, as though this were the first time he had ever put the words "community" and "college" together. "So, what are you going to do, Lucy? After community college?"

"I'm hoping to go to Old Dominion University," I told him.

"And after that?" he asked.

I shrugged. "I haven't figured that out yet."

"Perhaps you could teach."

"Oh, Jack, I have spent too many hours in the classroom as a student to even think about spending more time in one, even if I'm being paid to be there."

"You could be a nurse," he suggested.

"If I could stand the sight of blood, that would be fine." But then I thought of the hinted sexism in his vocational proposal. "Why not a doctor?"

"Well—"

"Why couldn't I be a doctor?"

"I'm sure you could—"

"A woman can do anything a man can do."

"Well, maybe not *everything*, but—"

"But why did you automatically think nurse?"

"What does it matter, anyway? You can't stand the sight of blood. Both nurses and doctors encounter blood and one time or another."

"I suppose you're right," I said, dismounting delicately from the high horse I was on. I slumped against the back of the bench. My companion was showing just a little too much victory in his grin. "Maybe one day I could work for Marconi Marine."

"First woman Marconi operator," he said laughing.

"Hey, why not?" I said.

"There will be a man on the moon before that happens."

Just then I saw a flash.

A blurry, black and white moving image developed in my mind.

A man in a puffy white suit stepped down a ladder. Over his face he wore a shield of glass. He looked like an albino ladybug descending from that ladder. There were two men in these white suits stepping around on a powdery surface—like a beach after nightfall. They staked the American flag into the surface of this shadowy world. A man with slicked-back, thinning hair took off his black-rimmed glasses. "Whew, boy!" he said.

"One small step for man, one giant leap for mankind," I heard myself mutter.

"What did you say?"

And then I couldn't recall what I *had* said. "Hmmm?"

"Something about a man, a step and a leap."

"I was remembering. Something. I don't know what it was." I looked up again at the smoke stack. "But you know, if man can build something this huge that can float on water, then why can't a man walk on the moon?"

"Or a woman," he said with a smile.

I smiled back at him. "Or a woman."

"You perhaps."

"No, not me," remembering the claustrophobia of the family Corpus Christi excursion. "I hate long trips."

We both decided it was too cold to sit out in the open air. It seemed very late, but I was not tired. I noticed Jack was looking sleepy and I felt slightly guilty keeping him up. However, when we reached the Marconi room, he said he'd feel better if he escorted me back to my cabin.

We veered off the deck and ducked into a door and there we were at the foot of the top of the staircase we had taken the night before. Seeing it again was like finding a finally recognizable landmark after being lost for many miles on a highway. I looked at the clock and saw that it was 1:30. There was such a tremendous silence all around that it seemed we were surrounded by sleeping souls.

By the time we got to the first landing, he told me that if we continued on down, we would reach the hallway that led to my room. Under the lights, I saw the fatigue in Jack's eyes and realized that the evening would have to come to an end soon or else *he* would be the one collapsing.

By the time we reached my floor, I realized I was beginning to recognize my surroundings and counted the doors down as we walked. B87, B89, B91, and my cabin, B93.

Standing at the door, we said our goodnights, but before I entered my room, Jack had something to say to me. His expression had turned very serious, his broad brow bearing down hard on his almond-shaped eyes.

"Lucy, usually on these crossings young women like yourself often find themselves with a self-appointed guardian, someone, usually a fellow passenger, who volunteers to see that they are looked after. But I don't see that you have such a person."

"Not that I know of," I said, my heart suddenly taking off in a sprint.

"Well," he said, biting into his bottom lip with a jagged incisor as he contemplated what he was going to say next. "Obviously I can't be with you at all times, since I am here to work. If Marconi paid us to escort lovely young ladies about, there wouldn't be a man left working on land. But I would like to let you know that should you need anything during the next three or fours days, I'll try to see what I can do to help you."

I smiled, overwhelmed by the sweetness of this gesture. "That's very kind of you," I said.

"Obviously, I won't be able to dine with you, or pay a call on you with any sort of regularity. But since you seem to be keeping odd hours, almost as mad as mine, perhaps when I'm finished with my work tomorrow night, we can talk again."

"I'd like that."

"I'm not certain when I'll finish," he said. "It could be as late as midnight."

"I'll wait up."

As I made this promise to him, I felt funny in my head, a little dizzy and very warm. A precocious jolt of electricity—a spark—was buzzing though me like a clumsy bumblebee knocking around my insides. I could feel something was happening in him too. His expression gleaned from the suggestion of our meeting-to-be was alive with excitement. We stood together, static from the rapture of a little joy being passed silently between us and we both seemed to be saying to ourselves, "Tomorrow will be better. Tomorrow there will be more time and we will know more about each other than we did before."

"I'll try not to make it too late, all right?"

"All right," I said. "I look forward to seeing you again."

He smiled. "Me too."

Impulsively, I reached to touch his hand. His fingers, stilled chilled by the night air, went around mine. I wasn't sure if this was meant to be a handshake or a last ditch effort to hold onto to the evening. Then I felt the drumming of his index finger against my palm. "Goodnight, Lucy," he tapped out.

I returned the reply on not on his palm, but on his pale left cheek and not with my finger but with my lips. "Good night, Jack," I said in a whisper against his skin.

He stood there holding my hand for the longest time, stunned and still. I wondered if this were really an end or the beginning of something else. I thought about asking him in, but something told me he would have said no.

"I'll send word by the purser about tomorrow night," he promised as his hand finally left mine. "Good night."

As I turned to put my key in the door, my head was seized by a tidal wave of dizziness. There was that voice again, calling from inside my head, sharp in its demands for an answer. *Lucy . . . Lucy . . .* The air around me stiffened and I felt myself blacking out.

"Jack!" I managed to say. "It's happening again!"

Through a heavy veil of gray, I saw the terrified expression on Jack's face. "Lucy! Oh, God, Lucy!"

My knees buckled under me and I tumbled to the ground.

"Lucy Cranston!" Mom was saying.

Light gushed into my squinting eyes. I could just barely discern her figure standing over me. As my vision improved, I could see that she was holding a book and I thought at first that she was about to hit me with it. But then I realized it was my Irish Folklore book, which I had been using to block out the sun.

"My God, Lucy! Didn't you hear me?" she asked.

My heart was pounding so hard that I thought it would rupture. I pulled the headphones off my ears and squinted at her. "Yeah, I heard you."

"What were you doing?"

"Reading. Listening to music. Getting ready for class." *Class! Oh, God, class!* I sprang up from the chair. "What time is it?"

"A little after one thirty."

Just like it had been in the dream . . .

I swung my legs over the side of the deck chair and trudged off towards the house, "Crap, I'm going to be late."

Mom was following me close behind. "Did you finish your chores this afternoon?"

"Yeah. Well, most of them," I said, continuing to walk.

"Which ones did you not finish?"

"The ones I didn't have time for. I had assignments to do before class."

"Is that what you were doing? Homework? Because it certainly looked to me like you were sleeping."

"Mom, can we talk later? I've got class and I haven't even showered yet." Normally I wouldn't have been so maniacal about getting to class, but if there was one thing my Music Therapy instructor was a stickler for, aside from giving us a daily rundown of the miseries of his homeland, it was attendance. We were quizzed each class on the material on the tapes and were allowed to miss only three quizzes before he started deducting points from our grades. I couldn't afford to get any further in the red. My average at mid-term was a 78. Anything below that would be non-transferable.

Mom was close on my tail. "Lucy, I think we need to talk," she said in her best, scary mother tone.

"Look, if it's about the house-cleaning, I'll get to it later. I really have to get going."

"Lucy, your father and I don't ask a lot of you. We know you're trying to finish up your courses at PCC so that you can transfer to ODU in the fall," she said, two steps behind me. "We don't ask you to work so that you can concentrate on your studies. All we ask is that you occasionally do us little favors, like helping to keep the house clean, taking Aunt Teese on errands . . ."

"I'm sorry," I said, as I reached for the back door, "I thought I would have time to finish up later. But I fell asleep. I was reading, it was warm and I got tired."

"Well, I can certainly understand why you're tired. Honestly, I don't know how you get by on fourteen hours of sleep a night."

I rolled my eyes and proceeded to the back stoop. Mom was still behind me. When we got to the dishwasher, I hopped up and hoisted myself over. Mom was in a skirt, too tight for her to play follow the leader.

As I was making my way through the kitchen, I heard her call my name in near desperation.

"Will you please stop for a minute and listen to me? Please?"

I decided to do as she asked before she got ideas about running around to the front door and ambushing me in the shower. As I turned my head, I saw something out of the corner of my eye, something that had escaped my notice before. Around the window over the sink, there was a small tuft of insulation sticking out like a pink cloud and right behind it was a minuscule patch of green wallpaper. It was a peculiar shade of avocado, the color scheme that had existed when we moved in all those years ago and remained in tact for much of my childhood. My thoughts returned to the dream I had just had. That episode I recalled about being fed peas in the old kitchen . . . that was a new memory for me. All at once I was immersed in the recollection of the kitchen as it was when I was a child, complete with the leaky faucet that literally poured buckets of water every day and the ancient Norge refrigerator that had been on its last legs during the Truman administration. And that avacado green wallpaper that made everybody appear seasick under the fluorescent ceiling light. Mom was talking to me, but I was not looking at her. My eyes were on the wallpaper and soon my fingers were on it too, defining its texture under a shellac of aged grime and grease.

Suddenly I was snapped back into reality when Mom's voice thundered into my head.

"You haven't heard a word I've said, have you?" she said.

"Yes, I have," I said vaguely, as I turned to face her again. Honestly, all I had heard were a lot of "do's, do's, do's" and "why, why, why's," but at least I knew the gist of that she was saying. It was the same old thing she always said whenever she feared her authority was being questioned. I decided to steer the conversation in a different direction.

"Mom, do you remember a time when Dad wanted to change my name?"

Mom's shoulders sagged. "What has that got to do with anything?"

"Not much, really. But I'm just curious. Was there ever a time when he wanted to change my name?"

She looked at me, completely baffled. At length, she said, "We discussed using Astral Weeks as your middle name, but then your Dad decided that he didn't like Van Morrison that much."

"But when Dad's friend, Roger McPease, died in Vietnam, did he ever want to change my name?"

"Why would he want to change your name because of that?"

"Because of Lyndon Johnson's daughter or something."

"Lyndon Johnson's daughter? Wha—?" and then her mouth flew open in sudden recognition. "Oh, Luci Baines. Yes, that does ring a bell."

"Do you remember anything else about that day? The day Dad found out about Roger McPease."

"Lucy, what are you getting at?"

"Just stay with me, Mom. What else do you remember about that day?"

Mom squinted and gave a short sigh. "Well, I think it was the middle of June. It was a very hot day."

"Do you remember what you were doing?"

"Well, it seems it was the middle of the afternoon when your father came in and told me. So I guess I was feeding you."

"Peas and carrots?" I asked.

Mom looked at me strangely, as though she were trying to figure out where all this was coming from. "It's kind of hard for me to remember exact menu items from twenty years ago, but I suppose I could have been feeding you peas and carrots. That's about all you would eat back then." She paused and said, "Have you been talking to your father?"

"No. There was something about this patch of wallpaper that reminded me of that afternoon."

"How could you remember that day? You were only about a year old."

"Yeah, I know. But when I was out in the deck chair, I was having a dream and in that dream, that memory surfaced for some reason."

I wanted to tell her more. I liked to think that I could confide in my mother about anything. But these dreams, I thought, would exceed the limits of even a mother's unbiased understanding. Concurrent with this doubt ran a slight hope that perhaps she would see where I was coming from, as her LSD salad days probably offered up many hallucinations that bore some resemblance to these dreams. Perhaps she did have some inkling of what I had been experiencing because her next question had a slightly psychic bent.

"Lucy, I don't want to ask you this, but I feel that I have to. I'm not even sure that I want to know the answer. But I do want you to be honest with me."

"All right."

She closed her eyes and sighed. "Lucy, are you stoned?"

"Stoned? What? Stoned? Mom, I don't get high!"

"Lucy, I know that your father and I weren't the best examples for you to follow when you were growing up and we did more than our share of illegal substances. But drugs were different back then. They're more dangerous now, much deadlier than they were in the sixties."

"Oh, right, Mom, like people didn't die from drugs in the sixties. Come on, Mom. I've read *Go Ask Alice*. I'm not going down that rabbit hole."

"I have more than ample proof that you're getting wasted on something. I know you've been sneaking beers at night because I've seen the evidence piled high in your wastepaper basket. Is that all you've been doing up in your room late at night?"

"OK, Mom, I may have two or three beers while I watch TV in my room, but that's all. I haven't smoked a joint since I was sixteen," I said, wondering how I had ended up in an After School TV special.

Mom drew in a surprised breath. "Who gave you pot when you were sixteen?"

I threw my arms up in the air. "Dad. Who else?" Then I turned and continued on through the house, leaving Mom screeching like a blue jay.

I made it to class on time, my hair still damp from the shower I took to wash off the smell of coconut. I sat there and squirmed in my desk, only taking my eyes off the clock to look down at the answers on the quiz sheet and to occasionally smirk at one of the instructor's mispronunciations. Watching him flit nervously between the lectern and the enormous English dictionary he kept open on his desk at all times was usually enough to keep me amused, but that day I had other things on my mind. The most recent dream left a lingering effect on me like a hot bath and I sat there, deeply engrossed in all the sensations I had felt while in it. The images I tried to bury kept popping up in my brain. My notebook was open to a blank page and it stayed blank, except for the margins. While lost in the memories of what had taken place in the dream, I doodled a series of words there. "A" deck, sea air, his lips, and Jack . . . Jack . . .

I was daydreaming—daydreaming about a dream. Not really trying to analyze it because it had been very clear. Rather, I was trying to assemble some reasoning behind how I could have picked up so easily where the dream the day before had left off. Somehow I was able to just cruise right back into it as though it had been waiting for me to wake up on the other side of consciousness.

Clearly I had been thinking about Jack the day before as I drifted off to sleep. I had just read about him and had begun to form some thought about who he was and what his position was on the ship. But how had I made the connection this afternoon, when the last thing on my mind before I dozed off was "Appalachian Spring?"

Think, Lucy . . . think lucidly.

There was no fear. I felt so wholly protected as though walking in a glass bubble down the corridors of that beautiful ship, that beautiful, doomed ship, never thinking, "This will all soon be nothing more than a giant scrap heap at the bottom of the ocean." It was as though that bit of significant information was being squirreled away in some secret compartment in my head, off limits to any reasoning. The ship's very name had become synonymous with all things disastrous. But somehow when I said it there and when I heard Jack say it, the name sounded majestic and proud. The adverse connotation was not there, as though the sinking had yet to happen.

It hadn't happened yet.

It must have been April 11 there as it is today. But an April 11 many years ago.

A perverse thought about the whole thing that had tried to enter my mind since the first dream came to full fruition.

What if I really had been there?

I smiled thinking about it, but my emotions were tempered by a self-aware concern. It seemed that my doubts about the concept were beginning to be outnumbered by sincere belief.

My God, what if I really had been somehow thrust back in time? What if that deck chair is sending me back through time?

The idea was just too off the wall, too insane to even admit. I was feeling a deep shame for myself, being twenty-one years old, and voluntarily giving credence to something so bizarre, so entirely fantastic.

I hoped that reason would kick in at some point while I was thinking all this over. I told myself, *You can't think these things, Lucy. You just can't. You're dreaming and that's all. So stop trying to reconcile what happened.*

And even as I told myself that, there was another small voice, hunkering in the corner of my mind, cheering on the collapse of all rationale.

But I told Jack I would see him again.

And why did I even say that to him? There was no assurance that I would be able to make my way back to him tomorrow or any other day. If I didn't come, he would be disappointed, or maybe even try to find me.

While I was thinking this, I had my pen in hand. I had drawn a heart around Jack's name. When I saw it, I almost gasped.

I felt a little twinge, a splinter of a lightning strike that touched off a series of quivers all over me. This quick jolt of corporal seismic activity told me one thing: I had a crush.

That was why I had been dreaming about him. I had a crush on him. That was nothing new. I had developed crushes on literary heroes before. Heathcliff, Rhett Butler and Jay Gatsby, just to name a few. These crushes were always quick and quiet, never lasting longer than the duration of time it took to read the books that contained them. It had taken me five weeks to read *Gone With the Wind* and for half a summer I had drooled over Rhett Butler. I would have moved to Charleston if someone had told me that Rhett Butler was alive and well and had forgotten all about Scarlett. And though thoughts of him occupied a large portion of my waking hours, I never remembered dreaming about him. Not like this, anyway. I never remembered feeling guilty that I couldn't make it to Charleston to visit him.

Oh, God! Why do I even care? These dreams aren't reality. They're just little plays my mind is putting on to entertain me while I sleep.

And then, from a small corner, a new, stronger voice was emerging from the crowd.

But what If . . . what if?

Suddenly I heard my name from the front of the class. The instructor was calling on me.

My teacher was standing there at the podium, the sleeves of his blue chambray button down pushed up to his elbows, dark rings of perspiration dipping almost down to his waist. He was looking at me, along with everyone else, and I felt as though while I was daydreaming I had been placed on a petrie dish.

"Miss Cranston," the instructor was saying, "Your thoughts, please, on Aaron Copland's *Appalachian Spring?*"

I cleared my throat. "*Appalachian Spring?*"

"Yes. That was the . . . the . . . piss we were putting our minds together in thought to . . . speak about today. How did it make you feel?"

There was a small ripple of laughter at his use of the word "piss" for "piece" and I was glad of that. It took some of the scrutiny off me and the words I had crammed into my margins.

I put the nub of my pen to the paper and began sketching another heart.

"I felt like I had been transferred to the past," I said.

The class ended and as I was filing out with the other students on my way toward the adjoining building for Irish Folklore with Johnny Mumphrey,

I stopped. I couldn't let myself walk any further with them. I stood there, watching them take their purposeful strides, the swarm of them parting around me as though I were an abruptly formed pillar. I couldn't see myself walking with them anymore. I knew that if I couldn't make it through one class without debating myself to distraction, I couldn't go another hour without thinking self-commitment to a psychiatric ward might be a good vacation plan. There was something I had to do. I needed some confirmation either for or against what I was thinking to be true.

I had to find out about that deck chair. The only person who would know would be the person who sold it to my father. Johnny Mumphrey would have to count me absent that day. I went to the nearest exit, plunged through the heavy fire door and headed for the parking lot, flea market bound.

CHAPTER THREE

On all our Saturday antique hunts, my father and I always ended up at Mr. Baumgarten's, located only ten blocks down from our house on Warwick Boulevard. The building itself had become a relic of sorts, the last remnant of a once thriving area that had given way to urban sprawl and decay. When my father and I started going there in the early seventies, there had been a donut shop on one side and a candy store on the other, so I always had something to occupy my time if Dad's searches went a bit long. Now the two-story building with its maroon and green striped awning and pumice stone facade found itself between a pool hall and a vacated convenience store.

Overhead a weather-beaten sign swung like an empty trapeze. I looked up to read it, though it was hardly necessary. It was the only sign of its kind on the block situated over the only store of its kind in all of Hampton Roads: Baumgarten's Flea Market, est. 19—

The last two digits in the date had been rubbed off with exposure to the elements, but I thought at one time the sign had read 1942 or 1952, but I couldn't really be sure. It wouldn't have surprised me if the date had been much earlier, like 1912.

The name flea market was a misnomer. To people like my father, Baumgarten's was the antique world's answer to Tiffany's, a vast warehouse of every possible item that one could ever imagine. I always thought of it as being sort of a rescue mission for people's discarded attic clutter, a continuous yard sale open daily from 10:00 a.m. to 5:00 p.m., except for Sundays and holy days. The store was immaculately kept, neatly organized and cleaned to a spit shine, reflecting the naval heritage of its owner and proprietor, Augustus Baumgarten, who had once sailed with the British navy. My father had told me once that Mr. B, as Dad referred to him, had come to Newport News in the 1940s to live with his sister, Edith Tinsley, a widowed war bride from World War II who lived in one of the elegant homes in the ritzy section of Hampton Roads called Hilton Beach. Mrs. Tinsley was one of those women who had her name engraved on brass plaques on park benches, hospital suites and church windows all over town. Her husband's family had owned the flea market originally and she took it over after his death. When she died, she left the shop to Mr. Baumgarten, who had been operating it for most of the latter part of the decade.

I went inside that day and instantly felt as though the last thirteen years of my life had vanished the minute I was in the door. I half expected to hear my father's voice right behind me, saying, "Remember, Lucy. Don't touch anything. Some things here are very valuable." When I glanced at my image in one of the display cases I was almost shocked to see my current self reflected in the glass, thinking I might have seen instead that little girl in pigtails and a red cardigan sweater.

As I shut the door behind me, I was immediately greeted by a large, white, shaggy-haired dog who wagged his tail and panted so enthusiastically it was as though he had mistaken me for his long lost owner. I stooped to pat the dog's small, angular head. I remembered that Mr. Baumgarten used to have a dog and this animal looked remarkably like that one, but I knew it couldn't possibly be the same dog.

"Hey, fella," I said as his head kept prodding my hand for another stroke.

A voice from the back called, "I'll be right with you."

While the dog kept trying to make friends with my hand, I surveyed the place to see if anything had changed. Here was the last resort for all things otherwise destined for the landfill: China dolls, china plates, Chinese art, chinamen dolls, Barbie dolls, kewpie dolls, cloth dolls, table cloths, kitchen tables, kitchenware, kitchen witches, mess kits, kitty cats, Chatty Kathys, lazy susans, lazy boys, soldier boy figures, figurines, canteens, soup tureens, soup spoons, souvenir spoons, spoon racks, spice racks, gun racks, magazine racks, *Life* magazines, *Boy's Life*, *Highlights*, headlights, stop lights, Christmas lights, lava lamps, *Lava* soap ads, adding machines, Coke Machines, Coke bottles, Coke platters, Coke cans, can openers, cans, candy machines . . .

With all Mr. Baumgarten carried in his store, somehow he was able to keep it all together in neat and fashionable order, with the smaller items all lined up on long, oak tables in soldierly fashion and the larger ones grouped Stonehenge-style in the back. To be sure, there was a lot of stuff crammed into a small space—about 40' by 20' this daughter of a contractor would estimate—but it never looked like someone's overcrowded closet. There were some antique stores my father and I used to go to that made you think if you opened the door, a dislodged basketball from the top shelf might conk you on the head when you entered, but this was not the case here. I wondered how Mr. Baumgarten was able to make such junk seem almost opulent and why, in all their talks, he had never been able to impart any of this wisdom to my father.

Waiting for Mr. Baumgarten to appear, I looked to my left and saw a row of Barbie dolls, all seated, with their slender arms reaching for the sky as though they were all participating in some sort of yoga class. Some were dressed, some were nearly bald from the work of some demon child beautician, but most were just as naked as the day they came off the assembly line. I wondered what thoughts crossed Mr. B's mind as he held these little nude beauties in his thick, callused hands.

As I was picking up one of the dolls, I heard the sound of a hard-soled shoe against the floorboards. The dog, which had been following me since I came in, sprinted over to the back of the store. My eyes traced his movements until he finally came to a halt beside a pair of legs clad in gray pants. I looked up and smiled.

There in the doorway was Augustus Baumgarten, a man whose image was so irrevocably tied to my childhood he may as well have been Santa Claus or the Easter Bunny. He could have been both, with his closely cropped silver hair and steady, but friendly, dark-eyed gaze. He had been balding rapidly when I was little and I was amazed to see that he was still able to maintain a convincing comb-over, though the overhead fluorescent bulbs did shine a flashlight on his shiny scalp.

"Hi, Mr. Baumgarten. You probably don't remember me, but I used to come here with my father when I was little. My name is—"

"Lucy Cranston," he said suddenly, his eyes alight with recognition. "I don't believe it."

"You remember me?"

"Of course, I do!" he said, coming to meet me halfway. "I could never forget one of my best customers. My, my, it's good to see you!" He was presently pumping my arm in a handshake rarely seen outside Republican Party fund-raisers. "What an unexpected pleasure this is!"

As he was shaking my hand, the dog insinuated himself between us and began licking my palm.

"This can't be the same dog you used to have," I said.

"This one? No. This is Spruce Goose III. You might say he's the scion of Spruce Goose II who was the son and heir of the original Spruce Goose, the one you remember. But he's just as lively and ready to please the customers as the others were."

"I can see that," I said, stroking the dog under his chin.

"This is just such a nice surprise," Mr. Baumgarten said. "Can I get you anything? I've got some tea in the back that I just brewed."

"No thank you, Mr. Baumgarten. I—

Mr. Baumgarten flashed an index finger in front of his face to silence me. "I know what you want." He went to the vintage Coke machine just a few feet away and turned the key in the door. Carefully, he withdrew one of the slim, eight-ounce bottles, flipped the top off with the precision of a veteran soda jerk, and presented the Coke to me. I took it immediately, too impressed that he remembered my childhood sweet tooth to ask if he had anything diet. But once the bottle was in my hand, I found that I was really thirsty and I drank down half the bottle.

Mr. Baumgarten was smiling. "You always used to ask for those when you came on Saturdays. More specifically, you would whisper to your father that you wanted one and then he would say, 'Now, Lucy, you know that if you want something you have to ask for it yourself.' Sometimes you would ask me, but you were so incredibly bashful at the time it hurt to see you struggle with the words. So the minute that you and your father made your Saturday appearance, I would automatically have one ready for you."

"I remember," I said, studying the bottle under the light. "I didn't even know that they made these anymore."

"They're not easy to come by. I suspect this may be about the only place in Newport News where one can find them these days. At least for this price."

I looked over at the machine and saw that eight years of Reaganomics and the decade of skyrocketing inflation that proceeded the Great Communicator's reign had not spurred Mr. Baumgarten to hike up the cost beyond the twenty-five cents the sodas always had been. He may as well have been giving them away. But then again, I had never seen Dad ever actually pay for one of them and Mr. Baumgarten wasn't asking for any money from me now.

"I keep them priced low for the youngsters at the Catholic school," he explained. "They come in here after school every day. And some days, to be honest, if it weren't for them I wouldn't see anybody at all. It's not like it was when you were little. At least I could count on your father and you to come on Saturdays and liven things up a bit. Tell me. How is your father?"

"He's fine. He's in Ohio now."

"On another construction site, I assume."

"That's where he is," I said.

"I often think about your father. You know, I haven't seen much of him in the past few years. Did he send you here for something?"

"Actually, I'm here on a mission. For myself."

"Oh? Is there something I can help you find, then?"

"It's about something my father bought from your store a long time ago. I was wondering if you could tell me a little more about it."

"I'll certainly try. But as I recall, your father spent a lot of time and money acquiring a lot of my inventory. I may not be able to recall the origins of everything he bought."

"This one you may remember," I said. "It was a deck chair. Supposedly from the *Titanic*?"

A mercurial smile appeared on Mr. Baumgarten's face. "Oh, yes," he said, "The deck chair."

"You remember it, then?"

"Yes, of course."

"I was wondering if you could tell me a little more about it."

Mom didn't expect me home until after five. By the octagonal clock fixed to the wall behind Mr. Baumgarten, I had at least a half an hour. This was ample time for him to spout off the fish story he was surely about to hand me and to fit in a salespitch for the canvas cover that originally came with the deck chair—a real bargain at $500. I had the time to listen. And if it was an interesting story, maybe I could include it in my journal entry for Dr. Schindler to show him that I had actually made an attempt at outside research.

I polished off the rest of the soda and placed the empty bottle in a bin of other empties beside the vending machine. Mr. Baumgarten asked me if I wanted another and I told him I did. After getting me another Coke, Mr. Baumgarten showed me around to his office, which was where he had conducted all of his Saturday afternoon bull sessions with my father. The two of them had a way of dealing with one another that to outsiders may have appeared unseemly. I often wondered if Dad had taken me along all those years just so that I could act as a witness in case anyone ever regarded these covert actions with suspicion. They would meet here, chat for a while, just to be polite, and then Dad would light in with, "Anything new this week, Mr. B.?" When I got older, I always secretly begged that he would begin his dealings with this question instead of pussy-footing around it, wasting time that could be spent at the beach or the pool.

The back room was more or less a storeroom where Mr. B. kept all the things that were too out of shape for display. Along the shelves were baskets full of chipped pottery, broken toys and amputee furniture. From where I was sitting, I could see the cracked face of a porcelain doll peeking over the side of a shoebox as though she were a tiny corpse emerging from a tomb. I sat in the same chair where my father had once sat with me on his lap and Mr. Baumgarten pushed aside some of the papers on his desk and sat there. Spruce Goose had followed us in and folded his legs beneath his long, shaggy frame, coming to a rest at his master's feet. Mr. Baumgarten reached down and stroked Spruce Goose a few times across the top of his flaxen head as he began to speak.

"A man came into the shop one day, one day late when I was about to close. He was getting on in years, about the age I am now, was very frail and reed thin. I could tell by his clothing that he was not someone accustomed to waking up in a nice bed every morning. I could almost see traces of the heat grating he had been sleeping on," Mr. Baumgarten said. "He was dragging along something heavy, sheathed in a black plastic bag. I brought him back here, got him a Coke, and asked him what he had. And after finishing his drink, he removed the plastic cover and there it was. The deck chair. There was nothing extraordinary about it; it was just a deck chair, a very old one that looked as though it had been discarded from the shipyards. When I asked him where he found it, he was not immediately forthcoming with the information. He said that even if he told me, I wouldn't believe him. I in turn told him that being in this business I was asked to believe all sorts of things. But finally, after I offered him another Coke and he drank that one down too, he was more willing to talk."

I was in the middle of taking another gulp of soda when he said this. Feeling suddenly self-conscious, I unsuctioned the rim of the bottle from my lips and set the soda down on the desk.

"He began telling me a story that was by turns fascinating and absurd," Mr. Baumgarten continued. "He told me that the chair had saved his life once when he was a young man and he hoped he would be able to employ it in that position again. He then went on to tell me that he had been a third-class passenger on the *Titanic*, and that when the ship sank, he had grabbed hold of the deck chair that was floating off at the same time he was and had clung to it with all his might as the ship slowly eased its way into the water. He held onto it throughout the night and eventually fell asleep from all the exertion involved in trying to stay afloat and alive. When he woke up, he found himself alone in an empty sea. He figured that he had drifted for miles until he was completely clear of the wreck and the victims it had claimed. Eventually a merchant ship picked him up en route to Newport News and that was how he ended up here. He further explained that he was never able to make a success out of his life here, alternately working at the shipyards and not working at all. But through everything he managed to keep the deck chair, regarding it as a symbol of his survival despite the odds. With his life nearing its close and nothing really keeping him here, he hoped to go back to Ireland to reclaim what he had lost so long ago. But first he needed the money for a plane ticket back, since he had sworn that he would never board a ship again."

Feeling that Mr. Baumgarten had reached a stopping place, I asked, "And you bought that story?"

"Of course not!" he said. "But I did buy his chair."

"Why didn't you just give him the money and send him off?"

"Because that would have insulted him. By paying for the chair, I was validating his story and that was all he really wanted. You see, Miss Cranston, I sell these things because they once were important to someone and may still be so. Some of these things just don't have a place in the owner's world anymore, but still occupy a part of that person's heart. When someone brings me something—say, a plain stoneware pitcher, all chipped and darkened with crazing, something that had possibly been in the family, as they say, for years and years, I don't look at the market value. You can't find the real value of such an item in a book. I look into the seller's eyes and see the trouble the person is having parting with the pitcher. That's where I get my numbers from. And if it doesn't sell, then it's not a real loss. At least it is in a place where people can see it and know by looking at it that it was well-used and probably even loved. If it does sell, then I've made two people happy—myself and the person who sold it to me because now it is in someone else's cupboard, or perhaps on someone's bedside table holding bright, spring flowers."

I could understand what he was saying and thought this kind of sales philosophy was quite beautiful, if not entirely practical. But, how on earth had he kept this shop going for thirty-five years paying handsomely for such junk when most of it, quite honestly, couldn't even be considered the cream of the crop of a dumpster? The only thing I could think of was that his sister must have left him a wad of cash and that he had one hell of a pension from the Navy.

"That deck chair sat in my store for years before your father came in and bought it," Mr. Baumgarten said.

"Did you tell him the story that you just told me?" I asked.

"The story made him want the chair even more."

"And was it the same story you just told me, word for word?" I had to ask him this because in my father's mind, to say that the chair was said to have come from the *Titanic* was the same thing as saying that it actually did come from the *Titanic*. He always had to go with the belief that there was always a chance that something he bought had some earnest value beyond being just someone else's garbage.

"Word for word," Mr. Baumgarten assured me. "Tell me. What exactly has sparked your interest in the deck chair? Your father has had it for years and years. You must have known about it before now."

"I've been reading *A Night for Remember* for my American History class."

"Oh," he said, "Good book. Are you enjoying it?"

"More than just about anything I've read so far this semester."

"It's very involving, isn't it?"

"Definitely," I said. "I'm especially interested in the chief wireless operator." Suddenly I found my mouth was very dry and drained the rest of the Coke.

"Ah, Phillips. It's strange that you should mention him, because when I read the book, I had a lot of empathy for him as well. Perhaps because what he was doing was so futile at the end, signaling out in the night, just hoping that a ship close by would hear his call and respond in time. Even when the captain released him from his duty, Phillips continued to send distress calls." He shook his head. "He must have been an extraordinary man."

"He is," I heard myself say. And when that response garnered a strange look, I very quickly added. "He must have been."

I wanted to ask this next question, but I wasn't sure that I wanted to know the answer just yet. I still had quite a lot of reading to do in the book and I wanted to find out at the end. But at that moment, I was very anxious to know if Jack made it into a lifeboat or not.

Mr. Baumgarten looked perplexed, as though he could hear the fear in my voice and wondered why I would be so concerned for a man years away from being my contemporary.

"Yes," he said, giving it some thought, "Yes, he does make it into a lifeboat."

The relief I felt was so intense it was almost draining.

"Oh, well, that's good," I said, pretending to be casual, but failing miserably.

When I told Mr. Baumgarten that I had to go, he walked me to the door with Spruce Goose tagging along. When we got to the entrance, I stopped just short of opening the door. I looked back at Mr. Baumgarten, his hand gently kneading Spruce Goose on the neck while the dog panted in appreciation. I looked at him and thought to myself, This is all he had in the world. Just the shop and the dog. There was no one and nothing else keeping him here. His Navy career ended and his sister deceased, these myriad objects around him and the stories that were told about them were all he had to sustain him. Before I left, I took one last look at the shop and I came to the conclusion that the real reason why everything looked as though it hadn't been touched was that nothing *had* been touched in a long time. Most of the residents avoided this area of town, preferring the strip malls on the other side of town. These modern day temples to the credit card faithful had been a plague coming on for decades. When the downtown looked as though it were dying, the city planners, rather than investing any thoughts into urban renewal, thought constructing a place where sportsgoods stores and lingerie shops could coexist in harmony might be a better idea. I just couldn't picture a store like Mr. Baumgarten's having any sort of meaningful existence in a shopping mall. It just seemed it would be completely robbed of its soul if it had to compete with the likes of Spencer's Gifts and Everything's a Dollar.

At the door on my way out, I told Mr. Baumgarten that it had been nice to see him again, and it had been. Being in his store was like briefly revisiting my childhood. Impulsively, I asked him to dinner sometime when Dad was home from Ohio and the kitchen was back in working order. I wasn't sure why I asked him this, because in all their years of seeing each other, Mr. Baumgarten and my father had never known each other on a social basis. The invitation was just one of those suggestions that I could almost see happening, but not quite. For about the next six months, I would pass his shop and probably think, "I need to call Mr. Baumgarten and ask him to dinner" and then never do anything about it. This would not be an intentional slight. I was certain that over time, the invitation would lose its importance in the grand scheme of things. Eventually I would coast by the shop and not pay any attention to that thought at all.

Before I left, Mr. Baumgarten made me promise that I would tell Dad that he said hello and I told him that I would, the next time I talked to him. He said good-bye the usual way, with a smile and the parting words, "Please come again, won't you?" as though acting the part of the genial host of a kid's Saturday morning cartoon show. Once I was out on the sidewalk, he fixed a closed sign in the window and let the Venetian blinds clatter shut against the door.

When I got home, I went again to the deck chair, convinced that whatever dreams I had been having were of my own making. Whatever magic I thought the chair once harnessed was bogus. The only power at play here was the power of suggestion. I even sat down for a bit to test it out and after fifteen minutes I was still in my backyard with the sun dripping lazily over the horizon and the evening cool setting in. I admonished myself for being so foolish and secretly cursed Dad for being taken in so easily. He may as well have come home with a truckload of snake oil, I thought. In defeat, I folded the chair up and put it back in the shed, resolved to keep a lid on my insanity for at least another day.

After dinner that night, just as Mom and I were tackling the remainder of the dishes, the phone rang and I was the first to answer it.

"Hello, Luce," the voice said. "You miss me yet?"

A wave of familiarity closed over my head as my ears caught the sound of my father's voice.

"Hey, Dad. Of course I miss you."

Mom turned to face me, eyes alight. "Is that your father?"

I grimaced. "No, Mom. Danny DeVito."

Mom frowned, snapped a dishtowel from one of the handles on the cabinet under the sink and started drying.

"How's Ohio?" I asked.

"Oh, you know. It's a little high in the middle and round on both ends. Yuck, yuck, yuck."

Yuck, indeed, I thought. Dad's jokes were always intended to please, but so old they made some of Henny Youngman's earliest material seem fresh.

"How's my girl?"

"Doing OK."

"Classes going all right?"

"Fine."

"Have you had your midterms yet?"

"Couple of weeks ago."

"Did you do all right?"

"Mixed bag. B's and C's."

"No F's though, I hope."

"No. No F's."

"Well, good then. 'Scuse me a minute," he said. I could tell he had cupped his hand over the phone and he was now speaking to someone who had walked into the room. I couldn't hear much of what was going on, until he was just about finished with his conversation. "Yeah, yeah. We got those Monday. We'll get them put up Thursday. Friday at the latest. All right, man. Take it easy."

"You calling from work, Dad?" I asked.

"Yeah. We're working late today. Trying to meet our deadline."

"Is it still May?"

"I don't think so. Not now. Maybe June or July."

Mom approached me, asking me what he said. When I told her, she rolled her eyes and sighed. "Always something, always something."

"Everything going all right at the homefront?"

"I think so."

"Your Mom sold that house yet?"

"She's closing the deal on Thursday."

"And your Aunt Teese? How's she doing?"

"Depleting the ozone as usual."

"You two getting along?"

"We're mostly avoiding each other. That's usually what works best."

"You be nice to your Aunt Teese, now. You know, she's not going to live forever."

Know it? That was my daily mantra. "Yeah, I know."

"Your money holding out OK?"

"Nope. Broke as usual."

There was a pause. "Well, I sent you some money."

"Oh, I haven't gotten it yet."

"You'll probably get it tomorrow or Thursday. Today's Tuesday, right?"

"Yeah, Tuesday."

"You'll get it Thursday, then."

"Thanks, Dad. You really didn't have to do that."

"Well, it keeps you from borrowing money from your mother and my having to hear about it."

"I guess you're right."

"Is she around?"

"She's right here."

"If you'd put her on, I'd appreciate it."

"Will do."

"Take care of yourself, Luce. Love you."

"Love you too, Dad."

The minute Mom seized the phone, instead of hearing the beginnings of a verbal *billet doux*, I caught a near growl of contempt in her voice as she lit in immediately with, "Dan, I have to talk to you. What's this about you giving Lucy marijuana?"

"What?" I heard Dad blast on the other end.

"Lucy said you gave her marijuana." There was a pause. "When she was sixteen."

Dad fired back, "Good God, Eve. That was years ago!"

"It doesn't matter how long ago it was. The point is that you were corrupting our child behind my back. We promised each other a long time ago that we would never force our lifestyle on Lucy. You know that." There was another pause. "I don't care if it was one joint or one thousand. You gave our child drugs and that's . . . I don't care. I don't care. Dan, I don't care. You shouldn't have shared it with Lucy."

I knew that I should have left the minute I heard that tempered pitch in Mom's girlish voice, so I quietly slipped out, leaving her to berate my poor father for that rather innocent transgression from my teenage years. It really wasn't that big of a deal. Dad had found a matured dime bag of weed crammed in an old toolbox and wanted to see if it still retained some of its 1970s potency. Mom had long since given up the habit and all of Dad's druggie pals had wandered elsewhere or were on the wagon. In retrospect, I think Dad was hoping that he might find something to unite us once again, since our days of antiquing were long behind us and I was all into that teenage doom rebellion thing. And it was just one joint, just a few puffs that scalded my throat and made me ravenously hungry. I figured I didn't need that. My appetite had always been pretty good and beer had become my controlled substance of choice by my mid-teens.

I didn't have to worry about this sort of argument putting a permanent rift in their relationship. Dad's long absences had a stronger chance of doing that and would have killed most marriages by now. I really and truly believed there were no other people on the planet better suited for each other, though at the time of their first meeting, any outsider would have thought otherwise.

Mom had been a very straight teenager. She was a dutiful daughter, an exemplary student and a first-chair flute player in the school orchestra. I know this because I went to the same high school and decades after she graduated, her teachers still remembered shy, prim Eve Jarnel who had a different colored twin set for each day of the week and matching hair bows for every one of them. All that changed when she encountered Daniel Christopher Cranston.

Mom, the ultimate help-after-school junkie, was working in the guidance counselor's office, running notes to students in class and providing tutorials after school. In the second semester of her junior year, she was told to meet a new student after school in the library for some extra help with chemistry. After the last bell rang, she went to the library and sat and waited for a half an hour. When she couldn't stay any longer, she gathered her books and headed out the door, walking right into this tall, gangly boy who seemed to be all limbs and hair. The minute she caught sight of his mangy blond mane and two weeks' worth of facial stubble, it was, she said, like two worlds coming together.

As they scrambled to the floor to retrieve their books, Mom picked up one of his three-ring binders and noticed that he had etched the name "Led Zeppelin" into the front cover. She asked him if he knew he had misspelled "lead." Dad chortled at her innocence and told her that Led Zeppelin was the name of a new rock band out of England that was destined to be the sound of the decade. She apologized for not knowing about Robert Plant and Company and that her fave rave was the Beatles, a band he admired as well. They found themselves a table and talked until the library closed, promising that they would get together again.

And they did, again and again, until gradually, Mom's neat sweater sets were replaced by crocheted ponchos and her bouffant hairdo was ironed and tamed into sleek strands going all the way down her back. The two masterminded the counter culture ring at the high school, took part in anti-war rallies, and rang the chimes of freedom on up until graduation. This was a complete turnaround for my Mom whose previous idea of rebellion consisted of using tape instead of thumbtacks to anchor her Beatles posters to her bedroom walls. Dad was a serial class skipper who openly thumbed his nose at authority by smoking in the halls and refusing to cut his hair, though at this time most of his male classmates still sported the buzz cuts of the previous decade. But, my Mom said, they were destined to be together. She often wondered that if her student hadn't been so late that day if she would have met Dad at all. And if she hadn't, she imagined that she would have spent the rest of her life looking for him.

When I asked for Dad's take on the whole idea of destiny playing such a huge part in their relationship, he said he knew Mom was the woman for him the first time she told him her name. "She just told me her name was Eve," Dad recalled. "And that's all she needed to say. It was like God was saying, 'Here's the person made from your rib, Dan. Here's your chance to be whole again.'" He added also that she looked really cute in her sweater that day.

Their argument via fiber optics didn't last long. When I came back by the kitchen fifteen minutes later, Mom was cooing into the phone and twisting her hair around her finger as though she were flirting with him. In moments like these I felt I was catching a glimpse of the high school sweethearts they had been and, in their minds, still were.

Mom must have seen my shadow pass as she was still talking to Dad. I heard her call my name and I ducked my head in the door, finding her face full of smiles and her hair in knots from all the twisting.

"Lucy, can you think of anything else your Dad needs to know?"

I couldn't at first, but then I remembered where I had been that afternoon.

"You can tell him I saw an old friend of his today," I said, loud enough so that he could hear me.

"Did you catch that, Dan?" Mom asked. She put the receiver on her shoulder. "He wants to know who."

"Somebody who still sells Cokes for a quarter," I said.

Mom relayed the answer to him. There was a pause and then she returned her gaze to me. "Do you mean Mr. B., he asks."

"Of course," I said.

Mom was back to Dad again. Then she gave a dramatic sigh. "Your Dad wants to know if he had anything new."

I laughed. "No, nothing new."

I went to bed fairly early that night. The evening was cooling down and since I had left my window open all day, my room felt almost air-conditioned. I slept better in the cool, with all my covers piled up on top of me. It was a rare treat not to have to sleep in a stuffy room.

I went to my desk and switched on the light. I picked up my book bag and got out my binder. Taking a quick look at the syllabus for my Post Colonial Lit class, I saw that we were due to discuss a book that I had not even started yet and couldn't even begin to find. Luckily it was a Derek Wolcott novel I had read for my Twentieth Century World Lit class four semesters ago and I still remembered enough of the plot to speak competently about it in class the next day.

I flipped a section ahead to Dr. Schindler's syllabus, though I already knew what the assignment was for the next. I had finished the assigned pages and then some. *Mustn't get too far ahead*, I thought to myself. *Wouldn't want to fool myself into believing I'm becoming an overachiever.*

I was behind in my journaling, though. I sorted through the rest of the books in my satchel and took out the slim spiral notebook I had designated for my reader's journal. I was feeling more tired than I had been, so I decided to write the entry in bed.

I liked writing in bed. With the cedar chest scent of my sheets all around me and the warmth of the reading lamp overhead, I sort of got that writing letters from camp feeling. There was a certain intimacy, too, about taking my work to bed, like I was actually making a commitment to what I was doing.

I flipped back to what I had written the day before. Going over what had happened, I was seized with a longing to be back there again. But I had to remind myself, over and over, *it just can't be . . . it just can't be.*

Another dream, this one slightly extended, more coherent. More about Jack Phillips. He came to my room. Seems he had to put me to bed the last time. We walked along "A" deck, had a lengthy talk on one of the upper decks right under one of the funnels. I wanted to stay longer, but time was short. I did that fainting thing at the end of my dream again. I wonder if Jack put me into bed?

Even though we made plans to see each other again, I don't know if I'll be able to. Mr. B confirmed today that the chair is a fake. But even though I know this, I keep thinking that I will see him again. Maybe in my dreams tonight.

I was so tired when I first got into bed that I was sure I was going to fall right to sleep. But the minute I turned out the light, I was wide awake. I really didn't want to take anything. Post Colonial Lit was a 9:30 class and I would have to be up by 8:00 to shower, dress and have breakfast. It was 11:30 now. I knew that if I took a sleeping pill it would be wearing off when I got behind the wheel of the car. But I really didn't see what choice I had. A medicated sleep was better than no sleep at all. And they were just over the counter tablets.

I got out of bed and went to the bathroom. Squinting in the bright fluorescent light, I groped, almost blind, for the box of Dozeaze in my medicine chest. There was only one left. I popped the pill out, snapped it in half and swallowed without water. I tucked the other half back in its foil blister and padded back to my room.

Sleep wasn't a problem after that. I think all I needed was the assurance of the pill to back me up in case I couldn't ease into sleep by myself. As I drifted off to sleep, I remember wishing myself sweet dreams and I was completely out.

CHAPTER FOUR

"Well, class," Dr. Schindler said from the podium at the front of the classroom the next day. "I hope that some of you are no longer of the opinion that *A Night to Remember* sucks."

There was some laughter over the novelty of hearing Dr. Schindler utter the word "sucks," as though he had just learned it in that context the day before. Also, surprisingly, there were strong nods of agreement.

"One of the most exciting books of this or any year!" shouted someone in the back.

Dr. Schindler smiled. "I see that one gentleman in the class had at least read the book jacket. I hope that he and the rest of you have read a little more than that. You should have read through the chapter entitled, *You Go and I'll Stay A Little While*. Is that where everyone is now?"

Most everyone mumbled yes. There were a few who did not, presumably because they had not bought the book or hadn't read it.

"I'm reading along as well," Dr. Schindler said. "And it just amazes me that even though I have read it many, many times, I still get angry every time. Has it had that effect on anyone else?" He walked over to a blond girl in the front row. She always sat there, right in the front, and sometimes when I got bored, I would write down the number of times she flipped her hair. There were 46 tick marks in the margin of my notebook paper before class ended.

"Did it make you angry when you read it, Miss Barnes?" Dr. Schindler was asking.

Hair flip one. "A little," she said.

"And what made you angry?"

Two, three. "I don't know. Everything, I guess."

"Something in particular?"

Four, five, six. "Not really."

"Miss Barnes, did you read to Chapter V?"

Seven, eight, nine. "No, sir."

"And why not?"

Ten, eleven. "Because when I got to the bookstore yesterday they were all out of books."

"How could that be, Miss Barnes? I ordered one for everyone in the class."

"Well, there weren't any left on the shelf."

Dr. Schindler was shaking his head. "You go back to the bookstore this afternoon, Miss Barnes. They don't always have all the inventory on the shelves. Ask them to check in the back for you. I'm sure someone will be able to find a copy."

Occasionally Dr. Schindler did make things fun by humiliating a worthy student. And he did it really well, as though part of his free time was spent watching Perry Mason in the mornings like Aunt Teese. Luckily for poor Miss Barnes, someone else raised a hand. This time it was one of the older folks in the class, a middle-aged man I had seen in a lot of my classes. He always wore a short sleeve button down shirt and a tie like some middle management schmuck.

"Isn't this a class in American History?" he asked.

"That is true," Dr. Schindler said, nonplussed.

"Well, I don't see how this book or the incident it was written about has anything to do with American history. It was, after all, a British-made ship, owned by a British company, with primarily foreigners on board. I just don't see what it has to do with the American experience."

"Mr. Hackman here has brought up an interesting point," Dr. Schindler said. "And perhaps it is one that some of you have taken up in your journals, which, by the way, are going to be graded. I think I mentioned that, but in case you have forgotten, I thought I would bring it up again." He gave us all a warning stare before proceeding. "Anyway, to address Mr. Hackman's question. True, she was British-made, but she was partly owned by American interests. Financier J.P. Morgan was one of the chief owners of the ship and would have been on the voyage, if not for the fact that he had taken ill and could not go at the last. But in the absence of this more notable American of the early part of the century, there were many more, including millionaire John Jacob Astor, Denver socialite Maggie Brown and the fabulously wealthy philanderer, Benjamin Guggenheim. These people were the celebrities of the day, before movies and TV, and they enjoyed lives of enormous wealth, due in part to the absence of any federal income tax. But the list of glitterati was small compared to the nameless hordes who dwelled in the ship's bowels. The folks in third class or steerage who were setting out for their own American experience, hoping to restart their lives in a new country. Those hundred of steerage passengers that were lost never did get to become part of the American landscape. Because their lives were unexplored here in the new world, their contributions were never made, so their losses were perhaps the most keenly felt."

"There was more where that came from," someone said.

The air in the room stiffened and there were a few mutters, but Dr. Schindler continued on.

"I hope that you all will be able to derive some sort of meaning from the story of what happened to these poor souls that terrible night, April 14, 1912. Now, as wonderful as Mr. Lord is at giving you the details of what happened, step by step, in an almost methodical way, I thought you might like to see pictures of some of the people you're reading about. So I went though my library last night and dug up a book that I thought would help put faces with the names in the text."

Dr. Schindler had in his hands a large book tagged with little yellow post-it notes. He put the book on one of the desks in the front row and the recipient began flipping through it casually as though breezing through a magazine. Dr. Schindler continued his discussion.

When the book got to me, the class was nearly over. Some students had dwelled over its pages more than others, especially after it was discovered that one of the unmarked pages had ghoulish pictures of some of the victims.

I let my fingers slide over the glossy, heavy bond pages, taking an equal look at each page Dr. Schindler had marked. The tragic cast of characters became more and more human as I looked into their sepia toned faces:

Look-Out Frederick Fleet, his mouth twisted and slack from saying so many things in Cockney English, including the fateful remark, "Iceberg, right ahead;" J. Bruce Ismay, Managing Director of the White Star Line, a severely mustachioed gentleman peering out sheepishly with his cold-eyed stare as though saying, even now, "I had nothing to do with what happened. Nothing at all;" First Officer William Murdoch, looking stiff and tall, his face a puzzle, as though subconsciously he had meant to convey to future generations his bewilderment that a tragedy of this magnitude could have happened on his watch; Thomas Andrews, the ship's chief builder, pictured looking off to the side, as though he were just receiving word that the ship had struck something; John Jacob Astor, possessor of one of the largest fortunes in the world, looking pensive in a uniform of some kind; Mr.

and Mrs. Isidore Straus, founders of Macy's Department Store, appearing elderly, tight-lipped, determined to stay together until the end; Mrs. Hudson J. Allison and her baby, Loraine, staring inquisitively as though the photographer had told her to watch the birdie and she was looking for a real bird flying in the air; Colonel Archibald Gracie, a man who appeared to be all mustache and eyebrows, who survived after clinging to an overturned lifeboat most of the night.

I turned the page once more and my eyes seemed to freeze up in their sockets. For a minute everything around me had suddenly come to a stop—all talking, all rustling of notebook pages, all fierce scribbling of notes, all of Dr. Schindler's endless, droning talk. My thoughts were turning slowly like dry leaves on the agitated waters of a genthly moving stream. I couldn't grasp them, couldn't catch hold of their meaning as they slipped one by one beneath the rapids of my churning mind. I was suddenly conscious of the fact that I wasn't breathing and hadn't been for several minutes. When I finally forced myself to take a breath, I took it with a large gulp some people in the class actually turned around and stared at me.

There he was, exactly as I had seen him. All the familiar features were there, just as they had been when I first had a good look at him, standing outside my stateroom. There was the serious stare of his eyes, proceeding over the orderly arrangement of his slightly rounded countenance, the curved plumpness of his lips, virtually pouting over his broad, flat chin. There was the dark hair, topped by the hat with its shiny bill and the embroidered oak leaf clusters circling an "M" which I had seen him put on that first night. That was him. That was most definitely him. Even if I had found the same picture in a book of anonymous mug shots, I could have picked him out, easily. "Yes, officer, that was the man I was with last night."

There was no mistaking something else: I had never seen this picture before.

How could I have dreamed him so accurately? I've never even read a description of him before!

There was a caption under his picture that read:

> *Telegraphist John George "Jack" Phillips, the only son of George and Anne Phillips of Godalming, Surrey, stayed and worked the wireless until the very end, never giving up hope that his pleas for help would be answered by a nearby ship in time to avert disaster. Mr. Phillips had just turned twenty-five years of age the second day of the voyage.*

I couldn't have guessed at that information. That's what he told me. He did say he was from Godalming. And he did mention sisters, but no brothers, which probably did make him an only son. But he didn't tell me it was his birthday. When was his birthday? The second day? That must have been yesterday, the last time I was in the chair. Why didn't he tell me it was his birthday? Especially one as important as the twenty-fifth . . .

I paged ahead, plunging feverishly through the book, until my eyes settled on another familiar face: Harold Bride, assistant Marconi officer. There he was, on page 147, just as I remembered him with his impossibly young, cherubic face, his droopy hound dog eyes. He was looking very serious for his official Marconi Marine pose . . .

"He says the most amusing things . . ."

Where was the captain? There had to be a picture of the captain in there somewhere. But as I was thumbing through, someone was poking me on the back, taking me away from all the confusion that reigned supreme in my head. "Are you finished?" the person whispered sharply.

I returned quickly from my flight out of myself and reminded myself that I was in class. But instead of feeling dull from boredom overload, I felt a hum going all over me.

I closed the book and handed it back to the person behind me. I looked up at the clock over the blackboard and saw that it was ten after eleven.

That's why I couldn't get there yesterday, I reasoned. The two times before I had sat down in the chair at approximately the same time. And it had been the same time in my dreams as it had been in real life, only twelve hours ahead.

There were only ten minutes left. Only a half hour to drive home, twenty if the traffic was light, fifteen if I broke the speed limit. I'd fly if I could. I thought for a minute I could fly if I just concentrated really hard and let my arms come up and catch the wind. Because at that moment, the impossible, the unfathomable became as real as my own existence, my own place in the universe as Lucy Cranston, student, daughter, resident of Hampton Roads, and now, apparently, accidental time traveler.

None of these people have to die. I can save them. I can save them all!

I can save them all, I can save them all.

I kept saying this to myself all the way down Jefferson. When my car came screeching to a halt at a red light, so did all my thoughts.

What if I can't remember what's going to happen?

In these dreams, one aspect remained consistent: I could not remember certain things. And when I did remember aspects of my life, it was as though they were being sorted by an unknown source. I thought perhaps that was my own conscience censoring my thoughts, but I couldn't be sure.

But it seemed also that I was remembering more in the last dream. I knew who my parents were, where I lived, and that I was in school. I also remembered Johnny Mumphrey, though I incorrectly identified him as a place in Ireland. But I had been thinking about Johnny Mumphrey and Ireland before I went into the dream. My state of mind before each episode seemed to have some bearing on what I could think about and talk about in the dreams.

God, I must sound like such an idiot to Jack. I knew International Morse Code because I took a class in early twentieth century communications four semesters ago. Why couldn't I have remembered that? And why can't I remember that the ship is going to sink? Why wasn't I preoccupied with that?

"I've known all along that the ship is going to sink," I said aloud, biting along the edge of my thumbnail.

The light turned green and I proceeded on, still nibbling on my thumbnail.

I did know what the ship was going to sink. I knew that from the first time I sat down in the deck chair. Why did I keep forgetting that in the dreams?

I remembered what I had been thinking yesterday. If I were there during the first days of the voyage, then the sinking, obviously, had not occurred yet. Maybe I wouldn't know about it until it actually happened. Maybe I would be doomed as well if I continued to go back.

"But *I* haven't occurred yet. I'm not even the proverbial twinkle in someone's eye," I told myself. "So if I haven't happened in 1912, why am I there? Why can I conjure up thoughts about my life when it doesn't exist?"

I was talking quite loudly with the windows rolled down as I coasted towards another red light. I would have been self-conscious about this if I hadn't been one-upped by a carload of teenagers beside me in a convertible, all screaming along to the Beastie Boys' "No Sleep Till Brooklyn" blaring on the radio.

"I could be just dreaming," I reassured myself.

That was my original rationale, but it was starting to make the least sense. In each dream, I seemed to be waking up there in the midst of things, as though everything were waiting for me to return. I had a life, another life in this realm and I was living it in my dreams.

"Maybe it's a parallel universe that I've entered. No, then it would be the same time as the present I'm living in now." I laughed at a sudden, delinquent thought. "Maybe the person back there is the real me and what I'm doing now is a dream."

For the first time in my life, I almost missed the turn off from Warwick to 66th Street and nearly plowed into a Dodge Caravan loaded down with kids in soccer gear and one very frazzled Mom at the wheel who probably would have given me the finger if she hadn't been playing chaperone that afternoon.

I pulled into the driveway and noted that Mom was still out. She had left me a note in the morning telling me that lunch was whatever we wanted again and that she wouldn't be home until five. I looked greedily at the clock on the dashboard. It was a little after eleven. If all went well, if my mind carried me to where I intended to go that afternoon, I could be there for hours without interruption.

I couldn't get to the shed fast enough, never thinking how bizarre my longing was or how foolish I may have looked to anyone looking on. There was a lump in my throat the size of a chestnut, steadily growing to grapefruit proportions. My anticipation for what could happen asserted itself in the loud pounding of my heart.

I found the chair and brought it back out into the yard, thinking an apology might be in order for ever doubting its power. When I set it down, I touched the wood with a reverential awe, letting the splinters scratch against my hand. I sat down quickly and slid my legs into position. My shoulders were tense, nearly drawn up under my ears. I had to relax. I had been relaxed before. Getting there was never in my mind before. I had been led by my conscience, allowing time to sweep me away. I closed my eyes to the bright noonday sun, hoping that midnight would greet me when I opened them again.

Slowly my mind began the task of rebuilding belief after doubt had left my faith in ruins. I began thinking things I hadn't thought about in years: make believe, playtime, the time I turned my bookshelves into Barbie houses before Santa came and gave the dolls a swinging bachelorette pad for entertaining Ken, G.I. Joe and Steve Austin. I thought of the pieces of glass I had found in the compost heap. Not precious stones, just broken glass, just trash. I thought of all the summers before when my family followed the sun-speckled green waters of the James River to the sea grass dunes and jagged coastline of the Atlantic that was Virginia Beach. I recalled the many times I had stood just where the ocean spilled foamy remnants of waves at my toes before recessing and reforming again, each breaker edging closer to high tide, the end of the day. I thought of all the time I spent on the shore, up to my elbows in sand, reaching for China down below. I could dig for it if I had the time, I believed. If my parents had let me stay there a while until I was beet red and blistered, I could have made it to China. But I was still a child then.

I'm a child in my parents' home, still a child in their eyes. As long as I stay here I'll be a child. I'll be a child . . .

My thoughts began moving in that slow, swirling pattern that drowsiness induces. My head was becoming vaporous.

The big tree swaying overhead, bows trembling, capable of breaking, capable of crushing me as I lay here, semi-conscious, oblivious to any pain as the branches tear my flesh to shreds, snapping my spine, leaving me paralyzed. I can't die . . . I've got all that homework for tonight. Johnny Mumphrey's class . . . I need to get the notes from someone because I missed the last class. Who can I ask to borrow the notes from? I need to borrow . . . borrow . . . I need to borrow something from Mom . . . maybe that typewriter she doesn't use anymore. Oh, no, she sold it. At a yard sale. The yard . . . so green . . . it's spring, it's spring . . . April on the coast, so great, so great . . .

The air around me was suddenly quiet and still. Everything was giving away, under me, over me, through me. The chair was slowly contouring around my body, turning from wood to silk. The wind, once gusting, was vanishing, giving way to a constant stream of warm, comforting air. The light outside my shielding eyelids was diminishing to near darkness and then complete darkness, enveloping me like a shroud. My shirt seemed to tighten around me, gripping me around my ribs, tighter, tighter. And then there was a hum, a distant hum coming from somewhere below. And then came knocking, persistent knocking, over and over.

I opened my eyes.

And I was there.

CHAPTER FIVE

I knew where to look for the light switch this time and turned on the bedside lamp before getting out of bed. A voice was calling my name from behind the door now, sounding much deeper than Jack's.

"Who is it?" I asked.

"It's the purser, miss. I've got a message for you from the wireless office," the voice said.

I made my way quickly over to the door. When I opened it, I found a middle-aged man standing there, slightly doughy and looking a little sleepy. He was holding a folded slip of paper and I took it from him, ignoring all the looks I was getting from him as I stood there, still in my gown from days before, my hair most likely a matted mess.

I quickly unfolded the message and read it in the sparse light.

> *I'm off at half past midnight. Do you still want to meet? Send word by the purser. I'll be waiting.*
>
> *Jack*

As I stood there, marveling at the note, examining it and reading it over and over until, in my mind, it sounded like the greatest four sentences ever written in the history of western literature, I realized that the purser was standing there too, waiting, probably going off to bed as soon as this last task of the evening was seen through.

"Is there a reply, Miss?" he asked, viewing me through heavy eyelids.

"Yes. Yes. Tell him to come down here when he's finished. No! Wait! What time is it?"

"It's midnight, Miss."

"That only gives me half an hour," I said, thinking aloud. I scraped my top teeth along my bottom lip and drummed my fingers on the folded note. "Tell him I'll meet him at the station at 12:30."

"Yes, Miss," he replied, readying to leave. And then he asked the obligatory, "Will there be anything else, Miss?"

A thought was coming to me now. *His birthday . . . yesterday was his birthday.*

"Actually, yes," I said. "I know it's late, but . . . my friend just had a birthday and didn't get to celebrate it. I wanted to do something special for him. A slice of cake, maybe."

"Regretfully, the bakers do not begin making pastry until the morning. But I shall see if there is something left over from tonight's dinner. Granted, whatever I find will not be entirely fresh."

"That's all right. Anything you can find that's decent, I'd appreciate."

"Certainly, Miss. And will there be anything else?"

What's a birthday celebration without a little bubbly? "Yes. Again, if possible, I would like a bottle of champagne." I wasn't sure who was paying for all this, so I added, "It doesn't have to be the best. Just whatever you got."

"Very well, Miss. And will there be anything else?"

There was something else. I didn't want to march all the way up to the boat deck with a bottle of champagne and day-old pastry wrapped in a napkin. Where would we go to have our little celebration? We could probably sit on one of the benches on the boat deck, close to the wireless shack, but the thought of sitting there in the open air with a bottle of champagne conjured up images of Bourbon Street at night. I didn't want that. I wanted something more intimate for Jack's birthday.

"I'd like for you to change my original reply, if you could."

"Yes, Miss?"

"Tell him to meet me down here at 12:30."

The man gave me a look as if to say, "Oh, now it all makes sense. The cake, the champagne, the unmade bed . . . The Marconi boy is in for some first-class canoodling tonight." I didn't want this man to think that. And I definitely didn't want Jack to think that.

"Wait!" I said once more. "Tell him that I'll meet him outside his office at 12:30."

"Yes, Miss," he said wearily. At this point all earnestness had left his voice until it was nothing but a hollow sigh.

I didn't have a lot of time to get ready. When I looked in the mirror, I saw that my hair hadn't improved overnight. Even with a half an hour, I'd never be able to get it looking any better than it already did. I fingered the combs. They would do, but I wasn't sure how to use them properly.

"Maybe if I had a hat," I said to myself.

I felt along the backside of the gown I was wearing, hoping to lay my fingers on some kind of fastener, and found a multitude of buttons, a virtual army of them, marching down my back. I started at my neck and worked my way down. Overhead was a shelf, lined with round and rectangular boxes. The first one contained a pair of small shoes that were the right color, but so small they could only have fit the feet of a Chinese concubine. Still, I put them aside just in case I couldn't find anything else to match. The second box held a straw hat with a black ribbon—not exactly what I was hoping for, but it was tons better than the next hat I found, an atrocious combination of cranberries and tulle featuring a large stuffed dove as a centerpiece. Still unbuttoning my dress, I went through more and more boxes, aware that time was leaving me. By the time my dress was on the floor, I had gotten to the last box which contained a pair of high-button shoes.

One gown in particular caught my eye, a deep blue silk gown with marabou flickering from tulle cap sleeves. Under the light, little studs of cut blue glass glistened on the bodice and on the fine mesh of the skirt. As I was wondering what to do with myself, there was a knock at the door and then came a young woman's voice from the other side, identifying herself as the stewardess. I told her to come on in, since I was nearly shin-deep in empty boxes and couldn't open the door for her.

A small girl entered, carrying a covered tray and two long-stem champagne glasses. The requested bottle was pinned snugly under her arm. She wore on her head what looked like a night cap and I wondered if I had gotten her out of bed as well, but when I saw she was wearing a matching apron, I just concluded that the head gear was part of her uniform.

She looked at me with a guarded expression, her shoulders slightly hunched in apprehension.

"Where would you like me to put these, Miss?" she asked cautiously in a soft, British clip.

"Over on the vanity table is fine," I said.

"I was able to find you an éclair. I hope that it's all right, Miss."

"I'm sure it will be fine," I said. "I hope you didn't go to any trouble."

"None at all, miss. I had just been down the hall, tending to a woman just about done in with seasickness."

"Are you going back to her now?"

"No. She's finally tucked away in bed asleep, I believe."

My face pulled together a frantic smile. "Can you help me, then?"

She nodded. "How can I help?"

I saw she had a gold watch dangling from her waist.

"You can start by telling me what time it is."

"Quarter past, Miss."

"I've got to get a move on," I said, kicking the boxes and shoes aside. "But I can't go anywhere without doing something about my hair. Can you do hair?"

"I can try," she said.

I sat down at the vanity and let her brush my hair. She asked me how I wanted it done, and I told her that I had no idea and that I'd let her experiment. I showed her the combs and the pins lying on the table and she thought she could put together a chignon fairly quickly. I hoped she was right and sat there feeling jittery as though I had just quaffed an entire pot of coffee.

"You have beautiful hair, Miss," she commented as she worked the first layer of pins into my scalp.

"You think? I've always hated it. Too fine."

"It is that. Like a baby's."

"By the way, my name is Lucy Cranston."

"Yes, miss. I know that."

"How did you know what my name was?"

"I've been assigned to your cabin since sailing day," she said, brushing out a length of hair before securing it to my scalp with a pin.

"But this is the first time we've met, isn't it?"

"Yes, Miss."

I blew out a breath. "That's good to know. I seem to be having trouble with my memory lately."

After a while she asked, "Are you meeting someone tonight, miss?"

"I am," I told her.

"Someone special?"

I smiled. "I think so."

"Someone you've met on the ship?"

"Yes. The first night."

"How lovely for you, miss!"

"Maybe you know him. He works in the Marconi office."

"Don't know any of their sort, miss. Is he a nice fellow?"

"Very nice." *He's put me to bed two nights in a row* . . . "Oh, no," I said, dropping my head into my hands.

"What is it? Have I done something wrong?"

"No, no, that's not it." When I faced myself again in the mirror, I was blushing. "I was just thinking about something that happened, or must have happened last night." I looked around at the bed. The covers had been turned down. I knew then that he had actually lifted the blankets and put me underneath them. In the rush to get to the door, I hadn't noticed that I had slept under the covers.

His words from the previous night came back to me in a whisper of remembrance. *I'll see what I can do to help you* . . .

"It always ends with me falling to the floor," I said, intending to keep the words to myself, but I had spoken aloud.

"Pardon?" the stewardess chirped.

"Oh, nothing. Something really embarrassing happened—again—last night and I don't know how I'm going to face him again."

"If you don't mind my saying so, I scarcely think you need worry about that. When he sees how you look tonight, he'll forget about what ever happened last night."

"You think?"

"I know so."

I did look sort of nice. My fly away hair had been tamed and corralled into a nice, neat bun on the back of my head. I had never once thought of myself as beautiful, but looking in the mirror, I could almost see how some people would consider me pretty.

Of course, in just underwear, many people would have considered me partially naked. I asked for the time again and she told me it was getting close to 12:30. I hurried over to the closet and picked up the gown I had chosen. With the stewardess' help, I stepped into it and let her do the fastening while I stepped into the blue shoes I had found. What a miracle! They fit.

She began collecting some of the things I had discarded during my search for the perfect hat. "You go and have a lovely time tonight, Miss. I'll get these things together."

"Oh, no. You don't have to do that. I'll do it when I get back."

"You'll be awfully tired when you get back, Miss. You haven't asked me to do a single thing for you since you've been here. I'll tend to this. You tend to your gent."

She had been so helpful I felt I owed her something, other than a polite thank you. I went over to the vanity, opened the left top drawer and found it was full of handkerchiefs and more long, white gloves. There were so many gloves, I wondered if I should be wearing a pair. I asked the stewardess for her opinion and she said yes, if not just for the look, for the warmth, especially if I were going to be outside for any length of time. She advised me to wear a wrap as well and I asked her to choose something for me. She took out a dark blue shawl that matched the glass stones twinkling in my gown. Meanwhile I pressed on in my search for a purse. In one of the bottom drawers was a black velvet covered jewelry box that opened to a hot pink interior. Inside was a small clutch shaped like a clam, filled with coins.

"I want you to have a little something for all you did for me tonight," I said as sifted through the coins with a gloved index finger. None of them looked even remotely familiar and I wondered if they were all foreign.

"No, miss. I couldn't," she said.

"Well, I want you to. Just because. Here," I said, popping two heavy coins into her hand. "For when you get to New York."

I knew that it had to be getting close to 12:30, if not past that time. I made a quick decision not to carry the silver tray and instead wrapped the éclair in one of the handkerchiefs I had found in the vanity drawer. I stuffed the bottle under one arm and pinched the stems of the glasses between my fore and middle fingers. In the other hand, I carried the éclair. The stewardess wished me good luck and went back to putting my things in order.

I thought I knew where I was going. If I went down the corridor I would find the B deck landing of the forward staircase. My surroundings were becoming awfully familiar, as though I were memorizing each nook and cranny of the ship in my sleep. I hadn't seen very much of it and if I had, I couldn't remember the circumstances. The first real occurrence I could remember was the first night in the Marconi shack being brought back to life by Jack.

When I got to the clock at the top of the stairs, the hands had passed the 12:35 position.

Oh, I hope he's still waiting.

I was up on the boat deck now, the fresh, sea air breathing life into me. The stewardess had been right to recommend a wrap. The air was tinged with the crisp chill.

As my feet clicked against the surface of the deck, I stared ahead, aware that the champagne bottle I was carrying had been well chilled and was presently chilling me. I shifted its position to my other arm, realizing I was not going to present myself to Jack in my most romantic light with two big wet spots under each arm.

Hopefully he won't be looking at my underarms.

I walked along a row of deck chairs and passed the area where we had sat the night before looking at the giant funnel. I knew I had to be in the right area, but I was absolutely sure. Just as I thought I had overshot my target, a door opened and Jack emerged onto the deck.

I felt my face breaking into a smile. "Hi!" I walked over to him, still battling the bottle. "I'm sorry I kept you waiting."

"You're forgetting I grew up in a house with three women. I know that ladies function on a different time schedule. I waited a few minutes inside figuring you might be running a bit late." He let his eyes do the talking for a few moments, examining me from head to toe, his curiosity settling on the bottle and the glasses. "What's all this?"

"Oh," I said, "For you. And if you could, take the bottle out from under my arm. It's really, really cold."

He did as instructed. A puzzled look fell over his face. "Champagne? For me?" And then came a suspicious look. "Why?"

"I heard it was your birthday yesterday."

"Yes, it was, but who told you?"

Now this was something I didn't know. So I simply made something up. "The captain."

"The captain told you it was my birthday?"

"Yes. At dinner. He told me that it was your birthday, yesterday. So this is a belated celebration. But it's the best I could do on short notice."

He stood there for a few minutes, letting the false information collect in his ears. Before he could question me any further, I presented him with the wrapped éclair.

"And there's this too," I said.

He unfolded the handkerchief very delicately. When he saw what was inside, he gave a laugh deep in his throat. Finally he said, "I'll give you this, Lucy. I never know what to expect from you. Now let's see if we can find a place to sit down for this."

He took me by the elbow, guiding me down the deck to a row of church-like windows. I couldn't see in through the frosted glass, but there seemed to be light shining within. He popped open a door and peeked in first, then motioned for me to follow.

Once I was inside, I noticed felt cloaked in warmth and then I was too dumbstruck to notice anything else but my own heightened sensation of what wealth really means.

The room was covered inch by inch, wall to wall in the most gorgeous polished wood that looked like obsidian under glass lightened to a burnt amber. The furniture was lushly covered in the most exquisitely fine fabric, bolts and bolts of it unspooled and tailored around handsome chairs and settees grouped together for conversations around buffed-to-a-spit-shine tables. Just around the corner past the entrance was a fireplace that glowed with a little fire, cheerfully blinking out its last few flames for the night. On one wall was a bookshelf overflowing with finely bound volumes, though I couldn't imagine anyone just coming to this room to read. This was a room to be savored on its own terms.

I was presently caught up in the image of the two of us reflected in the gilded mirror over the fireplace. I had a strange feeling come over me, as though I were seeing myself for the first time and not quite recognizing the person I saw. He must have seen how fixated I was and stood closer to me, preening and posing as though he were about to be photographed.

"We look well together," he said. "I love what you're wearing."

"Hmm?" I said, still studying myself in the mirror. "Thanks."

"It's a lovely color on you. Suits you quite nicely." He was making his way to one of the settees by the fire. He waited for me to sit down before taking a seat himself. "And your hair. You've done something different with it as well."

"The stewardess put it up for me," I told him.

"It's a very becoming style. Sort of shows off your face."

I laughed. "Some people would say that's not such a good thing."

"No, no. You're quite a beauty, Lucy. If you haven't been told that by now, you've been hanging about with the wrong sort of people."

"Thank you," I said. I think I may have even blushed.

"Are you feeling all right tonight?" he asked.

"Yes."

"I worried that you had hurt your head when you fell last night."

A felt that slash of embarrassment cross my face again. "Oh, that. Listen, I can explain—" Even though I really couldn't.

"No need, no need," he said. "I'm just glad you're all right. And glad you're here."

I smiled. "I'm glad I'm here too, Jack."

I watched as he seized the champagne and expertly maneuvered the cork until just the shallowest of pops sounded the opening of the bottle. He took a glass and poured until the round bowl was equal parts bubbles and beverage and then after the foam had receded, topped it off. He gave me the first glass and then repeated the process for himself. Once we both had our celebratory potables in hand, we clicked glasses and uttered "cheers" before taking a sip in unison. After that, he relaxed, removing the cap from his head and placing it beside him as he leaned against the back of the settee. After a few sips of the champagne, he got into the éclair, which he ate hungrily and without any hint of self-consciousness, as though he hadn't had a bite in days.

I wonder if he ever does get a chance to eat, I thought as I watched him dive in for another bite.

"Did you have supper tonight?" I asked.

"Just a bite," he said. "Probably nothing compared to what you had."

"I didn't go to dinner tonight."

He paused before taking another bite. "But you just told me that you saw the captain at dinner."

"Oh, right. I did go to dinner. But I didn't feel much like eating dessert. So I saved the éclair for you."

"Well, it was really very sweet of you to think of me."

After he had finished the éclair, he wiped his mouth with the handkerchief. I thought he had looked tired before, but the éclair seemed to be bringing on a sugar rush and all at once he looked energized and refreshed. He smiled over at me.

"Mmm. That was good. Thank you, Lucy"

"What's a birthday without a little celebration? Anyway, it must be hard for being so far away from your family on your birthday," I said.

"Oh, it's not something to be bothered about. I've been in service to Marconi since I was nineteen years of age," he said. "That's quite a lot of birthdays."

"And I'll bet most of them were spent alone or at work."

"For the most part, yes. But I don't place so much importance on birthdays anymore. Not like I did when I was a lad and birthdays seemed to mean something."

He took a thoughtful sip of his champagne and considered the glass in the light as he spoke. "I'm sure that if I were home, Mum would have something planned. Elsie would want to bake me a cake or a special pudding and make such a fuss about my being twenty-five. She'd probably sing something for me; play something on the piano that she had composed." He gave a little laugh as though tickled by a memory he alone was privy too. "Elsie. She's such a dear thing. Never let me out of her sight when I was a lad. Mum could always count on her to look after me when she was too tired or too busy. And she would do so without being asked. You see, and I think I've told you this, my family lives above the shop where my father works and when I was growing up, my parents had a bedroom at the back of the shop and my sisters and I slept upstairs. So we were all very close, my sisters and I. And even now that I'm at sea, I still feel the closeness I felt with my sisters when I was a youngster. They still want to know where I am all the time. We write constantly, letters, postcards and whatnot. I've got two postcards waiting to go out to them now that I've got to run by the post office."

"I'll bet they worry about you," I said.

"Quite a bit," he said, after swallowing his champagne. "I think Elsie more than any of them. At Christmas she kept reminding me to put my coat on when I went out in the cold. As though I were a child. She and Ethel and Mum made such a fuss that I was getting thin. 'You don't get enough to eat, you don't get enough sleep. You're going to be an old man by the time you're thirty.' They worry mostly that there's never anyone on board these ships who will take as good of care of me as they do. But if I'm lucky, sometimes a female passenger on one of the ships I'm working on will take an interest in me and stuff me full of sweets and fill me with champagne."

I knew that he was joking. There was a wink in his voice. "So this kind of thing has happened to you before?"

"Oh, all the time. It's become so commonplace I've just started scouting out women who I knew are alone and in need of seducing."

"So you think I'm in need of seducing?"

He turned to me and said with just a hint of naughtiness whipping his voice. "I don't know. You're the one who brought the champagne." He took one of my hands and brought it gingerly to his lips in a gentle kiss.

It was more than the tickle of his lips on my knuckles that made me laugh.

"Sweetheart, I'm not the Pope."

He looked at me like he didn't quite get my meaning.

"I'm saying that if you want to show me how you feel, don't make it seem like an official state visit to Vatican City."

When I looked into his eyes now, it was as though he was thinking of some immense, inevitable task that lay ahead and he was unsure about how to proceed. I felt a steady pulse against the back of my eyes. His face was drawing near mine. His hand went around to the back of my head. His lips were so close to mine, so close I could feel the kiss even before it struck my lips. It was in the air, in each breath we took, but not on my mouth. He took that ripe bottom lip of his into his mouth and it emerged moist and trembling. My head was swimming and I couldn't seem to keep it steady. I closed my eyes. Then I felt the polite pressure of his lips on mine, just briefly. When I opened my eyes again he was smiling.

"Was that better, your Holiness?" he asked, his lips still so close to mine I could feel the vibrations coming from them as he was speaking.

I sat listless under the lingering influence of the opiate of his lips. I couldn't move, couldn't think.

"That was all right," I finally said in a whisper.

We both found that our glasses were empty and he retrieved the bottle from the floor for a refill. After he did this, he settled back, extending his arm against the back of the settee, inviting me wordlessly to cuddle up next to him. And I did, resting my head on his shoulder, very aware of his breathing, his heavy, heavy breathing.

"You haven't spoken much about your family," he said. "I want to know all about you, and you're being stingy on the goods."

"There's not much to tell."

"You said you lived with your mother and father and I believe an aunt."

"Yeah, that's right."

"So what are they like? What do they do?"

"Dad works in construction. My mother sells real estate. And Aunt Teese—I don't know what she's doing half the time, but whatever it is, it's always really annoying."

"Your mother works?" he asked as though this were the most bizarre thing he had ever heard.

"Yeah. Just part-time, though."

"Why does she work?"

I shrugged. "Because she wants to. Because it brings in extra money. We're not millionaires. That's why I can't believe I'm sailing first class. I mean, I looked in my purse back in my cabin and all I had were coins. I swear some of them were subway tokens." I took a sip of my champagne kind of wishing I had ordered beer instead. He looked at me as though he didn't quite believe me. "Honest, Jack. I don't come from any money. I can't even keep a minimum balance in my checking account. I don't know how my parents could even afford to send me to Europe and then send me home on this big hunk of metal. As a matter of fact, I still don't know how I ended up here."

"You still don't remember sailing day? Nothing at all?"

I shook my head vehemently. "Not the least little detail. I still feel like I was somewhere else and then I was here."

"Where were you?" he asked.

"Hell if I know. It was a green place. There was a tree, a very large one. I was sitting under it in a chair, like the one you found me on. I swear, it was like I was there and then something or someone sucked me out of that place and put me here."

Jack had become very quiet. When I looked up at him, his face was stony and his eyes were unseeing. I would have thought he had slipped into a coma if it weren't for the fact that he was muttering something under his breath. "That's just . . . no, it can't be . . ."

"Jack, are you all right?" I said, jostling him by the shoulder. "You still with me?"

He blinked a few times. "What? Yes. I'm . . . all right. I was just thinking . . ."

My heart was in free fall to my stomach. "You think I'm crazy."

"No, I don't think that at all," he said, taking my hand again. "I think you're wonderful."

He set his champagne glass down. Then he took mine and put it on the floor also. He reached for my face and his mouth came crashing against mine.

We were kissing, holding each other in a wild, feverishly pitched embrace. I found myself pinned helplessly against the seat of the settee as he laid out layer upon layer of deep, soulful kisses, a dessert-happy little boy announcing his sweet tooth's satiation with a series of "Mmm's". His body was moving against mine, his hands running the length of my body. My hands went around his neck, brushing the closely shaved hairs there, pulling his face closer. His hands had made the trip to my breasts and he was flicking his thumbnails against the glass studs there. His mouth broke away from mine and I breathed deeply as his lips made a guided tour from my jaw line to my neck, all the way down to where my breasts peeked out from the top of my dress.

Just then, I heard the sound of a door turning on its hinges, followed by a woman's voice, ricocheting loudly off the walls. A man's whimpering tone joined in occasionally and Jack and I froze in our positions.

"I told you that this wasn't going to do!" the woman was saying. "None of this! It's all a half-hearted attempt to get me to stay with you and I won't do it!"

"Darling, if you'd let me explain—

"I'm tired of your explanations. You kill me with all your earnestness. The way you promise this and promise that and nothing comes as a result of any of it!"

The voices were getting closer. Jack looked up at me with a mixture of fear and amusement in his face and put a finger to his lips.

"Sweetheart, you're not being at all fair!" the man said, still closer.

"Fair? Fair! I'm grown tired of being fair. It's not enough that I've had to put up with your snotty relatives all these years. Your sisters with their hooknoses and hairy upper lips, always looking at me as though *I'm* the oddity in the family. Your mother with that awful temper, and *her* hideous sisters. Not to mention your father. God, your father. He tried to put his hand down my dress at our wedding!"

"Sweetheart, dear, it was all in good fun. He was in his cups."

"It was all what? In good fun? Oh, it was an amazing lot of fun! So much so that I forgot to laugh. You imbecilic, vulgar, impotent wreck of a man! I can't believe you even have a mistress. What could you possibly have for her? You must be paying her a lot of money. A *lot* of money."

Our bodies both went rigid as the couple now came into view. Fortunately, they were both so into their ranting and raving that we were still going undetected. I watched as the feather in the woman's headdress painted the air with angry strokes.

"I know I've been horrible in these last few months," the husband said, "And I can't begin to apologize for all the things I've done. But if you would just for a minute hear me out."

"It would take more than one minute, believe you me. Try a lifetime. Try a lifetime of your being on your knees. God knows I've spent enough time on mine."

Our eyes were following the couple as they arrived now at the mantle, just feet from where we lay. I wondered, should we watch? Should we look away? If we moved, then we'd make our presence known. And then what? Would Jack be in trouble for fraternizing with a female passenger? He *was* in a rather telling position, his face directly above my breasts.

"And here I had to pretend again. Pretend that we're so happy together in front of the Astors and all your filthy New York friends. I'm telling you now that this is the end. When we get to New York, I'm getting on the next train to Philadelphia without you!"

"Oh, darling, you don't mean that!"

"I certainly do. And you'd better find a good lawyer because when I'm done with you, you'll be a squatter."

"I wish you would calm yourself and listen to what you're saying."

"I am listening. And it makes damn more sense than any of the pitiful things you've said for the last ten years." The woman crossed her arms and looked away from her husband, but still staring daggers.

I gasped as I found her eyes suddenly trained on me. On *us*!

Her mouth flew open and she took a step backwards, almost into the fireplace. Her husband followed her line of vision until he too was looking at us.

We had been discovered.

"Hello," Jack and I said together.

The woman put her hand to her chest. "Oh—my—God."

Jack was scurrying to get to his feet, tucking everything back into place and smoothing out his uniform.

"Don't stop on account of us," he said. "We were just leaving," he said.

I carefully assessed my own clothes, finding my breasts still covered. I had lost my wrap and one of my shoes had come off. I groped along the floor for both, finding Jack's hat instead. I quickly hid it from view as I continued the search for the missing items.

"Here, Lucy. Here's your wrap. And your shoe," Jack said. "Don't forget your shoe." He turned to the couple and gave a nervous laugh. "She's always forgetting her shoes!"

Neither one of them said a word. But I noticed the husband was considerably more relaxed than his wife. I thought I even saw him crack a smile.

I slipped my shoe on, not really knowing how I was feeling. Shocked, afraid, a little inebriated. I had to follow Jack's lead because I wasn't sure how we were going to get out of this.

"We'll be going now. Hope everything is—Lucy, are you coming?—fine with you."

He had me firmly by the arm and I at least had enough wits about me to walk feebly as we backed our way out of the room. Jack kept genuflecting to the couple and apologizing while I looked shyly on, anticipating that we would receive at least a portion of the woman's wrath before we got to the door.

But she said nothing. We were able to make our escape as though it had never happened.

But it *had* happened. And as soon as we were safely out of earshot, the two of us burst into a roar of unbridled laughter. I don't know how long we laughed, but it was long enough to make me so weak that I had to go to the railing for support. My face ached and my eyes poured tears. Jack too was mopping a few escapee tears from his eyes as we both continued to laugh. We just could not stop.

"What was that?" I finally asked. "What the hell was that?"

"You can't pay for theatre such as that," Jack said. "I'd see it again."

I momentarily stopped laughing and tried to focus in on something more important, something I thought he should be thinking about.

"But Jack, what if one of them says something to the captain or one of the high ranking officers? You know, about us."

He shook his head. "They won't be able to identify me. They never saw the insignia on my hat. I think they were too shocked to get a good look at us. I'm not too concerned."

I had no idea what time it was, but I knew it had to be getting pretty late. I knew Jack had to be tired, but I didn't want to let him go. In the night air the champagne's charms were wearing off, but I was still glued to him, my arms wrapped around him as we walked the decks. The lights were low and the only sound that could be heard was the constant throb of the engines churning out speed through the night. Other than that the night was quelled by a fierce quiet. But then, just ahead was an area of the deck illuminated by a light source within. I heard first a smattering of human voices raised in laughter and then a familiar tune, etched in the air by the bow of a single violin. As I listened, I smiled. It was the overture to Verdi's *La Traviata*.

At my insistence, we took a seat by the door. Only a few passengers remained to hear the last few numbers in the orchestra's repertoire. The women were all dressed in long, flowing gowns, their large, Gibson girl heads adorned with plumage and pearls. The men were decked out in formal tuxes, none showing any signs of dishevelment even at this late hour. They were all seated in arrangements of white wicker furniture spread across a black and white checkerboard floor. The walls were lined in trellis greenery, with pots of palms springing up in every corner. In the center of it all was a quartet of gentlemen all decked out in midnight blue tuxes, keeping the evening alive with the mordant strains of Verdi's opera. It was as though we had stumbled upon a private picnic in the middle of the night.

"Do you know what they're playing?" Jack asked.

"Mmm hmmm," I said. And I told him what it was.

"That's opera, isn't it?"

"That's right."

"Don't get to the opera much."

"I don't either. We studied this in my music appreciation class a few semesters ago."

"You must have appreciated this one," he said.

"Very much," I said. "You know anything about it?"

"Not a thing."

"It's based on a play by Dumas. *La Dame Aux Camélias.*"

"And I see you've studied French as well," he said.

"Just two years. Anyway, it's sort of a boy meets girl, boy loses girl to horrible disease story. Violetta Valery, a courtesan, who has tuberculosis, is loved by Alfredo Germont. Violetta rejects his advances at first because she's not a big fan of commitment. But they end up together, spending this wonderful time in a country house outside of Paris. But when Afredo's father shows up, it's not pretty. He says he's dating a slut and is disgracing the family name. More complications ensue. Violetta throws a party. Alfredo shows up and is so cruel to her you just want to throw him out a second-story window. But in the end, he realizes how much she loves him but before the happily ever after she dies in his arms."

Out of the corner of my eye I saw him reach to cover his mouth. His jaw came open in a wide, silent yawn and he wiped his eyes. When he saw that he had been observed doing this, he offered a smile and a quick apology.

"You'll have to excuse me," he said. "That wasn't a comment on what you were saying. It's been a long day for me."

"I'm sure it has. But I appreciate you're staying up with me."

He smiled and took my hand. "It's not exactly as though I've been your prisoner tonight," he said brightly.

The music was building to its string heavy conclusion and the violins were becoming more insistent with each stroke of the bow. My hand was still nestled in Jack's. My head was resting on his shoulder. As the overture concluded, I felt the tip of his index finger tapping wildly against my palm.

"Did you get that?" he whispered.

I muttered no and he tried again. My mind clicked off each letter as the message was slowly transmitted into my open hand. . . (I) _ . . . . _. _._ (think) . . (I) ._ _ _ (am) . ._. ._ ._ . . . _ . . . _. _. (falling). The rest was delivered too quickly for me to comprehend. He thought that he was falling asleep? Was that what he was trying to say to me?

The taps began again. This time I understood.

I sat there numbly for a few minutes, watching the room clear out, watching the musicians slip their instruments back into their cases. My face felt as though it had hardened. My eyes were fixed in a stare. I was sure that the casual observer would have thought I had been given a mild electric shock.

I could feel his breath coming in hot rushes through his parted lips against the side of my face. "What is your reply?" he said, his words a crush of noise into my ear.

I turned to face him, finding pensiveness tempering his features. I put a hand on his cheek.

"I think you'd better tell me that in words."

He gave a lazy smile. He had the look of a schoolboy who knew the answer to his teacher's question, but didn't want to say it in front of the class. "I think I'm falling in love with you."

There was a sudden glaze of moisture forming on my eyes. I looked at him now through prisms of light. I felt the need to protest. I didn't know why, but I knew something was wrong about what he said. It wasn't that he was wrong to say it or that he didn't mean it, but that it couldn't be. It just couldn't be.

There were a thousand impulses coursing through me. One was to kiss him and tell him that I felt the same way. Another was to leave and run back to my cabin alone. Still another commanded me to chastise him for going too fast, for going too many steps ahead of me.

I very slowly slid out of my seat and stood up, bringing him to his feet. Then I said to him, "I think you should take me back to my cabin now."

"Not feeling faint, are you?" he asked.

I smiled. "Not a bit."

Moments later we were sitting on my bed. Both of his hands were resting on the covers. Mine were as well. There was about six inches of space separating us. My heart was thundering so I thought he could hear it. We hadn't said a word to each other all the way down to the cabin. I didn't even ask him to come in with me. I led and he followed. He seemed slightly flustered and kept looking at the things in my room. His eyes would go to the closet door, then to the vanity, lingering on my brush and my comb. He stared at the robe draped over the chair in front of the vanity. I didn't remember putting it there. I surmised that the stewardess had put it out for me to wear when I came in after my meeting with my special gent, as she called him.

I took a deep breath and looked over at Jack. He nodded and smiled and passed his hand through his hair a few times.

"Jack, do I make you nervous?" I asked.

"No," he said as his eyes dropped to his lap.

"No, really, Jack. Is it making you nervous to be here with me?"

He shook his head. I could see his chest rising he was breathing so hard. "Terrified."

"Terrified? Why terrified?"

"I don't know. I just think, well . . ." He sighed and scratched his shoulder vigorously. He was looking over at my robe again. "I shouldn't be here."

"You don't have to stay."

"That's the problem. I want to be here," he said, his gaze momentarily lingering on the bed. When his eyes met mine, they were hooded in desire. "You make it easy for a man to forget his place in the world."

"What's your place in the world?

"Nowhere near yours."

I put my hand on his knee. "But where are you now?"

Slowly his eyes made the return to mine. He covered my hand with his. His palm was drenched in perspiration. "Sitting next to the most beautiful woman I've ever seen."

"Oh, yeah? And where am I?"

"Here with me," he said. "Somehow."

I smiled, "Yes, you are." I kissed him on his cheek. I brushed his lips with my thumb and then kissed him there. "Where you came from, Jack. It's the same place I came from. There are generations and generations of hard-working people in my family and they all had to slave away and save for everything they had. Like I told you, I don't know how I ended up here. But I think there's a reason. And I think I'm looking at it right now. And I have to say, I'm terrified too."

I kissed him again. He kissed me back and as our arms went around each other, I knew. I *knew*. The clothes he was quickly divesting me of, the bed where we lay close to each other, the languid robe that held his attention so . . . none of these things were mine. These were all just props. The clothes behind that closet door were completely foreign to me. They had to be someone else's, not mine. I couldn't have owned anything as hideous as that fox stole or as grotesque as that hat adorned with the dead dove. This bed was borrowed. It was something I couldn't have owned either. I didn't feel as though I belonged in it, though I had grown to suspect this was where I was spending the bulk of my time, sleeping, dreaming of whatever that was on the other side of consciousness—that place far away, distant as the coldest planet, as still as an orchard in winter. But this young man, he was mine. He was all mine, I thought greedily as my mouth took ownership of his.

His body was undulating against mine. His breath was coming harder and harder, warding off evil spells by summoning angels praying with every kiss. There were no words, only sounds—a symphony of sighs and oh's. We were both physically incapable of doing anything but surrendering to each other completely. All our mutual needs had taken over until we were not ourselves anymore. We were so close that I thought at any minute he would break right through to my soul and find me weeping with delight.

And then he did. And there was such joy, not wrecked or split in two by any distracting thought, but a complete infusion of every dazzling sight and sound and taste and smell all at once. His lips were everywhere, his hands. I was made inert by the potency of each new touch, my bare flesh pocked with the prints of his fingertips. His mouth was by my ear, whispering my name. I felt everything that was I was, everything that I had been, going away, vanished by his swift handiwork of recreating my soul from the ground up. The spirits of the old, dead flesh fell away in shadows. I was all new in his arms.

There was one, final push, enough to send me tumbling into clouds of bliss. Jack's own plunge followed. His eyes were closed, his mouth jaggedly open to his ragged breath.

When he opened his eyes, he looked down at me as though he were seeing me all over again for the first time. His face took on a severe, almost panicked look. I tried to swab the seriousness from his face by drawing my hand down his cheek. I smiled up at him and very quietly said his name. It was then that he returned from wherever he had been in his mind and a lazy grin materialized on his face.

He fell beside me in exhaustion, holding out his arms for me and I took my place at his side. He kissed me on my forehead and I curled up as close as I could to him. In minutes his labored breath slowed and became deeper and steadier. As we lay there, both nearing sleep, my soul still sang. I carried my smile into sleep and woke to sunshine.

There I was in the backyard of my home, awaking from this dream, from this other existence. The horns from the shipyard sounded a shift change and a breeze tossed the buds in the giant oak. I was all alone.

Dinner was over.

Mom had slapped some salmon on the grill and the three of us felt as though we had eaten well. It was nice, having something fresh to eat, accompanied by a sweet Riesling and Mom's musings about the closing of the Marple place.

Mom and I were doing the dishes. There were just three plates to scrape, three forks and three knives to clean and one spoon to wash. I was the only one who dove into the thawed chocolate pie that night. Mom had developed a sudden dislike for dessert because she thought she was getting too heavy. Aunt Teese liked her dessert flavored with nicotine.

While drying a dish, I saw my reflection in the plate.

The most beautiful woman I've ever seen . . .

Had he meant that? It certainly seemed that way. Suddenly I was immersed in memory—how the room in which we made love whirled with the sounds of sighs and kisses. Being locked in his arms—we had lain together in such a frenzied state. How had we gone so quickly from two people chatting amicably on the boat deck to two panting, desperate creatures all over each other past two in the morning?

"You gonna put that plate away, Lucy?" Mom asked me. "I think it's dry now."

"Yeah," I said. I was thinking about the warmth of his mouth against my breast. I put the plate in the cabinet and remembered how his lips were such a sensual surprise everywhere they went.

"I hope you don't stay out too late tonight with Janet," Mom said. "Aunt Teese's surgery is tomorrow."

"Yeah," I replied, thinking about his hands, his fingers, how they went to all the right places.

"You know how she gets about appointments. She thinks that if she goes early, they will take her early."

"Uh huh," I said.

We went to sleep. At the last, he took me in his arms and we went to sleep together.

I thought about what he had said in the silence of my cabin as we sat thinking about what we were about to do. We were in different worlds. And the one I was in now was too far away from his. I wanted to be there in his arms again. I wanted to wake next to him. I wanted to see him sleepy, hair mussed, looking at me as we both came into consciousness. I wanted to go back to where we left off.

I looked at the clock on the microwave. 7:45. I had just fifteen minutes before I had to meet Janet. If I were running late, she would be running later. The kids, always the kids.

I felt myself moving toward the washer in the door. As one in a trance, I swept over the top of it and landed softly on the other side.

"Lucy, where are you going?" I heard Mom say.

"Outside," I replied, noting my voice had taken only a ghostly tonality.

I switched on the outside flood lamp. The light didn't reach as far as the deck chair. I sat down in the cold darkness. The leaves were stilled in the oak. I could hear the cachunk, cachunk, cachunk of the movement of heavy machinery down at the shipyards. As I looked into the darkness, I thought it would be nice to see a few fireflies punctuating the night sky, but there were none. It was too early for them. But through the fledgling forms of the oak's leaves and the sturdy branches, I saw the stars. I took one brief breath and closed my eyes.

My eyes opened slowly to whiteness—the vast expanse of a cream-colored pillow where my head was resting. Soft breath was flowing into my hair. An arm was over my shoulder, another around my waist.

I turned my head very slowly. There he was, sound asleep. What a sweet angel he was in sleep. I put my hand on his face, tracing the lines of his nose, his pillowy lips, the bit of boyish flesh under his chin. I loved his eyebrows, the way they felt like feathers under my fingertips. His mouth was slightly open, letting the air glance off his throat as it entered. There were no other sounds except the droning of the engines deep in the bowels of the ship.

All at once, Jack's arm came up over his head in a stretch. When his eyes fluttered open, he smiled at me.

"Good morning," he said groggily.

"Morning," I said.

I ran my hand through his hair. His breath smelled of champagne and the night before. He kissed me and called me sweetheart.

For a few moments we just stared at each other, silently recounting the evening before and how it had all ended here. Still virtual strangers, only knowing the barest essentials about each other, we had come together so perfectly and everything had seemed to right, so planned. It still struck me as odd that though I had just met this man a couple nights before, it seemed we had known each other for some time. It was almost as though I had encountered a boy who once taunted me on the playground for the homemade clothes my mother stitched together for me—those gingham prints, those shawls made from mismatched skeins of yarn. Only this boy had matured now and his thoughts had changed. He now thought me beautiful.

"What are you staring at?" he asked me.

"Your nose," I admitted.

"Why?" he asked, as he passed his thumb over his nostrils, "Do I have something in it?"

"No, I just think it's cute. It's one of the first things I noticed about you."

"Really?" he said as his arms went around me and he tugged me closer to him. "You know what I first noticed about you?"

"That I was asleep in a deck chair?" I asked.

He growled a laugh. "No. You smell like coconuts."

"I do?" I sniffed my arm. "I don't know why. It's not like I'm taking a bath in coconut milk every evening."

He swept a few strands of hair away from my face. "Why don't you seem a stranger?" he asked.

"I was just thinking the same thing," I said. "This is right, isn't it? And it's real?"

"It's real," he said as he stroked my cheek.

"Thank you," I said as I wrapped my arms around him. "I think sometimes I'm living in a dream world here. I still feel like I'm somewhere else when I'm asleep."

"Trust me. You've been here all the time. You woke me up during the night."

"I did? Oh, God, please don't tell me that I was snoring!"

"No, you were talking."

"I was talking in my sleep?"

He nodded slowly.

"What did I say?"

"Nothing I could really make out. Something about salmon and pie."

"Well, that makes sense. I think I dreamed I was eating."

"You must have been hungry while you were sleeping," he said, nuzzling my neck.

"I must have been," I said.

"Are you still hungry?" he asked.

"Starving," I confessed.

His lips were on mine. I could hear all his longings in his quick breaths as his kisses settled on my neck and his hands moved across my back. There were voices in the hallway, laughter. There was a constant flow of movement and sound, and I gathered all my neighbors on the ship were all heading for breakfast. I wondered naughtily if they could hear us.

But then suddenly my mind went blank. I no longer cared that there were people outside. I was seeing stars again, the heavens. I was revisiting all the places he had taken me the night before and was finding them all as wonderful as I had remembered them.

He was now saying my name rapidly as he was nearing his peak. I was getting close too and when we both got there, this time at the same instance, we cried out in unison.

Just then we heard a man's voice right outside the door as he addressed someone in passing. "Excuse me, sir. Do you have the time?"

"It's fifteen past, sir," was the reply.

"Fifteen past eight?"

"That's correct, sir."

Jack suddenly froze. His eyes went dark with dread.

He reached over the side of the bed and retrieved his vest from the floor. He fished around the inside of the garment for something, and pulled out a gold pocket watch. He flipped it open and then instantly snapped it shut.

"Oh, God!" he said in a panic.

"What?" I asked.

"I'm late." Everything he had taken off was on the floor on his side of the bed. As he hastened to dress himself, I wondered where that urgency was when I lay naked the night before while he remained nearly fully-clothed, in shirt, vest and trousers, his tie a wagging navy tongue against his white shirt.

As he was tying his shoes, I came up behind him and kissed him and on his neck. "Am I going to see you tonight? After midnight?"

"No," he said.

"No?"

He finished tying his shoes. He turned to me and we lay down together in a flurry of kisses.

"We'll have to start earlier tonight," he said, kissing me down my neck.

"All right. What time?"

He thought for a minute. "How about half past eleven?"

"Anytime. Anytime at all." I kissed him just beside his mouth.

"So eleven o'clock, then?"

"I thought you said half past?" I said, trying to mimic his accent.

"All right. So half past ten."

"Why not ten, then?" I laughed.

"Ten is good," he said. "Ten is much better." Then a shadow passed over his face and he became quite serious. "I will have to ask Bride first if he can come on a bit earlier. He's going to be upset with me this morning as it is."

"Just tell him that you have to perform another personal favor for the captain," I suggested mockingly.

"Pardon?"

"That's what you told the elevator attendant the first night when you were escorting me back to my room."

"Oh, right," he said. "Well, just between you and me, I would have been crushed if the captain hadn't asked me to escort you. Otherwise I wouldn't be with you right now."

"God bless Captain Smith," I said, my fingers drifting over his pale visage.

"Yes," he said. "God bless Captain Smith."

When he finally got up to leave, I asked him to grab my robe from the back of the vanity chair and I slipped it on so that I could show him to the door. It was decided that I should peek out to see if anyone was coming down the hall. From the sounds of things, the herd going to breakfast had thinned.

"I think you're safe," I told him.

"Right," he said, stepping quickly outside. He glanced at both ends of the hall and dipped his head inside the door for one more kiss. "Ten o'clock, then."

"Ten," I promised.

"It shall be the longest wait of my life," he said.

"Mine too," I sighed.

I watched him disappear around the corridor and I slowly shut the door. I fell to the bed, lying on my side, touching the empty space on the pillow where his head had been. It smelled like him, a sort of woodsy, natural smell. Then I noticed that his scent was not the only thing he left behind. There on the bedside table was his cap.

I sprang from the bed, wondering if he had gotten too far, or if he was realizing now that he was reporting for duty uncovered. I ran to the door, cap in hand, and when I threw the door open, there he was.

"Lucy, my—

"I know, you left your cap," I said.

"Thanks, Lucy," he said, grabbing for another kiss.

"See you tonight," I said.

He smiled as he positioned his cap on his head. "Tonight."

He left me then with the promise of the night in his excited smile. Once again alone in my cabin, I stepped around the room in pirouettes, letting my legs kick up the length of my robe like a dance hall girl. I brought my hand to my lips, kissing my own palm. A burst of fizzy rapture flowed through me as I spun around, feeling absolutely, ridiculously in love.

"Yes!" I said, stinging the silence with my own trumpeting joy. "Yes! Yes! I'm in love! I'm in love!" I happened to catch a glimpse of myself in the mirror after I said this. I hopped on over to the mirror and gazed at my reflection, bewitched by my own appearance. My face was ruddy and glowing. I smiled back at myself, resisting the temptation to kiss the glass. I leaned on the vanity table and kicked up my feet. I spun off into the middle of the room, twirling in one spot until dizziness ensued.

But now, along with the vertigo, was a voice, a raspy, familiar voice calling my name. The voice tumbled through the air, hitting invisible plateaus, and my mind was snared by a quick, pulverizing drowse. I was compelled to close my eyes and when I opened them again, a saw a gray mist walking towards me in a halo of light. I was in my backyard again, sitting in the chair. I blinked a few times, bringing the specter of Aunt Teese into focus.

"Didn't ya hear me calling you's?" she asked.

My mind was cloaked in the woolen affects of the dream and I came awake as angry as a child snatched too early from an afternoon nap.

"No," I said. "What do you want?"

"That girl is on the phone for you's."

"What girl?"

"That girl who's always calling here. Janice."

Teese handed me the phone and for a few minutes it was as though I had forgotten how to use it. When I said hello, I spoke with a voice I barely recognized.

"Lucy, did you forget about me?" said the person on the line.

Who is this, I was thinking, and what is she talking about?

"Lucy? Are you there?"

"Yeah, I'm here," I said slowly.

"Lucy, I've been waiting for you here at Danny's for half an hour. What's keeping you?"

Danny's! Drinks! Janet! I gasped, agog at my own forgetfulness. "Janet! I'm so sorry. I'm so sorry! I just got a little . . . wrapped up in something else. Ten minutes, give me ten minutes and I'll be right there."

"Lucy, is something wrong? You sound very strange."
"No, nothing's wrong. I'll be there soon. Just wait for me."

CHAPTER SIX

At Danny's, I found Janet seated in a booth by the window. When she saw me, she gestured toward her gold Movado watch and gave me an exasperated look. She was dressed impeccably in jeans I swore she had ironed, a yellow and navy print blouse and a pink scarf tied around her neck. Her short and spiky sandy blond locks were given just the right amount of gel so they stood up like peaks of meringue. To me, she looked just as she always had, but when I came closer, I became aware of the laugh lines and creases that early motherhood had brought on and I was reminded of just how much time had passed since age twelve.

"I'm so sorry," I said, greeting her with an air kiss, rather than risk being branded by her coral lipstick. I slid into the booth. "Boy, am I ready for one of those," I said, pointing at her beer.

"Well, this was actually your beer. I ordered it for you, and then you were so late in coming, I ended up drinking it," she said. "And I thought I was going to be the tardy one. Joshua just wouldn't let me leave tonight. I was almost out the door when he started crying. I mean, bawling his little eyes out. 'Mommy, don't leave! Help me color!' I told him that Daddy was staying with him and he would color with him, but that wasn't good enough. He wanted Mommy. Then Christina started crying because she couldn't find Miss Pretty. You know, that old velveteen cat she carries around all the time? I had to help her find that. Found it—where else?—in the laundry room. Joshua had dropped it down the laundry chute and it was about to be washed with all my undies and bras. Well, after I got them settled, my husband didn't want me to leave either when he saw how the evening was shaping up. So I fixed him a bourbon and coke and got the kids some peanut butter cups. I think they'll be all right for a little while." She gave a self-satisfied smile. "Anyway, that's my evening so far. So what's going on with you?"

How to begin? I decided to order a drink first and then I would tell her. And with her beer half empty, she would need another one as well.

After the waitress plopped our drinks on the table, I sat, trying to muster the right words to use, while Janet chirped on about the kids. When I was halfway through my beer, she implored me again to tell her what was wrong. All the way to the restaurant, I rehearsed several different ways I could tell her, but all the scenarios ended with her calling me crazy and storming out of the restaurant.

How can I tell her that I've fallen in love with a man who only exists in my dreams?

"Janet, I've got something to tell you and I don't know how you're going to take it," I finally said.

"OK," she said warily.

"Do you remember the other day when we were talking on the phone and I told you that I had had a really bizarre dream?"

"Yeah, I remember that."

"Well, I keep having them. It's a whole series of dreams. They all started when I found this deck chair my Dad bought from Baumgarten's Flea Market back in the seventies . . ."

I told her everything, every detail of all the dreams I had had since the first day, from my first appearance on the boat deck. I described all the conversations I had had with Jack, all the rooms we had been in, how kind he was to me and how we had become fast friends and then, just this afternoon, lovers.

"The first dream," I said, "was sort of like a quick shower that you take, just to sponge off. The second was like a longer shower, the kind you take when you have plenty of time to get somewhere. But the third and fourth ones, the ones I had today. These were something else. It was more like a long, hot bath that just melts you to the porcelain. And when you step out of it, there's still a part of you standing there steaming in the middle of the bathroom, wanting to climb back in for another soak. Do you have any idea what I'm talking about?"

Janet was staring at me from across the table with a look of astonishment on her pert, freckled face. "I don't know," she said. "I don't think I've ever dreamed like that before."

"Neither have I. That's what makes me think that something else is going on."

"Like what?"

"Well," I said. "I'm thinking that. I'm thinking that, these aren't dreams anymore. I think . . . what I'm trying to say is . . . I think I might actually be . . . going back there."

"Back there? Back where?" Her eyes widened. "You mean . . ."

I nodded slowly. "I think I might actually be going back in time."

All at once Janet's expression changed from horror to mild condescension. She had the tenderly patient look of a first grade teacher whose pupil had just informed her that his imaginary friend would like a juice and a cookie as well.

"You don't believe me, do you?" I asked.

"Well, Lucy, I mean, hey," she said, giving a little nervous whinny. "It's not that I don't want to believe you. It's just that it's very hard to believe."

"I know. And I couldn't believe it was really happening to me at first. I couldn't let myself. I thought that if I let myself believe that I was really time traveling, that I'd also have to admit that I was going crazy. But now I not only believe that I have discovered a portal through time, I want to believe."

"Why? What's changed?"

"Because I'm in love with him."

Janet dropped her head as though she thought viewing me from a lower angle would increase her understanding of what I was saying. "Oh, but Lucy!"

"What? You don't think I know my own feelings?"

"I'm not saying that. I just think it's kind of hard to fall in love with someone you've never met."

"But we *have* met. Haven't you been listening to me?"

"Lucy, you're dreaming! They may be really nice, really real dreams, but that's all they are. Just dreams."

"If these are dreams, they're unlike any I've ever had before. You know how when you're dreaming, there are these little clues that tell you that you are dreaming. Like, it's not unusual for, say, one person to turn into another person or something else entirely right before your eyes. Or, how sometimes you'll be walking someplace and suddenly you're somewhere else. Or somebody will say something really strange or in a really weird tone of voice."

"Yes."

"Well, none of those things have been happening in these dreams. Another thing that tells me what happening is real is that when I'm in the dream, events take place in real time. If I start the dream at 12:00 p.m. here, then it's 12:00 a.m. there. And feelings. I can feel the fabric of the clothes I'm wearing. I can feel the touch of Jack's hands, the weight of his body on mine, the velvety texture of his lips when we're kissing. I hear my heartbeat and I know it's mine. Now can you honestly say something like that has happened to you?"

"Well, not to me, personally."

"Then how do you explain what's been happening to me in the deck chair?"

Janet looked completely exhausted, as though listening to me had required every last ounce of her strength. She sighed and said, "I don't know, Lucy. I just don't know what to tell you. What do you want me to say?"

"I want you to say that you believe me. But if you say it, I'm not sure that you'll actually mean it. I know it all sounds fantastic and overwhelming and absurd, but think, Janet. I've discovered a way to see a world that has vanished, to meet people who don't exist anymore. And there's something else I've been thinking."

I could almost hear her saying to herself, *Oh, God, what? Please tell me it's something about the service here and not about the dream . . .*

"Maybe the reason I've been so unlucky in love is that I was always destined to meet Jack. That we're just from completely different times isn't an obstacle. Somehow we've found a way to be together."

Janet closed her eyes and rubbed the bridge of her nose. "Oh, God, Lucy . . ."

"There he's been, all these years, back in time, out of my reach, until the one day when I was curious enough to discover the portal that led me straight to him."

"Lucy . . ."

"Mr. Baumgarten was telling me about this man who sold him the deck chair. He said he was a *Titanic* survivor who needed the money from the sale of the deck chair to get back to Ireland and try to start his life over. Jack told me that he worked in Ireland, at the Marconi station in Clifden. What if that man was Jack Phillips? What if he was trying to find me then?"

"Were you even alive then?" she asked.

"No. So we had to meet this way. The only way that would allow us to be the same age at the same time."

Janet looked at me sheepishly as she folded her arms over the table.

"You know, Lucy, and I don't even know why I'm asking this, but here goes: do you know if this man actually does survive? Because with the way you've been talking about him, you're setting yourself up for a lot of heartbreak if he doesn't."

"Oh, no. He does live."

"How do you know?"

"Mr. Baumgarten told me so." And then there was a sudden, crippling thought, one that I had put aside since that day in the flea market. I had only asked Mr. Baumgarten if Jack made it into a lifeboat. I didn't ask him if he survived.

"Oh, God. Do you think . . . ?" And I couldn't finish what I was going to say.

"Do I think *what*?"

"Do you think he doesn't survive?" What reason would Mr. Baumgarten have had to shield me from the truth?

"What difference does it make anyway?" she asked. "Even if he did survive, he'd be over a hundred years old. He'd probably be dead now anyway."

"Yes, but . . ." It was getting hard for me to speak. My voice sounded tinny to my ears. "He just turned twenty-five."

Janet looked down at her beer and scooted the bottle across her napkin. When she looked up at me again, I didn't see the patronizing that had been there before. I saw a face full of worries. I had given her more than ample proof that there was something wrong with me, that my reasoning had skidded to the side of the road and spilled all of its contents into a ravine. But I couldn't understand that then. I was still thinking, *She doesn't want to believe me. She doesn't want me to be happy with Jack. She wants me to live the kind of life she's living and I don't want that. I want the kind of happy me that I am in my dreams when I'm with Jack.*

I hated myself for telling her. I wasn't angry with her for not understanding me, or for not at least being willing to lend an accepting ear. This was a lot to take in and I had not given her credit for having been taken off guard. I had not adequately prepared her for what I was going to say, nor had I let on in the past few days that I was experiencing something that went beyond belief. When I was sitting there with her, I knew that it was my job now to repair the damage. If I couldn't make her believe me, then I would have to convince her of something else.

"God, you're gullible," I said.

I saw a slight movement in her jaw. "What?"

"I really had you going, didn't I?"

"Had me going? What are you talking about?" she drew in a breath and exhaled her next sentence in a blast of hot air. "Lucy! Were you fucking with me?"

"Yes, ma'am. Ha, ha! I got you, girl!"

"Oh, Lucy!" Her head landed with a thud on the table and I was worried that she had hurt herself. She rolled her face around and looked up at me with a rush of scarlet embarrassment staining her white skin. "I can't believe you!"

Obviously.

She rubbed her eyes and said, "God, I was sitting here thinking, 'Lucy's lost her mind. Lucy's going to have to go to a mental institution instead of ODU in the fall.' Man, oh, man, Lucy. Am I on *Candid Camera* or something?"

"No. I did it for a class. My acting class."

"Well, somebody give this girl an award. Here," she said, sliding the saltshaker my way. "Will this do?"

The tension in the air had abated and left Janet the friend she had always been. Cheerful, engaging, full of chatter. This would have to be the way to go for now. We finished many beers together that night, but all the while all I wanted was to go home. In my mind I was already beating a path to my door, with one intention only: I had to find out what happened to Jack.

By midnight I had my answer.

I was up in my room, in my bed, book in one hand and beer in the other. Both hands were wet, one with the condensation of the cool bottle, the other moist with perspiration in the aftermath of reading four little words: *"Phillips disappeared walking aft."*

All thoughts came to a jarring halt. *How could he have disappeared? People just don't vanish.*

I read the sentence again and the paragraphs that had come before. Jack continued working through the uproar of the released steam and the people racing for their lives out on the boat deck. Harold Bride went in and got their belongings from their living quarters and when he came back out, he found a stoker trying to mug Jack of his lifejacket. Bride lunged at the stoker, Jack sprang to his feet and the three men thrashed around until Bride was able to get a hold of the perpetrator and Jack pummeled him into unconsciousness. The sea rolled in, prompting the men to finally abandon their cabin, the would-be lifejacket thief and the dead wireless to seek safety . . . but where?

All the lifeboats were gone, except for the collapsible on top of the officers' quarters, which wasn't anywhere near the davits and couldn't be launched properly. Some men were pushing it off and the boat landed on the deck, only to be washed off along with the men who had been trying to launch it, a motley group that included Harold Bride. But not Jack Phillips?

Where did he think he was going, walking aft? The deck had to be very steep at that point, nearly perpendicular to the waterline. What did he think he was going to find walking aft? He knew all the lifeboats were gone.

As my heart thumped audibly in my chest, I sat there trying to steady the book in my trembling hand. I took a few sips of beer in swallows that went down as easily as ostrich eggs. A calming thought entered my head.

Suppose that sentence had been written from Harold Bride's point of view? Maybe that was just the last time he saw him that evening until they were reunited on the rescue ship?

I flipped ahead, my fingers gripping the pages like fly paper. My eyes darted across each page, scanning the lines for his name. At 2:15 the sea gushed aft . . . bandleader Wallace Hartley dropped his violin bow on the beginning strains of the song *Autumn* . . . The bow dipped forward . . . People could no longer stand and were holding onto anything stationary . . . the lights flickered once, twice, and then out for good . . . the first funnel fell in a shower of sparks, killing many people in the water, but pushing the Collapsible Lifeboat B to safety . . . the bow was completely under . . . the ship settled into the water . . . as the water closed over the stern, there was only the merest of gulps over the flagstaff . . . Third Officer Herbert Pitman noted that the time was 2:20 . . . Bride found his way on top of Collapsible B . . . Hundreds of people littered the sea . . . some lifeboats went back to the scene of the wreck to pick up survivors . . . the people on the boats tried to stay warm, tried to come to terms with the reality of what had happened to them and their loved ones . . . the men on Collapsible B stood on the boat to counter the swell as the craft was in danger of sinking . . . Bride told Second Officer Lightoller of what ships were coming . . . one by one some men slipped off and died . . . the captain of the rescue ship *Carpathia* readied his officers and crew to take on *Titanic's* survivors . . . *Carpathia's* Marconi operator still tried to contact the long-gone *Titanic* . . . At 4:00 a.m. the *Carpathia* finally arrived at the scene of the wreck . . . the men on sinking Collapsible B were transferred onto nearby lifeboats . . . Lightoller lifted a lifeless body from B onto Lifeboat Twelve . . . Collapsible A's passengers were taken onto Lifeboat Fourteen . . . Managing Director of the White Star Line, Bruce Ismay, wanted to go "someplace quiet" and was taken to the doctor's cabin on *Carpathia* . . . In Lifeboat Twelve, Colonel Archibald Gracie tried to revive a lifeless body . . . Harold Bride was taken onto *Carpathia* and promptly passed out as he was being lifted onto the boat deck . . . *Carpathia* scouted around for more survivors . . . there was only one body . . . *Carpathia* steamed for New York . . . Bride awakened in a stateroom . . . *Titanic's* barber shop pole bobbed up and down on the debris-strewn North Atlantic . . .

And that was all.

Not one mention of Jack anywhere. Or was there? Could his have been one of the hundreds of cries heard that night from people struggling in the water? Could his have been the lifeless body taken off Collapsible B and brought onto Lifeboat Twelve? Could he have been the victim watched over by Archibald Gracie? Could his have been the lone body floating in the sea as *Carpathia* took one last look for survivors?

I threw the book down and took another swig of my beer. Beside the bed I found my cigarettes and I fished out two and lit one, tucking the other one behind my ear. Pacing the floor and smoking, I began to feel feverish as though a systematic virus were running its course all through me. The night was silent and dark, the only light supplied by my bedside table lamp. I went over to the darkest corner of the room, by the closet, and crouched there, continuously sighing through exhalations of smoke. My head was thundering with thoughts, some barely coherent, others all too clear.

What did Janet say? What does it matter if he did die? He wouldn't be alive today even if he had survived. I guess that's true. But it matters to me if he died. God, after meeting him and talking to him these past few nights, or days, whatever they were . . . just seeing him, talking to him, feeling so close to him . . . of course it matters!

The shock of what I had read had left me now. The warm and tumbling effects of the alcohol were permeating my brain with soft slugs of sentimentality. I had tears in my eyes and as I smoked and paced, I let them fall.

How in the world did he ever work through it? All the noise of people screaming and running in fear, his own fear? Why did he think it was even worth it, trying till the end to contact somebody? Was he punishing himself? He had the power to keep the ship from ever going into that icefield in the first place. He had received all the ice warnings, but they all hadn't been taken to the bridge. He told the Californian's *operator to shut up when the guy interrupted his work with an ice warning. If that message had made it into an officer's hands, the officer would have known the ship was headed straight for the icefield and the ship would have stopped for the night. Or even if the warning hadn't been heeded,* Californian *could have been contacted for a quicker rescue. But* Californian's *operator had shut off its wireless for the night . . .*

I closed my eyes as I imagined the guilt Jack must have wrestled with in those final moments. I thought of him sitting there, tapping out S.O.S. over and over, signaling to anyone who could hear. And the fight with the stoker who tried to take his lifejacket. I thought of those soft, sweet hands curled into fists, striking some sweaty, coal-encrusted brute of a man over and over until he collapsed. I thought of him in the lifejacket, chest deep in all that cold, miserable water, because there was no space for him in any of the boats. I thought of the two postcards he had written to his sister.

As I sat there in the darkness, feeling the claustrophobia of being trapped by my own unquiet thoughts, I slowly began to wonder if this was what the onset of madness was like.

I went back to the bed and fell onto the mattress, dropping my cigarette butt into an empty beer bottle. Through blurry eyes I looked over at the clock radio. The red numbers glowed 12:34.

CHAPTER SEVEN

I must have cried during the night in my sleep. I awoke, still dressed in the clothes I wore the day before, on top of my blankets, my eyes and nose swollen, my throat aching from choking down tears and smoke all night. I couldn't remember when I fell asleep. The last time I looked at the clock it was 12:34 a.m. Now it was 11:15 a.m.

11:15!

How could it have been morning so suddenly? How could it have become such a late morning so suddenly? The night had vanished and how there was this day with all this time to fill up. I couldn't waste a second. Not with Jack waiting. What time had I told him we would meet? Ten o'clock? He had already been waiting an hour and fifteen minutes, if he were waiting still at all. That was a long time for someone who could measure his life by the hours.

But there was still time to save him, save everybody.

I jumped out of bed. Through the open door I heard voices down in the foyer. Mom and Aunt Teese were talking very excitedly, but it didn't sound like an argument. In their raised voices I heard my name. When I was on my way down the stairs, I greeted Mom whose concerned expression dissolved into relief when she saw me.

"Oh, good," she breathed. "You're up. I was beginning to worry. Aunt Teese is all ready to go. Here's some money so that the two of you can go get lunch after she's finished. She'll need to go to the pharmacy to get her heart pills, but she has a check for that."

The cobwebs that came from sleep were still holding fast to my thoughts and I couldn't understand what Mom was saying. Then I saw Aunt Teese standing at the front door, dressed in something other than her pink robe. She was dressed to go out and her hair had been done.

A loud remembrance of a promise I had made clamored in my head: I had told Mom that I would take Aunt Teese to the doctor today.

"You forgot, didn't you?" Mom surmised correctly.

"Mom, I can't do it. I'm sorry." My tongue was thick when I tried to speak and I slurred as though still drunk. I hoped that Mom would see that I was in no shape to drive and would immediately volunteer to take Teese instead.

A hand went up on Mom's hip. She called down to Aunt Teese, "Why don't you go wait in the car, Teese? She'll be right out."

Aunt Teese shook her head and headed for the front door. I heard her mumbling, "Can't rely on her for anything. Anything at all. Stupid dishrag."

Mom returned her glaring eyes to me. "I cannot believe you. I cannot believe you! Aunt Teese asked you days ago to take her to the foot doctor and you promised her you would. You promised *me* that you would. We even talked about it last night."

"I know, Mom. But there's something else that I have to do this morning. It's very important."

"Something else that you have to do? Why would you make plans to do something else when you knew you had to this to do for Teese?"

"It just came up. Couldn't you take her? I promise I'll make it up to you somehow."

Mom shook her head. "Honey, today's the day I close the deal on the old Marple place. I can't take her. I'm supposed to meet with the new owners at 11:30."

"Can't you just drop her off on the way?"

"Dr. Fishburn's office is all the way on the other side of town. I'd be going twenty minutes out of my way and I'd be late for my meeting. How could you even suggest such a thing when you know how important this is to me?"

"Then can't she get a cab?"

"It's too late for that now. By the time the driver arrives, she will have missed her appointment all together."

"Then can't she take the bus?"

"A bus! Lucy! She's going to have to have surgery this morning! Show some compassion!"

Tears were thickening in the back of my throat as I realized I was losing.

"But Mom, if I don't do this thing that I have to do, it . . . it . . . it'll be bad. It's very important that I do this one thing!"

"What? What is so important that you'd let your father's only living aunt hobble around on public transportation?"

What could I say? That I had to abandon the reality of adult promises and commitments set in stone for a gossamer world waiting for me on the other side of consciousness? I couldn't tell her the truth. Perhaps twenty years before when Mom was still in her hippie-cum-earth mother phase, she would understand and maybe even offered a little advice. But this was a different time, a different mother, and yet still the same me, standing there wishing for stones instead of glass. I wondered how in four days' time how a man so far away in years, so deep in the past, had come to mean everything in the world to me, so much so that as I stood there, face to face with my angry mother, I couldn't feel any sympathy for her. I was only aware of the breaking of my own heart.

"I can't tell you," I said.

"You can't tell me. Well, that's just great, isn't it? Now listen to me, Lucy. And I'm going to say this very plainly. Your Aunt Teese is waiting for you to take her to the doctor. Not me, not some grumbling cab driver and not some bus driver either. It's your commitment and you have to honor it. You were the one who promised her that you would take her and you're the one who will take her. Understand?"

I nodded and said in a gravely voice, "Yes, Mom."

Mom sighed and twisted her watch around on her wrist so that she could read it. "Oh, God. Now I'm going to be late. I've got to get going and so do you."

She was now stomping down the stairs in her business heels, in all her business attire, making me suddenly sick to see her like that. I thought if there was a God looking out for me that morning that He would allow me to disappear, just vanish from the stairs or just get squeezed into nothingness by all the walls closing in around me.

The first dull thuds of a headache were pinning themselves between the skin and bone of my forehead. I kept thinking that in a minute I would start screaming, ranting and raving against the unfairness that I couldn't just disappear into the past where I stood, going right into Jack's arms.

I walked numbly out the door to the car. Aunt Teese was already in the passenger seat, puffing away, with such a smug, self-satisfied look on her face that I had to fight against a pugilist's urge to pound her paper thin flesh until it was raw and bloodied like a fresh cut of veal. It was as though she had planned it all along, or though she possessed some malice of foresight that today would be important and she was going to do her best to foul things up for me.

I sat in the driver's seat, not even attempting to start the car. I wasn't sure if I could or if I even should. The bitterness of the beer I had voraciously thirsted for all night had left me dry as a bone and aching with nausea. The smoke from Teese's cigarette seemed to be ignoring the fresh air outside the cracked window and was attracted only to me. I sat there, with anger percolating and popping in my ears, feeling boxed in by my own skin, my own existence, wanting to thrust my palms against the walls of the present time and burst through the other side. Or out, anyway, out of who I was, out of that car, out of all that I was doing and being all my life. I felt crammed into a hole, ten sizes smaller than what I needed for my own comfort, a root grown firmly into the ground until stymied against bedrock. This was it, this was all I was: Lucy Cranston, twenty-one year-old perpetual student, daughter, permanent resident of Hampton Roads, driving my father's aunt to the doctor.

"We're going to be late if you don't hurry," she said.

I said nothing as I slipped the key in the ignition and turned.

The doctor's office, any doctor's office, is a mean, ugly place, no matter if it's decorated like the presidential suite at a midtown Manhattan Hilton or a Greyhound bus terminal. No amount of fancy decorating can take away from the fact that one is sitting in a germ-filled petrie dish. This office had been done, inexplicably, in a mid-seventies bachelor pad motif with white vinyl chairs and beach scenes on the walls. Teese's podiatrist shared his practice with a dermatologist and there were gentle reminders about sun damage all over the place. Over the chair where I was sitting was a cheery photo of two toddlers holding hands as they walked along the surf. The caption read, "Young bodies need sun protection. The higher the SPF, the longer the life." On the opposite wall was a poster of a sun-lit beach with an overlay of calligraphic words saying, "The Ancient Sumarians worshipped the sun. Now they are all gone." Even the clock over the receptionist's desk was a public service announcement. Circling the circumference of the clock was a script that read, "Time to check your skin for melanoma."

From the minute Aunt Teese and I stepped into the office, I kept watch on that clock and its paranoid urging. It was 11:30 when we crossed the threshold, 11:45 when Aunt Teese was escorted back into the exam room. My eyes watched the clock as my feet took me back and forth between my chair and the drinking fountain with its endless supply of icy cold water. I was severely dehydrated. My brain had that dim bulb feel. I knew my blood sugar had to be extremely low as well. I could not stop shaking.

As I continued my jittery walks between my seat and the water fountain, I was being watched by the receptionist. I was the only one in the waiting room. Everyone else was being seen by the doctors. Teese's was the last appointment before the doctors broke for lunch.

Jack has given up hope on me, I thought. No matter how much he wanted to see me, I doubted he would have waited this long.

I could see him, waiting, looking at his watch. Did he know that as the hands made their sweeps across the watch face that his time on earth was slipping away? Of course not. That's why I had to tell him. I could see him in his uniform, in that nice, neat uniform, looking clean and sweet. I wondered if I would ever truly see him again.

On this last trip back to the chair, the receptionist called to me. "Miss, would you like a cup?"

She offered me a ceramic mug emblazoned with the names of the physicians and, in quotation marks, "Complete care from head to toe."

"Don't worry about your aunt," the receptionist said soothingly. "She'll be fine. Why don't you just sit and read for a while. It'll keep your mind off things."

I knew I wouldn't be able to read. When I was nervous and upset I couldn't concentrate. But just so she knew that I wasn't ignoring her, I went over to the coffee table and sifted through some of the periodicals there. Since it didn't matter what I was reading, because I couldn't read anyway, I picked up a women's magazine from February. All the articles inside were about Valentine's Day. "How to make your man think he's in seventh heaven on the 14th." "Will you be my Valentine? 10 ways to make that unattainable man yours." "I played Cupid for my best friend and shot myself with my own arrow."

Not only were all the articles about love and hearts, but the advertisements were also in support of the holiday. I ran across an ad for a jewelry firm sandwiched between a story entitled, "My most passionate Valentine memory" and a multiple choice quiz called, "Are you your own worst enemy when it comes to love?" I didn't even know that it was an advertisement for jewelry at first. All I saw was a close up shot, in soft focus, of a man and a woman on the verge of sharing a kiss. The woman's hand was weaving its way through the man's hair, displaying the reason for their embrace: a diamond solitaire. Underneath were the words: "This Valentine's Day, don't just tell her you love her. Show her you'll love her forever."

I shut the magazine, making such a noise that the receptionist flinched. I drank down the remainder of the water, got up and went over to the fountain for a refill. As I was walking back to the chair, I got a good look at myself in a mirror just left of the receptionist's desk. I looked God-awful, as though I had been living out of a car for six months. It was a warm day and I was certain I reeked like old onions and garlic. I combed through my hair with my fingers, remembering how I looked in the mirror with Jack.

I could picture him still out there by the station, smoking his fifth—no sixth—cigarette of the night. I could see him snuffing it out with the toe of his shoe, drawing his arms against his chest. It was too cold for him to wait any longer. He was walking now, towards the entrance to the Grand Staircase. I could see him walking down the hall now, trying the door, leaning close and whispering my name. He knocks again, a little louder this time. "Lucy, are you all right? Is something the matter?" *And then, after a few minutes, impatience moves him to try something else. He goes back up to the boat deck to see if we have missed each other.*

"Bride, have you seen Lucy?" *he asks his junior operator.* "Has she been here since I've been gone?"

"No, old man," *comes the reply.* "Perhaps she's found some other bloke she fancies. Someone more like herself."

Jack doesn't believe this, of course. But still, there is a little insecurity that allows him to think this could be true.

"She could be sleeping. She sleeps very soundly. She falls asleep quite easily. The first two nights she fell asleep right as we arrived at her cabin." *And then a sudden fear grips him.* "What if she's ill? What if she does have some sort of . . . sleeping sickness? Sometimes her mind isn't at all clear. She admits that. But then other times she seems just fine."

"I still say she had a blow to her head that first night. She could be dying from it now, if she isn't dead already. I'd fetch the surgeon again if I were you."

"I'm going to do just that," *Jack says.*

He goes to find the doctor. Where? In his office? In a stewardess' room? The doctor had a way with the ladies, I understood, from reading the book. He eventually finds the doctor in his quarters. The two men come to my room, find it locked, and try to rouse me, calling my name.

"Miss Cranston, are you in there? This is the doctor. I've a young man out here who has reason to believe you might have taken ill."

And then, total silence.

"Miss Cranston, please open the door and let us see that you're all right."

Jack chimes in at this point. "Lucy, please come to the door. We're worried about you."

Still, there is no answer.

The doctor turns to Jack. "Has she had any more of these sudden sleeping attacks since I examined her?"

"Yes. I had to put her into bed the night before last."

"And last night?"

The question solicits a sheepish look from Jack. He answers cautiously. "I went in with her."

The doctor looks impressed. "Third time was the charm, eh, boy?"

"Yes, right. At any rate, I think we should summon the purser to open the door. I don't like this."

The purser joins them shortly, master key in hand. He remembers me.

"Had trouble with this one the other night," he says. "Couldn't decide if she wanted her young gent to come down to her cabin or meet him up on the deck." He looks at Jack. "Were you the young gent?"

"Yes, I am."

The purser turns the key in the door. "I haven't heard from her or seen much of her since. It's as though she sleeps 'round the clock."

They are in my room now. I am lying motionless on the floor, dead to the world. The doctor is the first person to advance, although Jack wants to. The doctor pats my cheeks, calling my name, right into my ear. He pulls out a stethoscope and listens to my heart, proving to himself conclusively that I am still very much alive and still very much asleep.

"Why won't she wake up?" is Jack's query.

"I'm not quite certain. She appears to be fine. Pulse is normal, temperature is normal. Perhaps she just fell asleep."

Jack bends down close to me, touching my face. "Lucy, please wake up."

"Perhaps sleeping beauty needs a kiss to be her about?" the doctor suggests.

Though this proposal is made in jest, Jack takes it to heart. I can feel the softness of his lips on mine and I am zapped awake with one thought reverberating through my brain, and I voice it loudly, screaming, "Jack, this ship—

Fingertips drummed on my shoulder. When I looked up I saw Aunt Teese, all lanced, bandaged, and ready to go.

"I'm all finished now," she said.

"Not a minute too soon." the receptionist said. "Your niece has been very worried about you."

"Really? *My* niece?" Aunt Teese said, incredulously. "You were worried about me, Lucy?"

I looked at Aunt Teese and then at the receptionist, beaming up at us as though she were about to witness some sort of jubilant celebration in the aftermath of my aunt's successful surgery.

"Yeah, I was worried about you. But you're all right now," I said, taking her by the arm. "Does it hurt much?"

"Can't feel anything right now. The doctor shot my foot full of painkillers. You'll have to help me to the car."

On the way out of the doctor's office, Aunt Teese continued her mission of totally wrecking my plans for the day by reminding me that she would need to go to a drugstore to get her heart medicine.

"There's a pharmacy right next door to the medical complex," I said.

"Uh, Lucy, could you's take me to another one instead?"

"Why, what's wrong with this one?"

She was not immediately forthcoming with an answer. I derived from her hesitancy that she had bounced a check there.

"Well, here. Mom gave us twenty dollars for lunch. You can just use it to pay for your medicine and we can fix sandwiches at home."

She shook her head. "My prescription costs thirty-four dollars."

I sighed, knowing I didn't have the money to pay the difference. "Tell me, Aunt Teese, is there a pharmacy anywhere in the Hampton Roads area that doesn't have a sign behind the register that says, 'Do not accept checks from Theresa Kravitz?'"

"The one at Kmart doesn't."

"Oh, Kmart. The one on Warwick?"

"No," she said guardedly. "The one on Mercury."

The store she was referring to was all the way in Hampton, at least twenty minutes away. I would have yelled at her, but I was beyond that. There simply wasn't time for anything but going, going. There were more important issues to consider.

Jack was waiting.

It was nearly 1:30 when I pulled into the driveway that afternoon. Two epic hours had passed since Teese and I had left the house that morning. As I put the car in park, I couldn't comprehend how late it was, how strangely I was feeling, or how little I cared that I was going to miss my afternoon classes.

For a while I couldn't even get out of the driver's seat. It was as though when I shut the car off, I lost power. I was in shock from all that had transpired. First, the endless wait at the doctor's office, then the sojourn to the pharmacy on the other side of town, then the search for a fast food drive thru with the least number of cars. I sat at the wheel now with the lingering odor of Teese's fried chicken lunch and the smoke from her generic cigarettes threatening to do me in with their noxious fumes. But still I sat, windows closed, hands on the wheel.

I knew Jack hadn't waited for me, but I had to get to him. If I did anything at all that afternoon I had to get to him and tell him what was going to happen to him and to the 1500-some others. I knew that as soon as I was in his arms, I would remember. I would have to remember.

Now in the deck chair, I closed my eyes, fully expecting that when I opened them again, I would be in my stateroom.

Minutes passed. I opened my eyes to find that I hadn't left my backyard. I closed my eyes again. I had to overcome my own curiosity long enough to fall asleep. I tried to think about other things—the wind, how much homework I had for the next day, what Mom was going to fix for dinner. Still I wanted to open my eyes, just to see, just to *see*.

I tried letting my mind go blank.

I was still there.

I tried to relax. I kept telling myself that I just needed to relax. But just telling myself that I needed to relax was making me more nervous. There had to be something else I could do. I could read, I thought. I could read the book that had brought me to the ship in the first place.

I got out of the chair and went upstairs to my room where I had left the book on my bedside table under an empty beer bottle. I carried the book to the chair, sat back down again and began to read.

The first passage I came to had to be about Jack at a critical point of his mortality. It was late on the night of April 14, early April 15. The power was fading, the engine room was flooding. The ship couldn't last much longer. Women and children were being given first priority in the lifeboats.

Jack's own desperation leaped from the pages and merged with my own as I continued to linger in limbo. On page 43, Harold Bride draped a coat over Jack's shoulders and asked him where he had put his boots. Jack replied that he might not need them . . .

There were tears in my eyes, as though I were watching the events under glass and couldn't break through. I couldn't watch any longer. I had to get to him, get back there. Somehow.

Noisily chewing my thumbnail down until the blood formed a halo around the remaining nail, I remembered the half sleeping pill I had left in the box of Dozeaze upstairs. I could take that, I thought. That never failed me.

I jumped out of the chair and headed inside, tearing open the screen door with such force it sounded like a shotgun blast. From somewhere inside, Aunt Teese cried out, "Who's there?" Who the hell did she think it was? Santa Claus paying an early visit, so pissed off that we didn't have a working chimney that he was wreaking havoc on our back door? I charged into the house and brushed past her in the hallway.

"You nearly gave me a heart attack!" she said, clutching her chest for added effect.

Good thing you got those damn pills today, I thought angrily as I ran up the stairs.

My heart had been beating so fast for so long that it ached. I ripped open the medicine chest and grabbed the pink and white box beside my facial cleanser. I picked the pill out of the foil blister, sending it skittering down the sink. I retrieved it just before the drain could swallow it.

With the pill making its slow descent to my stomach, I went weakly down the stairs. The hands on the clock were arranged at a quarter to two. I was beginning to think I was never going to make it, and starting to feel a little foolish as well. By the time I reached the chair again, I was shaking.

I sat there in my backyard, under the tree, my body reverberating with the after effects of all that running, all that scrambling to do something that a day before had been so easy, so damn easy. I thought about what I was going to tell Jack and how I was going to tell him. I let the whole scenario develop in my mind, a hurried mental rehearsal for a final act that had to come off without a hitch.

I'll wake up in my stateroom. Then I'll run straight to his quarters. It doesn't matter if he's asleep. I'll ask Harold to wake him. No! I'll wake him myself. I'll just barge into his sleeping quarters and wake him gently. No, I'll shake him. I've got to let him know what an emergency he has on his hands. He'll be startled, of course, but by now he's probably assumed that I'm half-nuts. He can't think I'm being crazy this time, though. He's going to have to know what I'm saying is the truth and believe me. How will I make him believe me? I've got to come up with a way to tell him that will make sense to him. I'll take him by the shoulders and say, "Jack, I've got to tell you something. And I'm not saying it to frighten you. I just think you should know." No, I can't begin like that. It would probably be best to blurt it all out at once. "This ship is going to sink at 2:20 on Monday morning, but you can do something about it now!" No, he won't believe that. He'll know I'm being crazy then. I'll have to come up with some introduction, some way of softening the blow, while at the same time letting him know the seriousness of the matter. "Listen, Jack. You've got to believe me. Don't ask me how I know this, because I can't tell you, but you just have to trust me that what I'm saying is true." That sounds all right. "And I'm not saying this to shock you, or to scare you. I'm just telling you because you of all people need to know. This ship is going to sink at 2:20 on Monday morning." No, I won't have to mention that last part at all. I'll just say, "Jack, on Sunday night, you're going to get a message from The Californian. It'll be an ice warning. I know you're wondering how I know this and I can't tell you exactly why I do. You don't even have to believe me now. Just wait until Sunday night when you're working. The message will come to you just after eleven. You can't ignore this ice warning and you better make damn sure that the officers don't ignore it either. It has to go directly to the bridge. Put it in Officer Murdoch's hands. He will know then that the ship is steaming towards an ice field and will stop for the night or change course. Please, Jack. Don't tell me I don't know what I'm talking about. Don't think I'm crazy. I swear everything that I've said will happen. There's more I can tell you, but I'm not going to. If you just trust me on this, that what I've told you is the absolute truth, nothing bad will happen to anyone, not even to yourself. I know you'll be annoyed when the message comes through because you'll be working at transmitting all those backlogged messages and because Californian is so close, its message will momentarily deafen you. But don't be deaf to the warning, to my warning. Hear me, Jack, hear me. Remember when you found me, Jack? You asked me over and over if I could hear you. I could hear you, sweetheart. Every pitch-perfect note of your beautiful, musical voice. The soft whistles of you 'S' sounds when you whispered to me . . . the way you trim your 'R's and broaden your 'A's' . . . the way you say my name, putting such an importance on the 'U', making it sound otherworldly, imbued with all your seraphic sweetness. You make me feel like an angel, your angel. You took care of me, Jack. Even before you knew who the hell I was. And you reinforced that when you dropped me off at my door and promised to look after me during my journey. You saved me, Jack. And now I'm going to return the favor. Trust me. Just trust me . . .

    I seemed to be rising now, not from the chair, but from a place in my head. My thoughts were becoming brittle, frosted in drowse. I was falling upward, heading towards a clear, lighted surface overhead. I wasn't making any attempts at motion. Everything my body was doing was completely involuntary as I neared the light. My body was loose and wavy, my limbs falling in all directions. My mind was snared in a rush of instant wakefulness as I broke the thick surface of my emerging consciousness. I drew a breath.

There was a fresh presence in my mind, one that seemed to have sprouted instantaneously, a new lobe, with all of its receptors going mad, trying to process all the information flowing throughout. Adrenaline coursed through me and I felt energized by all my sensations being whisked by a new and vibrant force.

My head was alive with sounds. And then I knew. Then I knew!

"This ship is going to sink!" I said aloud.

I awoke on the floor of my stateroom, in my robe. It was enough to cover me on my journey to the boat deck. I wanted to think that he was still waiting for me, two decks up. I wished that I could have drilled a hole though the ceiling and through the walls to peek through just to see if he was still there. "I've got to tell Jack that this ship is going to sink at 2:20 Monday morning!" Even thinking about saying this brought such a heady infusion of relief that my knees got weak.

When I was out in the hallway, my feet felt strange. My shoes! I had forgotten my shoes again. This really didn't matter to me as I continued to think, in horror, *this ship is going to sink, this ship is going to sink* . . . I felt oddly exhilarated by this coming terror and I picked up the pace, though I couldn't be sure I were heading in the right direction. I found my mind was so bogged down with all that I had just remembered, I didn't know where to turn at first. Did I need to go to the left or to the right? I knew there was a stairwell somewhere. I didn't have time to debate the direction issue with myself. Jack was waiting.

As I flew down the hall, the intensity of my memory filled me with fear as though the halls I was walking through were already filling with icy cold water. It was easier to look at things when they were whizzing by my speeding form. I was seeing things now as I had always known them, from pictures I had seen: The strong pillars just ahead dissolving like sugar cubes, the light fixtures in the ceiling suspended by exposed electrical cords, as though the ship were hanging onto the last bit of her elegance, literally, by a thread, all the beautiful wood eaten away by the bottom dwelling sea life that had permanent residence in all the ship's staterooms.

I burst through the first door I came to and found myself out on the deck. The night air hitting my face heightened my senses. The office was at the end of the deck, right around the corner. In just a few seconds I would be right there. In full gallop, my feet slapped painfully against the wooden decks. Little beads of sweat were breaking out on my chest and my head was throbbing. My breath was coming faster as I approached the end of the deck, my lungs bursting as though I had sprinted the entire length of a football field ten times. I kept my eyes open for the door, just yards away. Just as I was about to get there, a figure materialized from the darkness. I was going too fast to stop and, with all my might, I barreled right into this person. I recoiled, nearly knocked flat on my back. All my limbs seemed to go everywhere at once. It was as though I had made a dive into too shallow waters and was instantly paralyzed. But I had enough feeling to know that someone was holding me with rough, masculine hands. I had not just merely walked into someone; I had encountered a force which blocked me with an unwavering shield.

I struggled to speak as my limbs fought to free themselves from this inescapable bind.

"Miss Cranston, no! I can't let you do this!" the man holding me said.

I identified him by voice long before my shell shocked mind allowed me to name him by his features.

"But Captain! This ship is going to sink!"

"I know," he said. I saw his face floating before me like a white mask in the dark. The darkness obscured his expression, but his eyes glimmered kindness in the milky white light of the ship's exterior lights. His grip became less fierce, his touch settled into tenderness; his words also. Calmly, reassuringly, he spoke to me.

"This is history, Miss Cranston. And no matter how it may break your heart, you cannot change a thing."

CHAPTER EIGHT

I was sitting now in a silent room, all white with little tables and chairs and sprays of greenery in each corner. A few lights glowed from an ornately detailed ceiling. My hysteria was beginning to peel away in cloves as I sat at a table across from the captain, awaiting an explanation, no matter how improbable, about how I came to be here. Oddly enough I felt perfectly safe. That in itself was unnerving. The captain seemed so at ease, as though this were the most normal thing, like we were sitting together, alone, in a church before all the other members of the congregation arrived.

"Here," he said, passing a handkerchief over to me. "I know Mr. Phillips has one of yours."

As I was buffing my nose, I asked, "How do you know that?"

"You are in my past," he said. "You're in my dream. A dream of my past. Since you have arrived, I've had access to everything you've been thinking and feeling. That trouble you've been having remembering things. You'll find that it's gone now. Let me show you. Where do you live in Newport News?"

"I live on 66th Street," I said.

"And what kind of automobile do you drive?"

"A Buick."

"And who is your American History instructor?"

"Dr. Presbyn Schindler."

"And what book are you reading in his course?"

"*A Night to Remember* by Walter Lord. About the sinking of this ship." I fixed him with a cold stare, feeling utterly violated. "You've been playing with my memories!"

"I've had to."

"But you had no right—

"I've had every right in the world, Miss Cranston. You're in my past and you're on my ship. I've been exercising a form of mind control in which my brain waves have been able to block certain information in your mind. I've been jamming your signals, if you will. Otherwise, you would have known from the first day about everything that's going to transpire in the next thirty hours. But I knew I could only exert this kind of control for so long." He rubbed his eyes as though his head were aching. "You're very head strong. When you started to remember the moon landing, I thought I had lost control of you then. But somehow I was able to regain my authority. I knew then that if you made it back this time, I would have no directive over your thoughts at all. I anticipated your arrival and I knew the person you would go to with the news." A secret, naughty thought hiked his countenance into a smile.

My face was doused in a red-hot gush of embarrassment until I knew my whole head must have been glowing like a traffic light.

"Don't be embarrassed, Miss Cranston," he said. "In many ways, I suppose, it's somehow right that the two of you came together. After all, you represent a future that he will never see, and he represents a past that you can only see in dreams." He shook his head slowly, a smile still hanging onto his whiskered mouth. "I knew you had fallen for him the day you came to my shop."

"Your shop?" *He doesn't mean* shop. *He means* ship. A runaway thought came crashing through my head like an errant pinball. I looked over at him, observing his head, the way it was shaped, how the minuscule threads of white hair desperately tried to cover the wide expanse of shiny scalp. Though he was outfitted in a uniform, he could have been any elderly man sitting anywhere in the world, whether here, or on a park bench . . . or in the back room of an antiques store, patting his dog's head while droning out a story for a curious inquirer who just wanted to know the value of something bought there. It was as though what he had said had sent a brick through the window of my mind and I was standing there, holding the projectile, reading the message attached.

"Mr. Baumgarten?" I asked.

He smiled. "That would be my present incarnation, yes."

"But how . . . what . . . ?" I sputtered, not knowing where to begin.

"We're never quite certain what our missions are, not until we find ourselves in them. All I can tell you is that one morning I woke up in Newport News. It was as though I had been sleeping for a long time. I was garbed from head to toe in heavy clothing in layers. On my hands I wore fingerless gloves. I thought God was having a bit of fun with me, sending me back as a beggar."

"Sent back? You were sent back?"

The captain flashed a warning glare, letting me know this was not going to be a question and answer session.

"On the streets sailors walked arm-in-arm with girls whose legs were painted with make-up. The store windows all bore reminders of using ration books and saving scrap metal and rubber for the war effort. I stopped someone on the street and asked if there were a war on and he looked at me as though I were out of my tree before replying, yes, there was. The Germans, the Japanese, the Russians, the Italians, the Americans, the British, the French in the theaters of the Atlantic and Pacific. The world, all at war. I couldn't fathom this. I found an electronics store where men were gathered listening to a radio. The announcer spoke in a flat voice about an allied beach invasion in France. There was a calendar hanging above the till at the counter in the store. The year was 1944. I asked one of the men for the date and he told me it was the sixth of June.

"I did not linger long with the men there. I thought to myself, if I were going to be a beggar in this life, then I better get on with it. I found a Methodist church where a soup kitchen was being run in the basement. I sat with a bowl of stew and a crust of bread alone on a bench. When I looked up from my solitary meal, I saw a striking red-headed woman coming towards me with a look of astonishment on her face. She put a hand to her heart as she approached and for a minute I thought she was going to faint. 'Gus?' she said, 'Gus, is that you?' I didn't know. Was I Gus? I didn't seem to be anyone else. And she certainly seemed to think I was someone named Gus. She sat at my side and took my hand. She put a hand to my cheek and continued to stare at me in utter amazement. 'Gus,' she said. 'Mother said you were lost. She sent me a telegram saying you were lost.' And then I looked at her and a wave of familiarity engulfed my senses. I thought, this woman is my sister. And somehow, I knew her name. 'Edith?' I questioned. And she smiled as her eyes began to pour tears, 'Yes, Gus. It's Edie. Your big sister.' She embraced me and began to sob and I held her and consoled her. 'Yes, Edie. I'm your little brother, Gus.'

"So it was on that sixth of June in 1944 in that church basement that I learned I had come back as a man named Augustus Baumgarten, a British sailor thought lost at sea, but found on Virginia's shores. Edie's own husband had died in battle in 1943. She had been living alone in their large home, and contemplating moving back to Leeds. But when she found me, she realized why God had put her in Newport News and left her to linger in her sad widowhood. It was to find me. She was a sweet lady, Edith Tinsley," he said, smiling and stroking his beard thoughtfully. "Charitable, loving, warm-hearted. I've never known a purer soul. Despite her appearance as a society matron and champion of good causes, she was, in reality, a very lonely woman. She regretted not having children with her husband and she hated running his family's second-hand store. She didn't need the income. The Baumgartens were a clan of wealthy landowners in Leeds who had come to Britain from Germany during the Age of Enlightenment, I learned. And when she married her young G.I. and he brought her to Newport News, she had quite the dowry. When he sailed away from her six months after their marriage and died shortly thereafter, she didn't know what to do with her time or her money, so she threw herself into volunteering for everything—scrap metal drives, U.S.O. functions, garden clubs, soup kitchens. I took over the second-hand store and she allowed me to change the name from Tinsley's to Baumgarten's. After a long day of her charitable works and my fiddling with knick-knacks, we would sit down over dinner and she would smile over at me with such warmth and such love. 'Oh, Gus. I'm so glad that you came back to me.' And I was glad to be there for her.

"We lived happily in that house for many, many years. The shop was doing well, Edith continued to fill up the city with benches and pretty flowers in the medians. And then her illness struck. I thought she was just working too hard, but the doctor said it was something else. A tumor was growing in her liver and had been from some time. She was told it was inoperable, but chemotherapy might slow the tumor's growth. So she fought it as best as she could, growing progressively weaker and more frail. At the last she was all of 85 pounds, I think. The morning she died—it was a Sunday, I recall—I took her hand. I told her that in all likelihood her real brother had died at sea and I had been sent back to look after her and see her through to the end. Her mind was already going over to the other side and in her altered state she believed me. She said she looked forward to seeing her brother in the next stage of her existence, but I had been just as good a brother as she could have possibly asked for. After that, she just drifted off peacefully."

The captain grew quiet. I wondered if he would now allow me to ask questions. But before I could say anything, he turned to me and said, "You want to know how you came to be here?"

"Yes, I would."

He shook his head. "The truth is, I don't know. I just know three nights ago, something changed about this place. Always in my memories of this time, everything is exactly the same. The events are always the same. The people I encounter are the same. But then, this time, there was something different. This time there was a new presence. I was having a glass of sherry in my quarters before bed. Something startled me. I thought, 'Someone's here. Someone's here who hasn't been here before.' A voice in my head told me, 'She's in the wireless room.' I very quickly got myself together. When I saw you, I recognized you right away. I was astonished. I couldn't imagine how you had made it from the other side. I'm still not quite certain. You must have been so locked into the events of the book you were reading that somehow your subconscious was sent to mingle with his."

"You mean with Jack's," I said, suddenly excited. "Maybe I was sent here to change the course of events. This time he won't have to die. No one will."

He offered a slight, crooked smile. His words were tempered with such patience I wondered how in the world he could be so calm with all that was facing him in the next thirty hours. I had to remind myself to breathe just to keep from passing out from all the anxiety I was feeling.

He stood up, pulling on his trouser leg to straighten out a crease. "If you would come with me, I'd like to introduce you to two people down in steerage whom you might be interested in meeting."

After a brief stop at my cabin to retrieve a coat and a pair of shoes for the nighttime air, the captain and I found our way around to the aft staircase, winding our way down, several decks deep, until we ended up in an all-white hallway. Apparently, the further down into the ship, the fewer the frills. I noticed none of the decorative flourishes that were omnipresent in the decks above—no brass wall sconces, no filigreed light fixtures in the ceiling, no plush carpeting. This area had the Spartan feel of the sleeping quarters of an aircraft carrier.

We walked down the colorless corridor until we got to a doorway leading out into the open air. Immediately I saw the wide expanse of a wooden deck spread out before us like a gymnasium floor. Directly ahead, I heard laughter. Under the glow of the ship's white exterior lights, I defined two figures, seemingly clamped to the railing where they were standing, looking out into the night. The captain and I kept a respectful distance and the pair didn't notice our arrival. I didn't have to get close to them to know whom I was seeing: two anonymous pilgrims sharing a corner of this quiet evening locked in an embrace as they watched the night deepen and head for morning.

"They come out here every night about this time," the captain said. "The man is Colm Tomlinson and the girl is Maeve O'Brien. Have you heard of either of them?"

I shook my head. "Should I have?"

"Miss O'Brien doesn't know it now, of course, but she is going to play a very important part in your family's history. Right now she's just enjoying the presence of her fiancé, whom she plans to marry in New York. He is to work for his uncle, a grocer in Brooklyn. It will be a job that will bring him some much-needed financial stability, but will never procure for him any personal satisfaction. Do you see what he's carrying there?"

I squinted into the darkness. "Looks like a violin."

"He's a musician at heart, if not professionally. That's what he would rather do with his life. But he has to be practical and realistic now with marriage looming on the horizon. He needs to think about how he's going to support Maeve and their future children. But something will happen tomorrow night to change all that. Maeve and Colm will make it to the boat deck just as the last boat is being launched. There will be no place for him, but there will be a seat for her and Colm will insist that Maeve take it. She will protest at first, but eventually she will be coaxed into the boat with the promise that he will find his way into another one. She will want to know that he is safe. He will tell her that she will know he is all right as long as she hears his music. And then he will take up his violin and play for her as he walks away. As her boat is lowered, she will continue to hear his music and will strain to pick it out of the uproar of people clamoring for safety, the bellow of the released steam, the din of the ship losing its battle to stay afloat, and the music from the band playing just outside the entrance to the first class stairwell. He will play for her in the exact spot where they are standing now and she will watch him from her place in the sea. And then she will not hear him or see him at all. He will have slipped off the steep deck into the sea."

A draft whipped up around my ankles and flew up my coat. I shivered and drew nearer to the captain.

"This next part," the captain continued, "I learned from your father."

"My father?"

"That's right, Miss Cranston. Your father. You see, very shortly, Miss O'Brien will find herself in a strange world where she knows no one. She will have to find work and take care of herself. Though her skills are very limited, she knows a little about sewing, cooking, keeping a house clean, that sort of thing. All matters that a married woman planning on having a large family would need to know. Fortunately, there are plenty of factories that need honest, hard-working immigrants. She goes out and finds a job at a factory that manufactures men's dress shirts. It is a hard job and she must work long hours, but she is able to live fairly independently. Sometimes she is even able to slip a few pennies into an envelope and send them back to her family in Ireland.

"One day while she's seated at her machine, just before lunch, a fire breaks out on the floor. All the exit doors are locked and the corridors are very quickly filling with smoke. As the fire begins to pour into the workroom, many of the other women start to panic and run, some heading right for the windows to jump to their deaths rather than face the agony of burning to death. Maeve, having lived through one disaster, is able to keep a clear head. She unspools a bolt of fabric and quickly fashions a rope. She then ties the makeshift rope to a piece of heavy machinery and begins lowering the women, one by one, to the ground, ten stories below. The process is agonizingly slow and the smoke is very intense at the last, but through her courage, Maeve is able to put all the women in safe hands. The last woman to be lowered is a young girl who has just turned eighteen. Maeve knows the young lady is to be married in a few weeks and insists that she descend the rope before her. With the room nearly ablaze it doesn't take a whole lot of convincing for the young lady to take her turn at the rope. On her way down, the young lady never takes her eyes off Maeve, who holds her head out of the window with the smoke nearly engulfing her now. As Maeve is about to lower herself, a fireball bursts through the window and shatters the glass. Maeve is not seen alive again. When the investigators comb through the ruins, they find her, crouched by the window, still holding onto the rope."

I stared at the couple the entire time the captain was speaking. I was trying to imagine all the things Colm and Maeve were thinking as they stared into the night sky. It probably seemed to them that they lives together were as infinite as the universe. I knew they were probably mapping out their lives, counting off coming milestones as though they were certainties. The first apartment, the first Christmas away from home, the birth of their first child, the child's first birthday, a second child, another Christmas, their own birthdays, more holidays . . .

"That last woman to be lowered to the ground," the captain said, "was a spirited, vivacious young colleen who had just found the man of her dreams and was going to marry him. She had met this young man at a Christmas Eve church service just the year before. He was a fortune hunter who had just arrived in New York eager to make his millions in the stock market, but he is destined for a more humble life working as a salesman. The young woman's name is Carrie; the young man's, Edward. In the spring of 1915, the two will marry and a year later will have a son, Ernest, and the next year, a daughter, Theresa. They will all live together in a five-floor walk-up in Brooklyn before moving to Queens where Theresa and Ernest will go to school. As all parents do, Carrie and Albert will watch with wonder as their children grow and become young adults in search of lives and loves of their own. Ernest will marry a young woman named Margaret Eleanor, affectionately known as Nellie by the family. Theresa will marry a man named Albert. Ernest finds work at the shipyards in Newport News where Nellie will give birth to their first and only child, a son, born one cold December night during a snowstorm. They will name the child—

"Daniel Christopher Cranston," I finished for him. I knew everything he had been telling me—every word. It was as though he had taken a recent peek at the endpapers of our family Bible and had absorbed all the details of all the deaths and births throughout the history of the Cranston family.

"So, in other words," I said, "If the events of tomorrow night don't occur, my family will never come to be."

He nodded, offering a sad, sympathetic smile.

Right at that moment, I had never felt so entwined by the heavy chains of history's burdens, or so much a part of their massive links.

There were sudden tears in my eyes. "I didn't ask to be here," I said.

"I know you did not."

"I didn't mean to—at first. It was an accident at first that I found I could come here. But if I had known . . . if I had any idea . . ." Tears were searing the back of my throat. Thoughts of Jack's caress and the sound of his voice came coasting into my head. "Oh, God, he means so much to me now!"

"I know he does. And I know that I am more than partially to blame. I did nothing to discourage your relationship. Now I don't know what I was thinking. It must have been what I saw in his face that first night. There was lightness in the air, something intangible that temporarily lifted the shadows that follow me to allow enough light for me to see that something was happening between the two of you. There was something in Phillips' face that I had never seen before. Almost all the times I've ever encountered him, he's been so serious and completely absorbed by his work. I saw him leaning over you, tending to you with such care and nurturing. It was as though he wanted to envelope you in his arms and protect you from all the harm in the world. And when I felt your presence again the next night, I returned to the wireless room and told him that I had seen you and you had been asking about him. I know now that I really shouldn't have done that, interfered in that way. I was unaware that the two of you would become so close. But once you began exerting your own power over your thoughts, there was nothing I could do but stand back and hope that you wouldn't get too hurt in all this. But I see that you have. If it's any consolation to you, you should know that he does love you. He's just not ready to tell you yet."

"I know," I said. "I love him too."

I was shaking through each sob, crying so loudly I was surprised the couple at the railing hadn't noticed. My shoulders felt the comfort of arms encircling them and I fell into the captain's embrace like a frightened child.

"For the record, I will try to save your young man. Many times tomorrow night I will try to convince him to leave his post. There will be nothing more for him to do. I think deep down he knows that is true, but he won't want to believe it. Of course, a lot of his actions will reflect his sincere belief that the technology he has invested so much of his young life in will not fail him. There remains the hope that there will be someone else out there who will hear the signal and come immediately. There will be another ship, not ten miles away. But she will not be responding tomorrow night. Her wireless will be shut down. Her wireless operator, sound asleep."

The *Californian's* operator, the captain meant, the one Jack had told in a moment of frustration and extreme fatigue, "Shut up, shut up. I am busy . . ."

"He must have been so tired," I said aloud, though I meant to only think it.

"He will be tired. He will have already worked himself into a state of exhaustion long before hypothermia can claim his life."

I broke away from his grasp. "Why did you tell me he survived?"

"I never told you that he survived. You asked me if he made it into a lifeboat, and I believe that he will. I cannot be certain, though. After I implore Phillips and Bride to abandon their work, I will not see either of them again. But given the extreme circumstances he puts himself through before he finds himself in the water, I imagine his suffering is not for long."

Suffering! I thought of Jack in the water, panicking and praying as the cold water soaked him to the bone. I thought of him clawing the water, reaching for out-stretched arms and the safety of a lifeboat. In my mind I put myself in one of those lifeboats. I could be there, just to tell him he was safe, just to let him know that I was there before he closed his eyes, before he . . .

"I want to be there when he dies," I said.

The captain frowned. "I'm afraid that is not possible."

"Why not? At least give me that!"

"You cannot be there because when the ship is gone, the dream is over."

A few tears froze on my face as I stood there, still not quite believing him. It seemed to me that if I had the power to be there in the first place, anything was possible. But suddenly there was a new urgency tearing at me. At that instant, the importance, the exuberance of the moment had never seemed so real. I wanted to go to Jack. I wanted to hide behind the looming shadows of the night and fight them back with the power of now. I needed to go to Jack. There would be no time for later. There would be no later for him or for us. For me there were many laters. I had laters to last me a lifetime. He had only enough to get him through the next day and he would be alone throughout that time. But not tonight. For this night I could go to him and be with him before time and infamy could snatch him away. I could be with him this night.

"Can I ask you two things?"

He nodded, warily.

"If I can't be with him anymore after tonight, then tomorrow . . . would you please tell him that I'm safe . . . that I've made it off the ship all right? Otherwise he might look for me."

"I'll see to it myself."

"And," I said, carefully preparing my next request so that it wouldn't appear unseemly. "Since I can't be with him in his last moments, I want to be with him tonight."

I saw the captain's mouth stiffen. A gradual scowl swept across his face like a rolling fog.

"Just to hold him," I said. "For as long as I can."

"I would allow that, but I must tell you that you will find your Phillips a changed man tonight. You see, the wireless broke down hours ago and he and Bride have been scrambling to fix it ever since. I'm afraid he will not have time for you tonight."

Hearing this made me wish I could have put the last few nights on replay. I recalled the first night, when I was so shocked by just being here that I couldn't speak. How I wished I could have said more things to him then. I barely even knew my name then or my circumstances. I didn't know how precious time was and the time I had spending with Jack would be counted only in hours and minutes. On the first night I was with him for just under an hour. The second night, maybe two. The third night had lingered into morning and we woke up in each other's arms. At least we had that night, even if most of it was spent sleeping. We had that night.

"I still want to see him. Just long enough to say goodbye."

The captain smiled. "I understand why you feel the need to do that. But I have to warn you that you may be putting your life in danger by staying on much longer. You may have noticed that is has become increasingly difficult for you to get here."

"Yes, it has. I thought I just wasn't concentrating hard enough."

"That could be part of it, but I think what's really happening is that our minds are becoming divided. The next time it is entirely possible that you may not be able to return at all. So you had better make certain that at the end of this dream you are in the place where you first found yourself at the start. At the first sign that you are being called from the other side, you must do all you can to get to that chair. That will be the only way you can completely sever your ties with the past."

"What will happen to me if I don't make it to the chair before I wake up?"

"Then you may continue to exist here, asleep and unaware of what is happening around you, as you have been each time you have awakened in your world," he said, the seriousness of the implications of his words muting his voice into a soft whisper.

But no matter how gentle his delivery, those words jabbed me directly in the heart, temporarily stunning it into producing labored thuds. "You mean I could die here without my conscious mind to tell me what to do?"

"That's right," he said at length.

I was reminded of the old myth that said if a person hits the ground in a falling dream, then in reality, the dreamer dies as well. I had never believed this, thinking it foolish to think that the events in someone's subconscious could have so much bearing on one's mortality. Now it seemed I had my proof.

"You know from past experiences that you are here only until external influences in your present time intervene."

"I know," I said. I thought about all that was happening in my reality at this moment. I could count on Aunt Teese being in front of the TV for most of the afternoon. She had plenty of cigarettes to get her through the day without having to borrow some from me. I wasn't so sure about Mom. If she closed the deal on the house as she had planned, it could take all afternoon for her to get together all the paperwork and have everything signed and notarized. If the deal didn't go through for whatever reason, she could be home within the hour. The way I saw it, I either had all night . . . or just a few minutes.

"The minute you hear someone calling you from the other side, you have to get to the deck chair," he said. "That is the only way you can make your transference permanent."

"How will I know which deck chair will take me back?"

"You'll know when you see it," he said. The captain reached inside his coat and rifled through his breast pocket before extracting a long, thin cigar.

"What do you mean? Aren't they all the same?"

He was taking his first puff. "You'll be able to recognize it without any difficulty."

"Captain," I said. "What's going to happen to you tomorrow night?"

He puffed thoughtfully at his cigar. "Same thing that always happens to me. So I'm going to enjoy this cigar for all it's worth. They just don't make these like they used to." He regarded the smoking end of his cigar with beaming admiration. "I want you to know something about the money your father gave me for the deck chair."

"Yes?"

"I never did anything with it. It's been sitting in a strong box in my back office, still in the bank envelope delivered to me by your father. I never wanted to take it in the first place, but he insisted."

There was so much more that I wanted to ask him, but I knew that I was allowing valuable minutes to escape unchecked the longer I stood there. I had to ask him one more thing before I took off for the upper decks.

"Why did you sell my father the deck chair in the first place?" I asked.

At length he said, "Because, Miss Cranston. He believed my story. Sometimes all we need is for someone to believe our stories."

I nodded and gulped down a sob lodged in my throat. While I was looking at him, I heard that same silent good-bye I had perceived before when I was in Mr. Baumgarten's shop, the day he had let the blinds of the windows snap shut just as I left. He's closing the blinds, I said to myself. He's closing the blinds . . .

I watched him turn and walk off in the direction of the two who continued to stand at the rail, with the night intensifying and time dwindling. I felt the minutes and seconds ebb with such a fine clarity it was as though I were standing on a timeline that had suddenly tilted down and I was sliding along with all the numbers into a vast blackness. I knew I couldn't stand there anymore. I had to go before I was gone as well.

In full flight up the aft staircase, I read that the time was 2:30. *2:30*, I thought. *Now he's got less than twenty-four hours . . . How long do I have?*

When I got to the boat deck, the captain's words came to be in a full warning. The splash of cold air replenished my head with fresh concerns. One in particular stopped me in my tracks.

I could die here.

In most of my dreams, whenever I received devastating news, the fact that I knew I was dreaming was always a buffering measure. But this was real. I supposed that I could chance it, go in and tell Jack what I knew anyway, and see if I still woke up with my family history intact. But then I thought too, no family history, no Lucy Cranston. I'd never wake up at all. This body, this consciousness would have never existed. I would just be a dream thing. Or maybe I would just disappear.

But people just don't disappear . . .

I was thinking very rapidly now, my mind tripping from one thing to the next.

What if Aunt Teese runs out of cigarettes and has to borrow some from me? She'll have to wake me up and ask me, unless she finds my purse first and gets them on her own. Oh, God! For once, Aunt Teese, I give you permission. Go into my purse, take anything you want. You won't find any money, though. There's no money in there. Dad was supposed to have sent me some money today and I haven't checked the mail. I've got to go check the mail because Dad is sending me some money. I hope it's at least twenty. I can get by on twenty dollars for a week. He'll want to know if I got the money because he hates sending cash though the mail, always thinks some psycho at the post office is going to use it to buy ammo and wipe out his coworkers . . . says that's not prejudicial thinking, that's just the kind of world we live in today. Dad, I'll call you as soon as I wake up and check the mail. I'll wake up soon, not too soon, though. What if Janet calls? If Janet calls, then Aunt Teese will wake me. "Lucy, it's that girl," *she'll say. Oh, please don't call, Janet. Please! If I wake up to answer your call, if I wake up . . . the captain said I could die here. There'll be no more thinking, it's so sad what happens to these people . . . I'll be one of these people! Only I won't even have a chance. I'll be asleep, unable to answer the door when the purser comes.* "Wake up, Miss Cranston. All passengers are being advised to don their life jackets and come out on deck . . ." *Only I won't hear that. I won't hear that if the next thing I hear from the other side is,* "Lucy, Lucy" *and I'm nowhere near . . .*

And there it was. Just as the captain said, I knew right away. I could pick it out of the entire line-up of its wooden clones. This one chair spoke to me, not so much in words, but in the way that it was. This was it, I was sure. It was certainly in the right position, just a few feet down from the Marconi station. I could see the door handle from where I was standing. And from where I was I could reach out and touch the wood, before the sea and time turned it gray, before my father bought it, before I ever found it and put it out in our backyard. I stood there for the longest time, thinking that this was it. I had to make the transference now, or I'd never have the chance again. Concurrent with that thought was Jack's next to last night, which he was spending just a few steps away, behind a closed door. I would never have that chance again to see him, to talk to him, to hold him. Most of the time in life there are no second chances and missed opportunities are always viewed with regret in retrospect. I knew there would be no second chances in either option I chose. I could get in the chair now and leave this world behind or stay with Jack and possibly never have the chance to leave, ever.

At that late hour, in that night so deep in the past, I had to make my decision. Looking down at the chair, I visualized how it was in our backyard under that giant tree, and the me in it who had spent her entire life under the oak's shading sanctuary in the safety of my backyard, under the protection of my parents. It was time to push away, burst from the bounds of that shady backyard and wander away, far away, to where ever this dream would take me.

I walked away from the chair and headed for the Marconi room.

CHAPTER NINE

I opened the door without knocking and proceeded inside just as though I belonged there. When I entered, I found only one occupant and that person wasn't Jack. Jack's assistant stood at a table strewn with disassembled parts of machinery. He was holding a headphone to his ear and didn't turn to see who was coming in the door. He seemed to think I was someone else.

"If it's more messages you got," he barked over his shoulder, "they'll have to bloody well wait like the rest. We've got a backlog here already and if that wench who complained before has anything more to say, tell her she can go to hell for all I care."

"Where's Jack?" I asked.

He spun around at the sound of my voice and jerked the headset from his ear. When his eyes identified me, he sputtered with embarrassment. "I'm sorry, Miss Cranston. I thought you were the purser."

I had been visualizing seeing Jack sitting there and when I didn't, I was taken aback. For a second I couldn't even remember the assistant's name, but soon I recalled the anger I had felt when I found out he had survived and Jack didn't, and along with that resentment came his identity.

Harold, why didn't you tell him that some men were launching a collapsible on top of the officer's quarters? Why didn't you tell him . . .

"Where's Jack?" I repeated in a firmer voice.

"Phillips," he called. "We've got company."

"Well, if it's the purser, tell him to sod off, we're up to our necks in trouble here." He appeared from an open door, just behind where Bride was sitting. His sleeves were rolled up and his tie was messily undone. I saw all his laborious efforts of the evening etched in deep lines on his face, all his frustration pinching his features, making him look like the old man he would never become. But the instant he saw me he was restored to newness and his eyes shined bright and clear as though the day were just starting and the sun was shining in a sky full of blue.

Something had told me that this was not going to be easy, but just how arduous this task was going to be was not presented to me until I saw his face. Having spent the past few hours thinking of him dead and now seeing him so alive, I had to tamp down the overpowering desire to cry out to him, "Sweetheart, you are standing in your grave."

"Lucy," he said quietly. "Oh. Lucy." He met me in the middle of the room and his hands went to my arms. A rosy blush appeared on his pale cheeks. "I didn't think I would see you tonight."

I couldn't say anything. There was a raucous sob forming in me that I feared would be unleashed if I were to speak. I could feel the tears in my eyes and I knew that he could see them.

"What's wrong, dear? You look so sad."

Oh, how I wish I could tell you. How I wish I could tell you everything I know, my love.

"Here. Let's go in here," he said, taking me by the hand and leading me to a green curtain drawn over a door.

On the other side of the curtain was a tiny room, not much bigger than the closet in my cabin. We sat down on the small cot inside. He held me close and more tears fell from my eyes as his sweet words conspired helplessly to console me. "Oh, dear heart, won't you tell me what's wrong? What's happened?" His kisses were on my forehead, on my brow, on my cheek. "Did someone hurt you?"

I shook my head.

"Then please tell me what's happened."

I hugged him close, putting my head firmly against his chest. I could hear his heart beating with a boxer's vigilance. I was beginning to realize the Captain's mind control had been more mercy than mercenary.

"Lucy," he said as he lifted my face with the crook of his index finger. "Lucy, dear, did you . . . did you think that I didn't want to see you tonight?"

I was bewildered as to why he would ask me such a thing.

"Did you not get my message?" he asked.

"Message," I managed to say.

"Well, yes, the message I sent earlier telling you the wireless broke down and I wouldn't be able to meet you as planned."

"I don't think I did."

"You didn't! Sodding purser! I knew I should have delivered it myself. I'm going to beat the stuffing out of that man when I see him. After he promised he would get my message to you right away. Oh, Lucy. What you must have thought when I didn't show!"

"No, it's all right," I told him. "The captain told me that the wireless broke down and that if I had been expecting to be with you tonight I probably wouldn't."

"The captain? Captain Smith said this to you?" he asked warily. "Does he know about us? That we're seeing each other?"

"He does."

Jack grew tense in my arms and his eyes held fear.

"But it's all right. We had a talk," I said. "Turns out he's good friends with my father."

Jack was still silent and he looked as though he were making an assessment of his career at sea and realizing it might be over.

"Honey, the captain said he did nothing to discourage us from seeing each other." I put a hand to his cheek. "We have his blessing."

"Always nice to have the permission of the man in charge when endeavoring in these things," he said at last. "But you still haven't told me why you were crying."

"Oh," I said, tracing the line of his jaw with my finger. "I just learned that something terrible is going to happen to someone I really care about."

"I'm sorry to hear that, Lucy," he said. "Is there something I can do?"

"Yes," I said. "Just hold me."

"That I can do, love," he said as his arms went around me.

I thought as he held me that if I had any control over this dream at all, I would will a rope to drop down from the future and we would both climb it to safety to and to forever, to days when this was all to do—just hold each other, be there for each other, love each other so much, even though we weren't ready to tell each other how we felt.

"I couldn't keep my thoughts off you all day," he said in a whisper close to my ear. "Every time I looked at my watch, ten o'clock seemed so far away. I took a rest this afternoon and I dreamed of being with you. I heard you laugh and saw your smile and felt the touch of your hands. When I woke up around 4, I thought to myself, 'Only six hours and I'll see her.' I sat and did my work. Every few minutes I looked at the time. Only four more hours, only three more hours, only two and a half hours . . . And then, at 9:30, Bride came in and said that I should be getting ready to see you. So I did and when I came back from the washroom, Bride told me that there was something wrong with the transmitter. I just knew then that I was in for a long night. I kept hoping that you would stop in to see me. Oh, I almost forgot." He got to his feet and kissed me quickly. "Be right back, love."

He went into the other room and I heard his assistant ask about me. Jack mumbled something in return and then the two began talking about the business at hand. In his absence, I looked around his quarters. The room had been designed specifically so that the occupants would not want to linger there too long. Over on the wall left of the window was a basin and a mirror, with a shelf for personal effects underneath. Next to that was a slim locker where I imagined he kept his uniform, his valise, maybe a pair of pajamas. Beside the bed was a small table on which there was a spill of coins, the handkerchief I had wrapped his éclair in the night before and a couple postcards. I knew I shouldn't have, but I peeked at what he had written. On one he had scrawled, "Dear Elsie, Sailing day. Beautiful weather and very clear. We could make New York in five days' time. Love, Jack." On the other was something that took my breath.

"Dear Elsie, I've met someone."

That was all it said. And it wasn't as though he had started the message and had been interrupted. It was finished with the sign off, "Love, Jack."

I checked the date. April 11. That was the second night, the night we talked out on the boat deck. I remembered very clearly what he had told me—he had two postcards to go out to his sister. These had to be the ones he was talking about, the ones he had dashed off before we even knew each other, before we had . . . Who *was* this someone? Was *I* this someone? Or was this person someone else?

Oh, God, I thought in boiling jealousy. *Is there someone else?*

I didn't know why I had been thinking that this young man had been floating around on these luxury vessels with his virtue mint-in-box. Having been virtually everywhere in the known Western world, I was sure there were many lovely ladies around the globe with whom he had shared cuddles and kisses that led to other things behind closed doors. He had made it clear to me the night before that he was no novice when it came to matters of the bedroom. But he had also made me feel like I was the only one that ever was and the only one that would ever be again for him.

I thought back to his trepidation as we sat on the bed in my cabin. Had he just been acting coy so that I would double my efforts to seduce him? That way he wouldn't come off as such a wolfish cad who found himself with a tipsy, flirty female of the first class. A sick thought made my stomach turn. What if I had allowed myself to be used yet again?

I heard his voice just behind the curtain. Just before he swept back into the room, I neatly shuffled the postcards back into their original place. He was holding something behind his back and grinning as he entered. When he stepped in front of me, he presented me with a small arrangement of blush and buff colored roses.

"Here, love," he said as he sat down beside me again. "These were for you. I suppose they still are. I got them earlier. I'm afraid they may have wilted a little."

"They're lovely," I said as I smelled their sweet fragrance and brushed the ripe blooms across my lips. I didn't want to ask him where or how he got them. This was the sort of arrangement one would find on a table in a slender, fluted, crystal vase. I imagined it very well could have come from a table in one of the dining rooms. He had probably brokered a deal with one of the stewards. "I'll send a message to your girl back home if you nick me some roses for my girl."

"You must get flowers all the time," he said.

"Not so often that I forget how special it is when I get them."

"Really? What's the matter with the lads in your town?"

I shook my head. "They're nothing like you."

He pulled me close and I let my head fall on his shoulder. With this gift of flowers and the sweet deliveries of kisses on my forehead and cheek, it was easy to believe that I could have been *someone*.

"Oh, Lucy, I'm so sorry the evening was ruined," he said.

"It's OK, Jack. Don't worry about it. It's nothing you did."

"I know, but—"

"Jack, really. It's nice being with you just like this."

"This is nice," he said. "But I'm afraid that I have to get back to what I was doing before."

All I wanted was his body next to mine, warm and alive, for as long as we had, now about 23 hours and counting. By this time tomorrow, he would be . . .

"I know," I said, reluctantly relinquishing my hold on him. "I know."

"Can you come back in the morning?" he said.

"It is morning," I reminded him.

"Later in the morning. When things are better here."

I didn't know. Could I? I was shocked to find myself nodding.

"You will?" he said excitedly.

"Yeah," I swallowed.

"You promise?"

"Yes, I promise," I said, putting my hand in his to seal the deal.

He escorted me out of his quarters and to the door of the station. I promised him again that I would see him in the morning. I walked slowly from the station with the flowers in my hands and the words of that one postcard in my head.

I've met someone. I've met someone.

That one little declarative sentence had my mind reeling as I imagined all that could have followed it. "I've met someone very special." "I've met someone here in Southampton." "I've met someone who knows how to tie a cherry stem with her tongue." "I've met someone who can sing 'God Save the Queen' while riding a unicycle and spinning plates."

When I got to my cabin, I didn't quite know what to do with myself. I was still thinking of the words he had written and all their implications. I took off my coat and put it on the back of the vanity chair and then sat down. I picked up the flowers and took a sniff as I looked over at the bed, still unmade. I visualized us there, in those creamy white sheets making love and then looked at myself in the mirror and saw confusion in my features.

Now, fully consumed in the mystery of someone, I paced the floor. I knew that if I were to have written the same words on a postcard, that someone I was referring to would have been him.

I looked at the small writing desk over in the corner. I went over to the desk and opened the top drawer. Inside I found plain, white linen stationery and an ebony Waterman's fountain pen.

I didn't even know what I wanted to write until I pressed the nib to the paper. But then the text just sort of flowed in.

April 13, 1912

Dear Miss Phillips,

My name is Lucy Jane Cranston. I am twenty-one years old and I live in Newport News, Virginia. I have had the privilege of getting to know your brother, Jack, during my voyage on the RMS Titanic. Tomorrow night, the ship will sink and your brother will die.

I have spent a great deal of time thinking about your sweet brother—more time thinking about him than I have actually been with him. This very simple, but somehow extraordinary man, your brother, Jack. There is certainly nothing on the outside that would lead anyone to think he was possessed of anything but what every other person has. I wonder if some time in his infancy or early childhood if something mythological occurred, some moment when others took notice and said in muttered unison, "That boy's going to be somebody." If there was such an incident, he doesn't seem to think that it's worth mentioning.

He has told me that you and your sister were teenagers when he came into the world. Your parents must have been middle-aged and had probably given up on ever having a son. I imagine that your family lived a quiet, staid existence before Jack's arrival. You had most likely all settled into what you were as a unit, never thinking that your family life would ever be changed. But then, an announcement. A baby was going to be born. A brief hope—maybe it would be a boy. Maybe it would be a boy and your little family circle would be complete. How your mother must have fretted. She must have known she only had that one last chance. Her childbearing years were dwindling. Your father must have told her, often, that it didn't matter. He had his two girls. Twins! A rarity. But your mother still felt that in the back of your father's mind dwelled a secret wish for a son. He didn't talk about it, but he didn't have to. She knew that longing was there. And then all the questions she had to deal with, from neighbors, from friends and family—are you hoping it's going to be a boy? And the automatic answer, always: "We don't care, as long as he's—or she's—healthy."

Then the day came, early one April. A boy. A boy at last, a dark-haired, blue-eyed baby with the palest skin that nearly matched the hue of his eyes. I think about those first few minutes when your mother was handed that squirming newness of life, when she looked down into his face and caught the clutch of his tiny fist with her index finger. Oh, he'll be a titan, she must have thought. He'll be the master of worlds. But then he was just her little boy.

I imagine your mother in those early months, getting reacquainted with the rhythm of uneven nights—one sleepless, one quiet, one cut up into periods of rest and then extreme exhaustion. Your poor mother, emerging from her bed, half-asleep, propelling herself somehow through her depleted energies to the cradle where the baby cried. Your father harrumphing from the bed, "Can't you do something with him? I've got work tomorrow." Then she would take the child up the stairs to your room. "Could you please do something with him?" I imagine it was you, Elsie, who would take the child, try some milk at first with his stubborn mouth and then a song. A sweet lullaby. And he would sleep in your arms and you would wake together. In time, you came to think of him as being your little boy too.

He was someone's little boy. A mother's only son. Your mother took him into her arms on that first day and wanted only to protect him and keep him safe from all the ills of the world, just like any other mother. But she must have known then that she could only protect him for so long. One day he would grow up and want to be, not just someone's child, but the person he had to be, that person the wanderlust in his heart kept instructing him to be. But he would always stay in touch, always come back to see her and the family. There was always home where he could be someone's little boy again.

There's a black day on the horizon for you and your family. The news at first will be too horrible to believe. First there will be hearsay, emanating in dark, whispered waves of rumors from the town's post office. Someone—a neighbor, perhaps—will happen by, eyes foretelling something bleak that your family can't begin to guess. There's talk about the Titanic going down. The neighbor will know that Jack was on it. The news will be received with a calm reserve as your family will collectively bargain against the truth. And how your family will wait, trapped in that awful limbo of not knowing, not wanting to know, but desperately needing some confirmation all the same. More news reports will follow. You will hear that one wireless operator has survived and was transmitting messages from the rescue ship. This will give you hope. You won't know that there were two wireless operators on the Titanic and the one who has survived is not your Jack.

And then the official news will come. A message delivered from the post office, perhaps from Marconi himself. Words scribbled on familiar paper with Jack's company's name embossed at the top. "Regret to inform young Phillips not among the survivors of the RMS Titanic."

And still, your voices will rise in protest, your mother's chief among them. But the montage of stony, grief-stricken faces before her will tell her that what she has heard is true and there will be no homecoming. She will never see her little boy again. He has died alone with no one there even to hold his hand.

I know you will never receive this letter. The vessel that is carrying it to its destination will perish and all letters with it. I'm just writing for my own peace of mind, to tell you and myself that if there were anything in the world I could do to save your brother and everyone else here, I would. But apparently, all I can do is save myself. And *though I didn't believe it before, I'm someone worth saving. Your brother has taught me that.*

*Sincerely yours,
Lucy Cranston*

Having finished my letter, I stuffed it into the envelope. I went over to the mirror and found my face red and my eyes puffy. My nose looked twice its size it was so swollen. I was beginning to notice that I had a slight odor. What I needed was a hot bath to put a fresh perspective on things. I had not found a bathroom yet. There was bound to be one somewhere. I padded around the room until I found a slender door. On the other side of the door was a small bathroom, replete with commode, wash basin and a clawfoot tub. The black and white tiles were sharply cold under my bare feet and I could hardly wait until I was up to my neck in warm, sudsy water. I turned the faucets on, finding that the stream was weak, and even though I had the hot tap turned to scalding, the water was still chilly as I swished my fingers underneath it. I realized it would be quite a long wait before the tub was completely full and I had too many things to do. I removed my robe and sat in the cold, shallow water, suppressing a yelp as I did. I shivered as I doused myself in the water just barely trickling from the faucet and reached for the soap, just taking care of what needed the most attention. In just a few short minutes, the skin under my nails turned blue.

I emerged from the bath damp and trembling. I thought about the promise I had made to Jack—I would see him sometime this morning. I plunged into the closet and sorted through the dresses, hoping to find something appropriate for morning, which was something new for me. Here I was always looking for something to wear for the evening, for my time past midnight's hands on the clock in the arms of my special gent. I did have some long skirts, I was glad to see, that I could probably put on without help, and there were billowy, high-necked blouses too that I could button by myself. I chose a burgundy skirt made from combed cotton and a white, button-down blouse. I dressed quickly and began to hear the ship coming to life. There was movement in the hall now and voices too.

I didn't know what to do with my hair, so I just combed it out, parted it down the middle, and spun the length into a bun on the back of my head, which I fastened between the two combs on the vanity. My face was still pale, but the cold water had reduced the puffiness to a degree. I uncapped the pot of rouge and smeared some on my mouth. I smacked my lips together and blotted them on one of the handkerchiefs in the drawer. After tucking away a few stray hairs, I felt that I was as ready as I ever would be.

As I was going to the door, something caught my eye—a small slip of folded paper.

I bent to retrieve it and opened it quickly.

> *Dear Lucy,*
>
> *I'm so sorry to tell you this, but I won't be able to meet you tonight. The wireless has broken down and I'll be all night trying to fix it, most likely. Do try and stop in. Would love to see you.*
>
> *Jack*

So I *had* gotten his message. In my haste to leave the cabin earlier, I hadn't seen it. The note was written as though the ink contained his disappointment that he wouldn't be able to see me that night. I wondered what kind of evening he had planned. As I opened the door, I could almost see him there with the flowers and the promise of the night on his face. "I'm not ready yet," I could imagine myself saying. "That's all right," he would say, before lifting me off the ground and carrying me to the bed. "This was the first thing I had in mind for the evening."

I went down the hall, still carrying the note, still thinking about that someone. When I emerged onto the boat deck, the ship was just coming awake. A crewman was washing down the deck with fast strokes. Two officers in their dark navy uniforms were chatting near the rail.

In the radio office, I found Jack hunkered down over the wireless. And though it was just the beginning of the day, already he appeared tired, as though the workload were prematurely marking him for exhaustion. His finger kept a steady, rapturous tapping at the key. The room was filled with the sounds of electric noise and the light of the sun beaming down from the skylight above. I just stood there, frozen at the door, staring at him, creating mental souvenirs to take with me.

I thought he had been too immersed in his work to notice my arrival, but after his transmission was complete, he spun around in his chair and beckoned for me to come over to him.

"Here," he said, "I want you to hear something."

I stole behind him and he swiveled the chair around. I let out a slight yelp as he grabbed me and put me on his lap and removed the headset from his ears and placed it, carefully, on mine. I listened attentively to the faint code fizzing in my ears. I tried to translate, but my mind was too frazzled to identify even a single word.

"What is it?" I asked.

"It's the last transmission I made. I asked the old man to read it back to me twice for good measure. The wireless is still not functioning as it should."

I handed the phones back to him and he dropped them to the desk. He encircled me with his arms buried his head in my chest. I touched his hair. It felt slightly oily and smelled of the spice of pomade applied in preparation for our aborted date the night before.

"What are you going to do today?" he asked.

I'm going home. "I don't know," I said, sliding his hair between my fingers. "What about yourself?"

"With all this?" he said, crooking a thumb towards the overflow of messages in his inbox. "I'm going to be a very busy man for about the next twenty-four hours. As a matter of fact," he placed a light kiss on my shoulder, "I don't know if I'll be able to get away tonight. Or tomorrow night for that matter. But what I was thinking was, since you're going to be in New York and I will be as well, perhaps you could tell me where you'll be staying and I could come see you."

I could hardly believe what he was asking me. How could he still believe that we were going to make it to New York? But then, I thought, why would he have any reason not to? This problem with the wireless was thus far the only wrench in the works of an otherwise perfect crossing. How was he to have known that this trouble with the radio equipment would soon join the list of other if only's that would make the night's tragedy seem, in retrospect, one of the most preventable disasters of all time?

He could see New York, see himself there, as he had been dozens and dozens of times before. This time would be different. This time he would know someone there—a girl he had just met on the way over. An educated girl of the first class, a girl with long blond hair and azure blue eyes, a humorous girl with a naughty wit. She would be staying at the Plaza and he would go to see her.

Impulsively, I murmured, "I'm not going to New York."

His shoulders froze and he looked up at me quizzically. "No, we *are* going to New York. Remember? You were so excited about it."

"What I mean is, when I get to New York, I'm not staying. You see, my Dad's going to pick me up and take me straight home to Virginia. I've got school and he has to go back to work."

"Oh," he said. "I hadn't considered that."

I had just thrown a wall up where once there had been a window. And while I knew it was impossible, I kept thinking to myself, "Maybe Dad won't have to leave right away. I can always skip classes," as though the miracle that had brought me to him would keep me with him for all time.

They would begin corresponding, by postcard at first, then by letter, anything that would go through the mail. Her letters would be long and full of news about herself, about her family. His would be short, a few lines here and there whenever he had a chance to sit down with his thoughts. Sometimes it would be just a phrase, just to let her know where he was. "Off the coast of France now. Sunny and clear. Miss you very much . . . Went to Gibraltar yesterday. Wonderful weather for now. May pass storms tomorrow. Would love to see you."

"Hmm . . ." he said. And then again. "Hmm . . ." He scratched the back of his head. I reached for his hand and we laced our fingers together. He fanned my hand out in his, kneading the pressure points of my palm with his thumb and stroking my fingers. "I do travel quite a bit. There is a possibility that I might come 'round to your town, but I don't know when that will be."

And then one day the postcard would arrive, "Sailing to Norfolk, Virginia. Can you come to meet me? I miss you and would love to see you again." And she would go to the port. She would get there just in time to greet the ship as it arrived and wait as each person got off, hoping that the face she kept in her memory matched one of those she saw passing by. And then she would see him. She would see him, after all that time, after condensing all those too short messages into one long promise that she would wait for him for as long as she possibly could. When they would see each other for the first time after all those miserable months apart, they would embrace in full view of everyone and string together all those kisses they had been dreaming about into one, long, breath-depriving kiss. He wouldn't know how much time he had—maybe a day, maybe just a few hours. But no! The ship was being detained for a day or two to correct a problem with the propeller. That could take days, maybe a week. He would have all that time to be with her and he would spend all that time with her—every second of every day. He would come to her house for dinner, sit at her table, by her side. They would hold hands under the table while the food was passed and the father asked questions. "So you're a wireless operator, Mr. Phillips?" "Yes sir, I am," he would say proudly. "Sounds like fascinating work. But do you think it will last?" would come the rebuttal. "Yes, sir. I believe that radio is here to stay." There would be questions and he would sail through all of them, effortlessly providing the right answers to every one. They would smile a lot. Because this was their time together. And at night, while the rest of the family slept, she would creep from her bedroom to his. She would allow him to remove her night gown she would lay back and let him touch her all over. She would sigh and stifle her moans with the back of her hand and shudder in his arms. And when he lay tired beside her, she would whisper, "I love you." And he would say, "I love you too."

But I wasn't that girl. I may have bourn a passing resemblance to that girl, but that wasn't who I was. That was who I was in that time, in *his* time. If he saw me in my own time, he wouldn't have recognized me in my slovenly, denim cut-off existence. There was so much about me that he didn't know, so much that I couldn't tell him. In that way he could never really love me, because the girl he knew only existed for him here. I had only materialized for this brief time period and then I would be gone. He would not have time to let me linger in his memories because he too would soon vanish. He would just disappear, walking aft, towards the stern, on a moonless night in the North Atlantic.

"No matter," he said, kissing me. "We've still got tonight. I may not have as much time to spend with you tonight as I have in the past four nights, but I'll try to get away for a bit, even if it's just to come down to your cabin and tell you goodnight. We will see each other tonight."

But we wouldn't. When he would finally catch up with all the messages that had piled up during the time the wireless had been down, the ice warnings would be coming in, the iceberg would be coming near, and the captain would be coming in with an edict to send a CQD . . . require assistance immediately . . .

I reached over to the desk and retrieved the pad of Marconigram forms lying there. I looked at the space designated for the message the sender intended to have transmitted. All those careless, breezy shipboard sentiments . . . "Wish you were here . . . having beautiful weather . . . will arrive on Tuesday . . . Having the most wonderful time . . . Perfectly smooth trip all the way . . . Reports of heavy pack ice and growlers ahead . . . are slowing course a bit . . . passed some ice this evening . . . are stopped for the night on account of ice . . . We've struck a berg . . . It's a CQD, old man . . . We've only got about an hour, maybe two . . ."

But from those blank lines came sudden inspiration.

"Can I send one?" I asked.

"If you wish," he said. "But I must tell you these others have priority over any incoming ones. It may not be until tomorrow that I can send it."

"That doesn't matter," I said. "I just thought maybe I'd send a message to my parents, letting them know that I had met someone."

My last words stirred something in his mind. He gave me look, equal parts scorn and comprehension.

"You read my postcards?"

I nodded sheepishly, letting my gaze hit the floor.

He sighed heavily. "Lucy, I wasn't going to tell you this."

My stomach was instantly in knots as soon as I heard these words. "What, Jack?"

He exhaled a long breath. "I didn't know if I should tell you, or if I should tell you. I didn't know how you would take it."

"What, Jack, what?" I demanded, now nearly hysterical.

He began to say something, but then thought better of it. "No, I can't tell you. You'll think I've gone daft."

"Jack, after all the insane things I've said to you, you're afraid *you're* going to be runner-up for the crazy crown?"

He studied me for a second before he said, "All right, I'll tell you." He took my hand and clamped it between his. "The first night. When I came out of the Marconi station."

"Yes?" I said.

"I . . ." He pursed his lips. "I just came out for a breath of air. I just needed to clear my head before bed. I got out a cigarette and lit it. Whilst smoking by the station, a young couple walked by, arm-in-arm. They were laughing, talking excitedly. I nodded at them as they walked by and they said hello. But it was as though they were in their own little world and they stepped out of it just long enough to greet me and then they were right back into it. I just remember thinking how nice it would be to have someone on this trip. Someone to talk to, and not all about work. Someone to spend some time with. And then I looked round and I saw you. And I didn't know how I had missed seeing you before. You were right there, not ten feet away. I really thought I was seeing things. And then I came over to you, and you were so cold when I touched you. And then you just sort of wilted in the chair. I thought to myself, 'Blimey, here's the most beautiful woman I've ever seen and she's dead and I didn't even get to say hello.' And then when I escorted you to your room after you came 'round, I thought, 'Blimey, here's the most beautiful woman I've ever seen and she doesn't want to talk to me.'" His hand came up against my cheek. I wouldn't have been surprised if his hand got singed, as my face was suddenly hot as a forge. "So when you told me that you were certain you had been somewhere else before and just seemed to reappear here on this ship, I found myself thinking, 'Maybe she's right. Maybe she did get pulled out of her world into mine somehow.'

I could never imagine such a thing happening because I'm a man of all this," he said, pointing to the wireless apparatus. "But if it could be true . . . if it is true . . . Whatever occurred that brought you aboard, I'm grateful for it."

"I'm grateful too," I told him. His face was shimmering before mine as my eyes filled with tears. "For everything we have had."

"So as you can see, that's quite a lot to write on a postcard. I'll just have to wait and tell my sister everything when I see her. Well, perhaps not everything. But she'll be happy that I had someone to spend my birthday with."

"So you were writing about me?"

"Of course I was. Who else?"

"Well, I didn't know."

"Well, you should have," he said, giving me a light tap on my bottom.

I smiled and threw my arms around him, hugging him tightly, holding him for all the people who would never embrace him again. "Yes, I should have."

I hopped off his lap and he handed me a pencil with two double helix-type zigzags of teeth marks curving towards the top. I wondered if he had been the eager beaver.

I went over to an adjacent table to write out my message. He laughed at my attempts at secrecy, telling me that he would have to read it eventually if I wanted it transmitted. It only took a second to put down what I had to say in seven, simple little words that summed up everything. How I felt about him, how I would always feel about him. I folded the paper in fourths and carried it over to him. I couldn't have picked a better moment. Just then a rumble sounded from a pneumatic tube on the wall and a scrolled message shot out of the end. While he went to get it, I put the message just outside the inbox to make it look as though it had fallen out or had been dropped in the wrong place by mistake. It would be a surprise for him later in the day when he had had his fill of other people's messages.

When he returned to his desk, he said, smiling, "Finished?"

I nodded, a few tears glistening in my eyes. "Yeah. I'm finished."

When he sat back down, he took up the headphones again and went onto the next message. As I watched him begin tapping away at the key again, I found myself thinking the most random things. I'll never hear what his voice sounds like on the phone . . . I'll never see him on the other side of the screen door on my front porch . . . I'll never see what he looks like in a T-shirt and a pair of jeans . . . I'll never see what his face looks like in my den with the reflection of the TV on his face . . . I'll never step with him across a sleek dance floor, my head on his shoulder, his arms snugly around me as we sway to the music . . .

Music!

My mind flipped through the images from the previous night as though putting on its own slide show. The moonlit deck on the stern, the two lovers embracing by the rail, the violin clutched in Colm's hand. And then I remembered the captain's words: *He's a musician at heart, if not professionally. That's what he would rather do with his life . . .*

There was still that stubborn thought in my head that resisted being put away. The completion of the journey, the arrival in New York. It would never happen and it couldn't happen. "*Since you're going to be in New York as well, perhaps you could tell me where you'll be staying and I could come see you.*" That tease of a suggestion was all I could think about. In my mind I put myself in his arms, under soft lighting, in a room full of people dressed to the nines, dancing.

"Jack," I said, surprised to find excitement in my voice. "What would we do if I stayed in New York?"

"Mmmm?" he said, continuing his work at the key. "I don't know. What would you like to do?"

"Could we go dancing?"

"Of course."

I leaned in close to him. "Can we go dancing now?"

"Now?" he said. "Lucy, I don't know if you've noticed, but I'm a bit busy right now."

"I know, Jack, I know. But could we? Go dancing? If I set something up?"

He was writing something down. I waited until he was finished before I tried the same question again.

He jerked the headphones off his head and leaned back in his chair. He rubbed his face until his flesh was pink. He looked up at me suspiciously.

"In the morning?"

"Yes!" I squatted down in front of him, my elbows on his knees, my hands in prayer.

"I don't think there's a place we could go on a Sunday morning on this ship to dance. Unless you know of a dance that goes along with 'Rock of Ages.'"

"I know a place." I said. I reached up and kissed him. "Will you come with me?"

"I can't go *now!*"

"What about when Harold gets back?"

He took up the pencil and began rapping on the desk, ignoring my pleading face. His eyes were aimed squarely at the inbox and its promise of long, labored hours ahead.

"Please, Jack? I just want to dance with you. You know I'm not going to be able to stay in New York. I just can't. We can't take long walks down Fifth Avenue or go see the Statue of Liberty or tour a museum here, but we can dance. We can do that."

He exhaled a long-stored breath from his nose and returned his gaze to me. A look of gradual resignation broke across his face.

"What did you have in mind?"

I told him to meet me down at the stern in thirty minutes. From the passenger list I found Colm's name and the location of his cabin. With that information in my head, I dashed out the door, heading straight for steerage, winding down the Grand Staircase, plowing deep into the ship. I was strangely giddy and I ran in a girlish gallop. I had to stop and ask a puzzled steward for directions and I was on my way to Colm's.

At his door I was greeted by a sleepy-eyed man who was not Colm, but one of his bunkmates. I asked for Colm immediately and the man went back into the room briefly to rouse him for bed. Colm came to the door bashfully, combing through his ratty brown curls with his fingers and blinking away sleep.

"Hello," I said. "You don't know me, but my name is Lucy Cranston. I'm a passenger on this ship. I know that you're a musician and I'd like to know if you could play something for me and my friend this morning."

He had been yawning as I spoke but all of a sudden he stopped, his mouth maintaining a perfect "O" as he seemed to be determining to himself what kind of sick joke this was and who was playing it on him.

"This mornin'?" he asked.

"Yes. If you could. I've got money. I'll pay you whatever you want."

This intrigued him. His eyes glowed with the promise of cash for his song.

"Where do you want me to play for ya', Miss?"

I instructed him to go to the stern in twenty minutes. I wanted him to play the song I thought Jack would know. The only song I could think of was "Let Me Call You Sweatheart." Colm told me he knew it and said he would be waiting for me at the stern, violin in hand.

Back in my own cabin, I rang for the stewardess and she appeared ten minutes later. I was finding myself in a time-crunch again, tearing gowns from the closet and ransacking boxes for shoes.

I found a sleeveless ivory dress that fell to the floor in cascades of burnished silk with a fitted bodice dotted with seed pearls.

"How's this?" I asked.

She made a face. "Fine, miss. But it's not much of a church-going dress, is it?"

"Oh, I'm not going to church," I said. "I'm going dancing."

"Now, Miss?" she asked.

"Yes, now."

I could tell what she was thinking: heathen girl. Spends all night gallivanting about with her gent and then dances instead of repenting. I didn't care what she was thinking. I didn't care what anybody thought or whispered behind my back. This was my time with Jack and it was going to be our most perfect moment yet.

The stewardess wanted to help me put my hair up, but I said no. Jack seemed to like my hair down. With a brush she tamed the matts into soft curls. I thought I looked divine.

Once I was outside, I observed that the ship's last day was blessed with a glorious morning. Under the light of the new sun, she appeared golden, looking every bit like the Millionaire's Special her builders' claimed she was. I was happy for her, going out looking so beautiful in her Sunday best.

With my heart pounding, I walked to the stern. Jack was right where I told him to be, standing near the rail. Beside him, Colm Wilkinson was tuning his violin. There were knots of people here and there, bundled up in shawls and heavy coats to fight the cold morning air. Tonight this would be the place where those left on the ship after the last lifeboat was launched would cling for their lives as the ship made its final plunge. Now it was just a gathering place for those in steerage who greeted my arrival with stares and hushed whispers. Who is she? What is she doing here? She must be lost. I pulled my wrap tightly around me and continued ahead.

Jack had been staring out at the ocean trailing behind, one leg up, and his arms crossed on the top of the rail. Colm saw me first and let him know I had arrived by motioning with his violin bow. Jack turned around, his eyes widening as I made my approach. I had evidently made the right selection in choosing this dress.

We had a brief discussion about what dance we would be doing. I had taken a class years ago in ballroom dancing and thought that I remembered enough of the box step without making myself look like a fool. He confessed that he wasn't the best dancer in the world, but he would try to keep up with my help.

He offered his hand and I took it. His arm went around my waist and mine went around his back. We were exactly the same height and I could look into his eyes as we swayed to the music.

"I can't stay for long," he said softly. "One dance and I shall have to go."

"One dance is all I want," I said. "But I want you to do something for me."

"What's that?"

"When you have to leave, I don't want you to tell me because I hate it when you tell me that you have to leave. So when the time comes, I just want you to tap it into my hand."

Colm asked us if we were ready to begin and I told him to start playing. Just three notes into the song, Jack's face was alight with recognition.

"Oh, I love this song," he said. "It's one of my favorites."

"Mine too. Now."

Our feet were gliding along the boards, independently mindful of not getting tangled together. Jack's eyes were trained on me continuously and he was the unwavering focus of my stare as well. This was the first time I had seen him in the sunlight. He virtually glowed before me.

While dancing, I began to get the sense that we were engaging in something beyond the physical. With our eyes locked, and our bodies entwined, it seemed that we were off in our own little world, suspended in space by the tune lilting in the air. There was nothing but us, nothing but the two of us loving the moment, loving each other. Everything else fell away. Even the sky seemed to have disappeared and the massive backdrop of the ship. This was all about us. And if it were possible to lay a bookmark on a specific time, I would have placed mine there on that moment so that I could always return to that feeling. This was what being in love was. My body felt the rush of every conceivable emotion jamming into every hollow space inside me. In this bright morning when everything seemed new and fresh, my soul was being lifted and I was in the full embrace of love.

In his arms, it was so easy to pretend that this day was over and the coming night had passed without incident. We stood perched on the forefront of a new phase in our relationship. But as much as this felt like a beginning, it was actually our end and in the context of this dazzling sunny morning, it seemed exceedingly cruel that this would have to be our final good-bye.

Jack's index finger was circling my palm, landing squarely in the middle. The taps began slowly and I picked out every word as though the message were going straight into my head. Once he was finished, I nodded. He kept me in his gaze. He seemed to be seeing something else now. All the emotions I was trying to hide, all the secrets I was trying to conceal, all the pain I was feeling from having to let him go. In those black magic eyes I witnessed an inner knowledge. I thought with both fear and hope that he finally realized why it had been so important for us to have this dance this morning. In the space between us was a silent good-bye hovering in the air. He heard it and I felt it as his lips brushed against my forehead.

"Thank you for being my someone," he whispered.

My hand went around to the back of his head and I kissed him softly. "Thank you for letting me know that's who I am."

I closed my eyes, effectively shutting out the sight of his departure, leaving only the sound and the feel of his arms slipping away from mine.

The music had stopped. Colm was beside me, wanting to know if we were finished here. I told him yes and to do me a favor. I wanted him to tell me when Jack was out of view. Then I could open my eyes again. I stood for many minutes, feeling like a ribbon rippling in the wind. Above the ocean's roar, I could still discern the sound of his footsteps. My hair flew in my face, teasingly tickling my closed eyes. Soon I couldn't hear anything except the sound of distant whispers, laughter. And then Colm's voice was in my ear, letting me know that Jack was gone.

As I took my place in the chair, I knew it was right. This was where I had come in. The caning in the seat was a little more structurally sound than how I remembered, the wood new and sturdy, but overall it had the familiar feel. There was that fear that it might be as hard for my mind to shuttle back home as it had been for me to find my way into my dreams. Did someone actually have to be calling me from the other side of consciousness? Would I just wake? And though I knew that I had left things with Jack the way they should have been, the way they had to be, my mind kept flipping around pictures of him, reliving little snatches of our time together. I was remembering the way he smiled, the way he smelled, the way his hair looked after he had been wearing a hat, the way he kissed me that first time, the way he kissed me the last time. The last time . . .

I could see him now, returning to his work, replacing Harold at the transmitter. Harold was looking at him with that secretive grin. It was the look of a younger brother who knew something shocking about his sibling's behavior.

"So Cad Phillips returns from another victory, eh, old man?" Harold said. "This I cannot believe. In the middle of the bloody North Atlantic, you still manage to get laid."

Jack shrugged, not wanting to be engaged in this line of conversation but knowing he had no choice.

"Oh, and if there are any more messages to go to the bridge, I shall continue to take them. I imagine you might be having a bit of trouble walking this morning."

"I'm walking quite fine this morning, thank you," Jack said curtly.

"Don't be so defensive, old man. I'm happy for you. This one's got quite a bit more class than the usual sort you muck about with."

"Bride, please—"

"So tell me, because I want to know. How was she?"

"Bride, I'm busy—"

"Just tell me, Phillips, for posterity's sake. How was your experience inside first class?"

Jack ripped the headset from his ears. "Bride, I'm not going to see her again!"

The junior wireless operator was suddenly mute from his senior's outburst. At length he said, "You what?"

The realization hit him hard again as it had out on the stern and it was tough for him to hide the emotion in his voice. "I'll not see her again," he repeated.

"But why? Did you have a row?"

"No, nothing of the sort."

"Then what happened?"

Jack stared into the inbox and all the messages it contained, thinking of all the hours it would take to transmit them and all that time without her. "I don't know. But as sure as I'm sitting here, she was saying good-bye."

"I'm sorry, old man. I thought you were getting on so well."

"We were. Very well. But I think it was just for this time."

"Well, cheer up, old man. You may see her again on one of these crossings."

As Bride began sifting through the messages waited to be transmitted, Jack had some doubt about this. "It'll be a miracle," he said grimly.

Bride saw the one message, folded in fourths, lying outside the box, and he picked it up, but he did not read it just yet.

"I think it's safe to say that it will be a bloody miracle if we manage to send all these. There must be a million of them just in this morning." He began unfolding the message. He thought it was odd to have found a message there like that, but supposed that it had just fallen out of the box. He read it just once and then shook his head. "If they're all like this one, we may have an easier time of it than we thought."

"How do you mean?"

"Well, there's no name, no address, no indication of who's sending it. All it says is, 'You're the man of my dreams.' That could be intended for anyone and from anyone. I suppose in addition to being magicians, we're expected to be mind readers as well."

"That's the way of it," Jack said.

"Strange. I don't remember taking in any messages like this. All folded and everything. Wasn't even in the box or on the spike." He looked at it one last time before crumpling the paper in his hands. "All right. In you go." And then he unceremoniously dropped it into the wastepaper basket.

Once he had finished with the message he was currently sending, Jack paused as his hands touched the next message. He looked down at the blank message pad there and observed the ragged edge remaining from where he had torn off a sheet that morning for Lucy.

"Bride, did you say it wasn't in the box or on the spike?" he asked.

"That's what I said."

"Then where exactly was it?"

"Right here. Beside the box."

Jack looked over at the place Harold was referring to. He saw how easy it would have been for someone to just put a message there while he was distracted. *A message had come through the tube while she was here,* he thought. *And in the time it took to go get it, she had finished writing. But she never gave it to me . . .*

He removed his headphones and wheeled himself over to the waste paper basket. Right on top was the crumpled note, compressed into a ball, lying among discarded orange peels and the remains of a sandwich. He began unraveling the ball, careful not to tear the fragile paper with too-eager hands. He straightened out the wrinkled message, ironing it with his hands on the desktop, mindful of not smudging the penciled words. There was no mistaking the sender once he read the message with his own eyes. There was no question as for whom the message was intended. By the triangular tear on the top right corner he knew this was the sheet of paper he had given her that morning. But beyond that he knew because she had been trying to say it to him all along. Only at the last did *she know exactly how to tell him and what words to use. This message was just for him, for her sweet angel whose life was history, whose future was his past, for the incredibly brave boy whose deeds this night would give him an immortality all his own, for this boy, just twenty five years old, whom she took into her heart in this long ago place, from a girl who had only begun to love him, who would have liked to have known him forever, but had simply run out of time.*

I was not there to hear his reply.

I was already in my backyard.

— — —

The next afternoon on April 15 at about 2:20 p.m., Augustus Baumgarten was found collapsed in his shop by the girls who regularly came in after school to buy their sodas. By the time the paramedics arrived, there was nothing they could do but pronounce him dead at the scene.

After all those years, the dream had finally ended for Mr. Baumgarten.

CHAPTER TEN

On Saturday morning Mom informed me that the project my father had been working on had temporarily shut down due to budget concerns and Dad would be arriving at about five o'clock in the evening at the Norfolk airport. Since Dad had not been home in a long time, and Mom wanted to make his return to the fold as welcoming as possible, she would be spending the afternoon cooking a special dinner for us at a neighbor's house and needed me to go the airport. She would be waiting for us with food on the table at six.

At 5:15 I was still waiting for Dad's plane to arrive. The monitors overhead proclaimed that his flight was on schedule, so I assumed that his plane was hovering overhead awaiting clearance for landing. Being a Saturday and a busy travel day, the place was packed. Mostly I saw young people, close to my age and younger—the backpack over one shoulder crowd. I was reminded that many schools were letting out for spring break. I could only imagine how many of these kids were headed for the Carolinas or Daytona. Lucky them, I thought. How sweet to be going somewhere else.

I was wondering too what kind of mood Dad would be in when he got off the plane. Mom had told me that he hadn't taken the news about Mr. Baumgarten very well, but didn't elaborate any further. I could understand why he would be upset. He had probably told Mr. Baumgarten that he would see him again soon the last time he saw him and now that time would never come.

Mom had acted really strangely about Dad coming home, and I couldn't quite figure out if she were annoyed by or just unprepared for his sudden visit. She had been on such a high ever since she closed the deal on the Marple place. That Thursday her coworkers had taken her out for drinks and she didn't come home until after 1:00 a.m. The next morning she was in the kitchen, gloriously hungover, twitching in front of the coffee maker, still caught up in all the delirium of all that immediate extra cash and all those White Russians poured one right after the next.

I supposed that Mom could have been perturbed at the notion of having two gloomy guses underfoot in the midst of her sudden prosperity. I had not been myself since Thursday night. One minute I felt exhilarated by my own youthful exuberance, the next I felt ancient and defeated, frightened by time. My mind was still, irrevocably, on Jack. I would think of him while doing the most mundane things, like going upstairs to my room or sitting on the sofa watching TV. And sometimes, when I was alone, I would say his name, just to hear it. "Oh, Jack," I would whisper to myself when his image would suddenly materialize in my mind. "Oh, Jack."

Although Mom seemed concerned that I was sleeping more than usual and eating less than a bird, she hadn't reached out yet. I knew that if Dad sensed that something was wrong, I would have to tell him, something. Mom was very good at putting the "What's wrong with you?" question to me in a variety of ways and getting nothing from me. Dad was more the type who would say, "I want to know what's bothering you" and getting everything.

At 5:30, I turned around in my seat and viewed the gleaming flank of a US Airways fuselage moving by slowly, nosing its way to the gangplank which would carry the passengers into the terminal. This had to be Dad's flight, I thought. I took a notion to call Mom and let her know that we would be late, but I didn't know the number of the neighbor's house where she was cooking. In a few minutes, a trickle of people started to flow from the mouth of the gate. I was convinced that these were all folks making connections, since they looked too anticipative of tropical weather in their cool blues and bright fuchsias to be vacationing on this part of the Atlantic. And in this throng, I saw my Dad, weaving his way through, an eager needle through this staid tapestry. He looked at me and smiled through a head bob.

Most children linger under the delusion that their parents will never get old. I could almost assure myself that age would never affect my father and that he would always look exactly the same. Other members of his generation wore their gray, thinning hair in ponytails like the tattered remains of their hippie battle flags. Dad's hair was still the same sun-kissed blond it had always been, hanging in slight rebellion over his azure eyes, the same tint as mine. In his forties, he was still slim, still walking with the assured gait of someone who always knew where he was going, though he had spent half his life wandering.

He hadn't changed out of his work clothes, I observed: Levis the color of white chalk smeared against a blue blackboard, bargain bin flannel shirt, holey T-shirt from Danny's, sandy-colored lug-soled work boots. When we hugged, I caught the aroma of a mingling of sweat and airline food.

"Oh, Lucifer," he said, aiming a kiss at my cheek. "Thanks so much for coming to get me. Where's your Mom?"

"She's cooking." I said. And the minute the words left my mouth, I was instantly sorry. I hadn't checked with Mom beforehand to see if the meal were going to be a surprise or not.

"Really? At home?"

"No, at a neighbor's."

Dad laughed, putting his arm around my shoulder. "I didn't think she'd mastered the microwave in this short of time. Tell me, Luce. Should I begin genuflecting to her the minute I hit the back door or should I just enter with tools in hand, ready to go to work?"

I just smiled at this. Normally I would have had an answer, but I honestly didn't know what to say. This didn't seem to bother Dad. He pulled me a little tighter and drew a breath.

"God, it's good to see you."

Five minutes into our drive down the long, black ribbon of the James River Bridge, Dad tried to engage me in some kind of conversation. I felt like a non-participant, listening to our voices, sounding louder than they would normally, straining to be heard over the engine noise and the long dip into the tunnel. At first he wanted to know about my classes, how they were going, nearly reiterating what he had asked me on the phone days before, and I used the same pre-programmed responses.

"So school's going well?" he asked.

"Yeah."

"You don't have much longer to go. About a month, right?"

"Yeah."

"Not a month too soon, huh?"

"Yeah."

"Any classes giving you any trouble?"

"No."

"None at all?"

"They're all pretty easy."

"Your Mom said one professor was giving you a fit. That fake Irish guy, I think."

"Johnny Mumphrey." I wasn't going to tell him that I skipped Mumphrey's class on Thursday, how I'd probably end up with a "D" average because I had missed too many classes.

"And then there was someone else your Mom mentioned. Schlessinger, Schick, Sheridan, Sch—"

"Schindler, Dad. Presbyn Schindler."

"For American History, right?"

"That's right." I wasn't going to tell him that on the day before, I had visited Dr. Schindler after class in his office. I had to tell him that I didn't have my journal, the reader's journal that we were supposed to have been keeping. I had, of course, written it, but at the last minute decided that what I had written was not meant for his eyes or anyone else's. The passages were too personal, too close to the bone, too close to sounding like the realized ramblings of a mad mind. I had told him that I would write the journal over the weekend, and he replied that he would not accept it, since I was supposed to have been writing in it all along. Now my final grade on the unit was dependent on how well I did on the test Monday, but the best I could hope for would be a "D-."

Dad wanted next to talk about Mr. Baumgarten and all the details of his death. All the details I knew, anyway, which didn't amount to much.

"Poor Mr. B.," Dad said. "God, I just couldn't believe it when I heard. I mean, I knew he only had a few good years left in him, but . . ." He shook his head. "Say, Lucifer, did the obituary mention his age?"

"I don't remember," I told him.

"I think he was in his 80s, but I could be wrong. The man never seemed to age. Any family listed?"

"No. No survivors." *703 survivors, or somewhere along that line.*

"That's strange. I could have sworn that at one time he had mentioned a niece back home in England. As a matter of fact, I remember once when we were there in his shop one afternoon, he told me that you reminded him a lot of his niece."

I only nodded.

"I guess she could have died before he did, since he had some age on him." Dad was staring straight ahead at the road. He began drumming a little on the dashboard like a little kid and I thought that if he continued, I'd have to use my parental voice and make him stop. He did stop, finally, on his own. My annoyance must have ricocheted off the windshield.

"Mr. B. Good ole Mr. B.," he murmured. "You know, Lucifer, when I heard that he had died, I was thinking that I couldn't remember when I saw him last. I don't think I've been in his shop in—Oh, I don't know—five years at least. Could be longer. I was thinking that, probably the last time I saw him, I never imagined that would be the last time. It's just so strange . . . it's just so strange how things happen sometime."

I knew I was seeing him for the last time. I knew when I looked into that bright, beautiful young face that I was seeing someone who was about to vanish from my life and become a memory. And in the fine, ebony glint of those mesmerizing oblong eyes, I had detected the same look reflecting back at me. We both knew that would be the last time we saw each other. If I ever do see him again, it will only be in dreams.

"Luce?" Dad was saying.

"Yes!" I answered, more abruptly than I should have.

"I'm sorry. I was just asking you a question. Did you hear me?"

"No."

"Then let me try again. Did Mr. B. seem sick when you saw him a couple days ago?"

"No, he seemed fine."

"Didn't look overly tired or anything?"

"He looked just the same as always, Dad." Why all the questions, I thought. Did he think that I had something to do with Mr. B's death? Had the county coroner's office appointed him an adjunct investigator? I just wanted to get back into my own head and mingle with my own thoughts. I needed to think of Jack.

Dad was looking at me now, trying to figure out the message behind all the curt responses and lengthy silences. If he had been the type of parent to say such a thing as, "I don't like your tone, young lady. Not one bit", he would have said that then. But he wasn't like that. All he said was, "Are you all right, Lucy? You seem a little . . . I don't know. Not yourself."

I kept my eyes fixed on the road. "I'm fine, Dad."

"No. no. Something is wrong. And it's not about Mr. B., is it?" he asked.

"Dad, I need you to tell me something," I said slowly and steadily. "About the deck chair you bought from Mr. B."

"The deck chair? What about it?"

"Did you ever find out anything about it? Like, was it real? Did it really come from the *Titanic*?"

"Hell no, it didn't come from the *Titanic*. It wasn't even from that era. I took it to a dealer one time and he told me that it was most likely a prop from one of the movies made about the ship in the 1950s. That's all. Just a prop."

And then, with my emotions running the gamut from uncontrollable rage to silent grief, I felt the sob that had been forming in me since Thursday building to a climax and I was almost knocked breathless by the sheer force of it as it seemingly splintered the bones of my rib cage and rose to my throat. As my mouth opened, involuntarily to let the sob out, I pressed a closed fist to my lips and my face was seared with an onslaught of insurgent tears.

Above the uproar of my own emotions, I heard my father speaking to me, rushing to hush, but not putting a stop to the ferocity of my sudden meltdown. His hands went to my arms, to comfort me, I thought, but then I realized he was trying to help me steer as the car veered ever closer to the shoulder. I snapped to attention, mashing down the remaining sobs, and guided the car back to where it needed to be.

After a while, he said, "You need to go somewhere to talk?"

"No," I said. But then I looked over at his concerned face and felt his callused hands massaging the nape of my neck. That touch . . . I remembered when I was little and Mom was tired or at her wit's end, how I would wake from one of those horrible, heart-pounding nightmares, convinced that what I had lived inside my head had been real. He would come to me, lift me from all that terror, and lead me to safety just by taking me into his arms and saying everything would be OK. I needed to know what had happened to me. I had always counted on him to help me see the difference between the real and imaginary.

"Yes."

"OK," he said. "We'll go someplace and talk."

"But Mom. She's waiting."

"Never mind that. I can deal with my wife. Right now I need to be a father to my daughter."

That was my father. My troubles were always worth his time, even when they may not have been worth the grief he would suffer at home when supper was served cold.

We had pulled off the road to Huntington Beach, a stretch of shoreline just up the road from where we lived. Night had fallen fast and the air had a certain, sullen tone as though light had only unwillingly given up its hold on the day. We were seated side by side on a bench on the pier there. Beneath us the James River lapped like the dark manes of a hundred head of black stallions. Just a few feet from us was a seafood restaurant and the aroma of freshly steamed mussels, shrimp and scallops hung in the air. All around us, dozens of people were taking advantage of the summer-like weather, staking out the pier with fishing poles hoisted in the air or dangling over the rails. Whole families paraded by with their catches in hand. I had been here with my father many times. But never like this.

Once seated on the pier, with the introduction of his arm behind my shoulder, he punctured a bladder, stored deep and bulging inside of me, full of everything I had been feeling. I had cried, confessed, all but stated by madness in a series of hallucinogenic, meandering monologues. And with the events, so lately lived, playing encores in my head, rediscovered in my speech, I felt awed by the dreams all over again.

Like the fireflies that emerge on a summer's evening, the dreams came out flickering in my recollections of them, and I found myself being enchanted once again by all I had experienced for the duration of those four wonderful, wonder-filled nights. I remembered everything and I told my father, everything. Everything seemed so precious, so rare, I had to share it with someone who would understand and that person had to be my father. Although I did find myself censoring some of the details out of respect for my father's feelings, I tried to be as candid as possible so that he would see how this person had been such a ray of sunshine in my life that in his wake I seemingly walked in shadow now. Just so he would know how deeply my feelings ran for this man in my dreams, I did tell my father that the ultimate knowledge I had of Jack was carnal in nature, though I spared him the details of the night we spent in my cabin.

And when I had finished, after I had stretched the story to the four corners of the canvas, what emerged was the full portrait of what the dreams had been in their entirety: a blissful, exquisite journey, taken by an unsure pilgrim, who now, seated on the shore of reality, looked back into the sea she had sailed and wondered, could it have all been true?

After a painfully extended lapse of incalculable time, he did speak, more or less. At first I heard a long "Hmm" followed by a series of staccato "M's."

Then he said, "I guess the easiest thing would have been to have asked Mr. Baumgarten, since you seem to think he was at the helm of things, so to speak."

I shook my head. "No. I couldn't do that. I thought of it, but I couldn't bring myself to it. I wouldn't know how to begin to ask him even if he were here today."

"I don't think I would know either, to tell you the truth."

"Daddy, weren't you furious with him when you found out that the chair was a fake?"

"Not too much. I didn't pay much for it, so it didn't bother me that it wasn't authentic."

"Didn't pay too much for it? You used my college money to buy it!"

"Huh?"

"The money that was in my savings account for my tuition!"

"Lucy, I didn't use that money to buy the deck chair."

"You didn't?"

"No. Lucy, your old man may act like a crazy fool sometime, but I'm not an idiot." He suddenly couldn't look me in the eye. "I cashed out that account to make a down payment on Mr. Baumgarten's business."

"You what?" This was like finding out the Mustang Dad used to drive was actually a rebuilt Maverick.

"Mr. B was going to sell the shop to me in the early seventies. He was tired of running it and thought it would be best to go back to England. There was really nothing keeping him here except for the shop. It wasn't making him any money and the neighborhood was becoming increasingly dangerous and shops were being boarded up and shut down left and right." He shook his head slowly as though feeling the shame for a deal gone wrong. "That was the only payment I ever made on it. I bought the deck chair around the time that I gave Mr. B the money for the store. That's why you probably remembered that I had spent it on the chair. You were really young then, couldn't have been more than five or six."

"But Daddy, you only made that one payment?" And then I thought, *Well, I only had the one account to dip into . . .*

"That's about as far as that business venture went. I realized if the shop wasn't making Mr. B any money, then it wouldn't bring in any real profit for me, either. And I had you and your Mom and Aunt Teese to support. I had to face reality." He paused to chuckle at himself. "The things we do when we're young and think that life is never ending and there will always be money."

"But when you decided not to buy the shop, why didn't you ask for the money back?"

"I guess I always thought that one day I would be able to complete the transaction."

That was Dad. Never giving up hope that one day he'd be rich doing this or that or one day he'd win the lottery and not have to think about money or one day someone from 'Antiques Roadshow' would come rambling through and declare the contents of the garage priceless. Meanwhile, we'd still have a kitchen we couldn't use.

"You know, in the dream, Mr. Baumgarten told me that he never did anything with that money. He said it was still in his shop," I told him.

"He did? Well, I'll be."

"He said he didn't want to take the money from you in the first place. Is that right?"

"No, he didn't want to take it. But I told him I'd be back in two weeks with the rest. I don't think he believed me. And then when I got home and your Mom nearly picked me up and threw me out the front window for what I had done, I thought, 'Well, maybe this isn't such a good idea.' Again, the things we do when we're young." He pulled me closer to him and placed a kiss on my forehead. "How old was this man in your dreams?"

"He had just turned twenty-five."

Dad winced and shook his head. "Poor boy."

"He was so sweet to me, Daddy. It was just weird being with someone who was so considerate and so caring. He told me I was beautiful." The back of my throat began to burn.

"Well, you are beautiful, Luce."

"A daughter would expect her father to tell her that. But not someone you haven't known for very long. And won't get to know hardly at all." I needed to be looking into his eyes when I asked him this. I needed him to be completely honest with me. "What do you think, Dad? Am I crazy? Have I absolutely lost it?"

"No," he said at length. "I don't think you've lost it."

"But do you think that what I experienced was real? Could it have been real?"

There was silence again from his end. He was thinking, taking his own time. His eyes were engaged in a pensive stare as though he were outlining his thoughts on an invisible screen. At last I heard another "Hmm" sound coming from deep inside his throat.

"Lucy, it just seems to me that you've been asking yourself the wrong question. The whole time you've been thinking, how could this have happened to me when you should have been thinking, why did this happen to me? Why did you reach out to this boy in your dreams? What did he have to tell you, to teach you? What can you learn from it all and how can you grow from it? I know now you're probably kind of dazed by the whole experience. You haven't had that much time away from it to figure out why things went on the way they did. You keep saying to yourself, 'How?' as though if it weren't a real experience then all of it wouldn't matter. You wouldn't have known this Jack Phillips person at all. End of story. But you'd continue to feel the way you do. You can't deny your feelings and I'm not going to tell you that the loss you're dealing with right now isn't the real thing, because I can tell by your tears that it is. Ultimately you're the only one who really knows how you're feeling. And ultimately you'll have to figure out a way to get over this . . . loss, somehow. I only wish there were some way now that I could comfort you."

"There is, Daddy. There is. Just believe me. That's all I ask. I just need you to tell me that you believe me, that you don't think I'm crazy." My eyes were filling with tears again. "I really loved this man, Daddy. I loved him so much. I can't stop thinking about him. I can't stop thinking about the people he left behind. If I feel this way, having just known him for the short time that I did, I can't imagine how they must have felt when they learned about what happened to him. You do believe me, don't you? You don't think I'm making this up?"

"Lucy," he said, as I settled back into his arms and my head reclaimed its position against his shoulder. "I'll tell you this. When you were first born, as you've been told time and time again, no one expected you to live. I just remember the look on your mother's face when she came running to me with your stilled form in her hands—in her hands! Not even in her arms. You were too small to be cradled like that. I couldn't believe that what she was holding was a baby. Our baby. It just seemed like some terrible, unfunny joke. We took off in that old Mustang. I looked over at your mother, saw that awful look in her eye. She wanted me to do something, help her somehow. She was sobbing, kept saying over and over again, 'Don't die. Please don't die.' I didn't even know if you were alive. But I remember at some point during the drive, the car went under a street lamp, and I looked over and saw something. Under your Mom's fingertips, I saw your little chest rising. And I knew that you were breathing. I knew then that you would make it. Even when the doctors at the hospital told us not to count on your being around very long, I had seen you taking your first breaths, struggling so hard to get air into those tiny lungs, and there was no question as to whether or not you would live, at least in my mind."

Dad reached up to rub his eye. Was he crying? I didn't ask him. If I had, he would have blamed it on moonlight dust or something. I felt his arm draw tight across my shoulder and the light tap of his kiss on my forehead. "If there's one thing you've given to me since day one, it's the power to believe the most incredible things."

On the day of Mr. Baumgarten's funeral, fickle April pulled one of her mean tricks and decided to be cold again, with many brisk winds coming out of the frigid north and I realized I would have to wear something warm, something from the winter section of my wardrobe, now pushed to the very back of my closet with my spring things hanging cheerily out in front. I had to crawl all the way back into the closet where my Barbie dolls and baby clothes were stored in giant, see-through plastic bins to find something appropriately somber enough for the occasion. I was moving slowly that afternoon, as though any sudden moves or accelerations might insult the dead. Dad was anxious to leave and kept shouting up the stairs every five minutes or so, "Lucy, you have five more minutes!"

After I had finally decided on my navy blue wool skirt and matching tunic, I heard the front doorbell ring. I didn't rush to answer it because I knew that Mom or Dad would get it first. Mom had installed herself in her newly restored kitchen with all the appliances now in place after Dad had pulled an all-nighter trying to get everything installed and Dad was with her. My bedroom door was open, so I had a perfect vantage point through which to eavesdrop, anyway, in case it was something important.

Oddly, when I heard the doorbell, my immediate thought was, "Maybe it's Jack." This was not an isolated incident. Since that Thursday whenever the doorbell rang, my thoughts were snared by that same idea. This, of course, was ludicrous and my mind knew that. But still, every time, my heart sort of pounced on the idea and thumped excitedly as though it had a dreamy mind of its own.

"Oh, Jack," I said aloud as I went over to my dresser for a slip.

I continued to dwell on Jack as I listened, half interested, to what was going on in the foyer.

I wonder if he would like this blue outfit. He seemed to like that blue gown I wore that night we celebrated his birthday . . .

"Hello. I'm looking for Dan Cranston," a gruff, masculine voice was saying from outside on the front stoop.

"You got him," my Dad said. "Can I help you with something?"

I'm so sick of this outfit. So sick of my winter things. My spring things aren't so great either, but at least I haven't worn them for a long time so they don't seem as relic-like as this old ancient blue thing...

"I hope you can," the man from outside was saying.

"Well, sir, it it's something I can help you with, I hope it won't take long. I'm on my way to a funeral, you see."

I don't have anything black, at least not something I could wear to a funeral. If only I had that closet I had on the ship. So full or gorgeous gowns. I saw a lot of black in there.

"I'm on my way to the same funeral. My name is Leon Baruski. I'm the owner of the building where Augustus Baumgarten kept his shop."

"Oh, Mr. Baruski. Come in, come in."

I wonder what happened to that closet? Did it disappear with me or did it go to the bottom...? Oh, come on, Lucy. Think, Lucy! Think lucidly. It was never there to begin with. It only existed in your mind...

"This won't take long." The stranger's voice was now louder, trumpeting in the hollow openness of the front hall. "I have something for you. My wife and I found this in a strong box in the back storage room at the shop. It had your name on it."

My thoughts were now drawn to what was going on downstairs. I paused in the middle of the room, my head feeling suddenly hot while my eyes froze in their sockets. *The money!*

"I don't know what's in it," the man continued. "But if it was something important, I know Augustus would want you to have it."

"Oh, my God," Dad was saying slowly. I imagined he had opened the envelope by this time, but was keeping the contents to himself. "I don't believe it. After all these years..."

"It looked real old," the man said. "Like it'd been there for at least a couple decades."

"Yes. Yes, almost twenty years exactly. I don't know what to say. Thank you, Mr. Baruski. I just don't know what else to say."

"Well... I'm just so glad I found you. When I found it, I just took a chance and looked in the phone book and there you were."

"Well, I appreciate your detective work. This is unbelievable... I just can't imagine why he would have kept this all these years."

Dad went outside with the man and I went to my front window to try to get a look at the stranger and, perhaps, what he had brought my Dad. But I knew exactly what it was. And I knew exactly where I had learned about it.

"It was in the dream. He told me about it in the dream," I was saying aloud. "He told me about the money in the dream! Which means it wasn't a dream at all!"

When I looked out the window I saw the man, a ridiculous, graying pompadour atop his head, a mint green sports jacket over sloppy pants. He made Dad's khaki pants and white oxford short ensemble look like an Armani tux. Dad was holding the envelope, still marveling at what it contained, still thanking Mr. Baruski, giving him repeated pats on the man's back while all the while there was undiluted, showy heroism on Mr. Baruski's face.

When Dad came back into the house, my mother had come to investigate and I listened again.

"I just don't believe it," Mom was saying in that little girl voice of hers. "It just doesn't make sense. Why would he keep it?"

"I don't know. It's a lot of cash. You'd think a retiree like Mr. B could have used it at some point or another. But I guess his pension from the navy and the money his sister left him kept him well-fixed. To tell you the truth, I don't think he ever made a penny from that store. It just gave him something to do each day, I guess. A way to wile away his twilight years."

That was true, I thought. He had told me that.

"God," Dad said, "No wonder you were pissed at me. There was enough here to put a down payment on a house in those days."

"There's enough here for a year's basic tuition at ODU for Lucy, though."

"You think?"

"Definitely. Which is kind of ironic when you think about it, because that money came from her college fund."

"Yes, I know. I remember you screaming at me to the top of your lungs about twenty years ago in this very spot about that very thing."

I was on my bed, shoes in hand, just listening to them talk without moving an inch. I was just letting the words fill my ears, bounce off the walls and land with a splat. And then things just sort of froze up around me and became silent as though I had found myself suddenly sealed up in a vacuum.

I looked around my room and it was as if I couldn't recognize anything or didn't want to anymore, didn't want to associate myself with the things I saw. Everything looked as though it belonged to someone else, someone younger, someone who had gone away and left everything just as it was. I looked at the crevices around where the posters didn't quite cover all the space on their allotted walls, noticing the way the room was straining to be pink, still. I looked at the pink gingham coverlet on the bed, the matching dust ruffle, the lampshade tilted like a lady's bonnet. I thought about the dolls inside the closet, piled one on top of the other in a bin like unidentified murder victims in a mass grave. When I went into my closet I could see their faces, plainly, straining against the clear plastic, looking forlornly at the empty dream house where they once lived. Like most dollhouses, its furnishings were much grander and much better kept than anything in our house. Living in the shadow of that tidy little mansion with its faux damask wallpaper and Louis Quinze furniture, I always felt like our house should have been condemned. From the time I was four up until the time I finally put that little house away in my closet, I never stopped dreaming that I would someday be able to reduce myself in size just enough to walk around in those tiny rooms, share clothes with the little girl in the play family, and eat crumbs on their Empire style dining table.

I looked at the area over by the he window overlooking the yard where the dream house had been when it was still the reason I rushed to be in this place in the afternoons after school. A steamer trunk was there now, but I could still see a faint, dark stain from where Janet and I had spilled coke after trying unsuccessfully to fill the dolls' tiny dinner glasses with soda.

There was a time when I couldn't fathom speaking about things having occurred twenty, fifteen, or even ten years ago, like my parents and grandparents and aunts and uncles, but now I could. Now I had reached that age where youth is still there, sometimes angrily so, and at its most ephemeral. Giving my room the once-over, I saw for myself that there was nothing there that would tell anyone looking from the outside that an adult lived here, not even a young adult, really. This was the place where I had once dreamed Barbie dreams and built presidential hopes in Lincoln log cabins, but that was all a long time ago.

When I was on that ship in my dreams, in that idyll, I had come to think of myself as being close to God in my power over the destinies of those 1523 souls who would die on April 15, 1912. With just a few words, I could have prevented that tragic event from happening. But I couldn't do that and still be alive. And I was alive.

Thoughts of Jack came coursing into my head, but in a different way now. He had been someone's little boy and he would forever be someone's little boy. He could have stayed there in his hometown and no one would have known who he was. He would have been just the Phillips boy. I thought of him going away from home, going far away from home. It was the bravery that made him take that first step away that I admired.

I had been afraid of being that next thing for fear that I wouldn't recognize myself and that the people in my life wouldn't either. But I *had* to go on and be the person I needed to be, otherwise I'd be trapped forever in the life of this person I had come to dislike.

The time had come. I couldn't wait even a second longer. I had to tell them then.

"Is there enough money there for a deposit on a small apartment?" I asked my parents from the top of the stairs. I had been thinking so hard about what I was going to say, how I was going to say it, and how it was going to be received that I, honestly, was as shocked as they were to find myself standing there.

Mom and Dad both looked up. They had that awe-struck, slightly dumb look of people watching fireworks. But then, simultaneously, their expressions changed to utter disbelief, no doubt matching the one Dad wore when he first saw the contents of the envelope.

They were both too startled to say anything and I could almost see them conferring with each other using their invisible parental antennae.

"If I'm going to ODU in the fall, I want my own apartment," I said, with such a sizzling determination in my voice I barely recognized it as my own.

"Well, Lucy," Mom said, with the most hopeless look on her face, "Having an apartment is a lot of responsibility. I mean, putting a deposit on an apartment and the first and last month's rent is one thing, but keeping up with the rent each month? Are you sure you can do that? I mean, you'd have to find a job."

Mom had used the "Honey-are-you-sure, something-or-another-is-a-big-responsibility" bit as a roadblock before. And I had almost always replied the same way—"I don't care." This time I did care. I felt the fear in my gut.

"I can do that," I said.

I was coming down the stairs now. Mom and Dad were still seemed shell-shocked and hadn't moved. Dad was still holding the envelope in his mannequin-stiff hand. And as I stood in front of him, he looked at me as though he knew about the revelation I had just had. A smile appeared on his face and it was as though the two of us were simultaneously drawn back to our talk on the pier.

"She's right, Eve," he said. "It's her money. She should do with it what she wants to."

"If it's my money, I'll take care of it. I'll put is somewhere safe. Somewhere Aunt Teese can't find it. I know just the place." Truth be told, I didn't know where I was going to put it. The experience of having it in my hands was so new, so unexpected. I thought maybe I would just stick it in my purse for a while, carry it around, maybe go to the bank and open a savings account. A savings account! What a grown-up thing to have.

I walked to the back of the house. When I got to the back porch, I was out of breath. Normally I would be panting from the exertion of having lifted myself over the dishwasher, but the dishwasher was gone. I stood there on the porch, the envelope pressed to my smiling lips, and suppressed a squeal. I had done it. I had told them. I knew this wasn't the end of it—discussions would follow, many late night talks in the dining room under the Tiffany lamp would take place, but at least I had made a start.

This was my beginning.

At the memorial service, the cold continued, and a stiff breeze was coming off the gray green water of the bay. The sky was bright though, necessitating sunglasses, standard funeral garb anyway. The service was not so much a funeral mass as it was just a chance for a few of Mr. Baumgarten's acquaintances to get together and say good-bye. Mr. Baumgarten had wished to be buried at sea so the memorial was held in Norfolk just outside the Naval base there. A speedboat tethered to a dock awaited the conclusion of the service. This small craft would take the remains of Augustus Baumgarten out to waves and into a watery eternity.

The sadness of the event was augmented by the low attendance. I got the sense that this was a gathering of strangers early on in the service, a swatch of Hampton Roads locals creating a motley crew. There was an older gentleman in a tweed suit with no necktie that I recognized as the butcher from the Food Lion not too far from where I lived and he was there with a woman about his age whom I assumed was his wife. There was also a man in a grungy trench coat who I think worked at the liquor store two doors down from Mr. B's shop. Another man I had seen just recently in my front yard, his heavyweight pompadour treating the wind like some frisky new bantam in the ring. There was no mistaking the identity of the five young girls present, so freshly-scrubbed and mall-haired. These were the girls from the Catholic school, all wearing floral print spring dresses under long, winter coats, all shivering through their impatience for the new season to come and stay this time.

It occurred to me as we were all standing there, that we were all mourning a different person, a man the minister described as someone many people could call by name, but few really knew. To the butcher, he was probably the distinguished looking and sounding older gentleman who never neglected the niceties of "please" and "thank you" when placing his order and who used phrases like, "Have you any of that lovely ground round this morning" or "I'd like some of your delightful sirloin if you have some that's not too terribly fatty." To the liquor storeowner, he was the sounding board and confidant for many a bad business day with too many unruly customers or perhaps no customers at all. For the schoolgirls, he was the kindly older gentleman who was always at the ready in the afternoons with a cold soda, maybe a word of advice here and there on a particularly difficult subject. To Dad, he was somewhere between a father figure and the realization of everything my father wanted to be—happy in his shop with all his things, seemingly independently wealthy, a knowledgeable dealer in his trade.

My feelings were complicated by what I believed I had been through with him in the past week. Angel of death, mortal soul made immortal by God's punishing hand, forced to live out eternity dreaming that same dream over and over, never able to make it right. No future, no real present, only a past revealed in a series of reoccurring nightmares. I liked to think that somehow I had played a part in setting his soul free, that by finding someone to listen to his story and believe it wholeheartedly, this ancient mariner had finally been relieved of his duty.

Ultimately for me, he would always be the man who, by showing me his dark past, held a lamp which illuminated my own present and future and gave the disaster that cold April night in the North Atlantic a human face and a human heart.

EPILOGUE

I was running late again.

The clock on the dashboard read 5:15. I pressed the accelerator with the toe of my work pump and was grateful that the sign for 66th Street was well within reach of 5:16.

Turning into the driveway of my parents' home, I saw Dad's Mustang parked proudly in front, covered in a tarp to protect its new paint job and complete overhauling from passing birds and bad weather.

I parked right behind Dad's car and got out. When I heard the squeals of my child, I smiled and went to the backyard.

Dad and little Lucie were playing their usual game—hide and go seek. I saw my child hiding behind the garbage cans beside the garage and she saw me. She suppressed a giggle as her grandfather pretended not to know where she was.

"Where is she? Where is she?" Dad questioned as he ambled around the backyard in his khaki pants and light blue oxford shirt.

Mom appeared on the back stoop. She folded her arms and smiled. "They've been doing this all afternoon."

I wasn't a bit surprised.

"You have time to come in for a drink?" Mom asked.

"No, I've got to pick Paul up from work. His car's in the shop," I said.

Mom looked disappointed, but nodded her understanding.

My daughter was quickly discovered, but Dad made it look as though it took him ages to find her.

"There you are! There you are!" he picked her up and tossed her into the air, catching her under her arms.

"Pa Dan, it's your turn," my daughter said.

"No, I think turns are over today," Dad told her. "Your mommy's here."

"But I don't want to go," my daughter protested.

"I'll give you five more minutes of playtime with Pa Dan and then we have to go," I told her.

I went into the house long enough to retrieve Lucie's lunch box from the top of the dryer in which a load of clothes spun. "She didn't eat the snack you packed," Mom said. "She ate some grapes that we had."

There was so much the smell of fabric softener and so little of cigarette smoke. I didn't live there anymore. And neither did Aunt Teese.

I had just a quick glimpse of the chair where Teese used to sit, watching "The Price is Right" and cheering on contestants. Aunt Teese died five summers before, suddenly, in her sleep. She asked to be cremated. There was nothing left of her now except the chair where she used to watch TV.

"You look tired, Lucy," Mom said.

I sighed. "I am. Had an afternoon of parent-teacher conferences."

"They didn't go well?"

I shrugged. "A lot of parents are angry that their children aren't doing as well as they should. They blame me."

"Well, I hope that you showed them your teacher of the year award."

"Oh, like that's going to impress them."

I heard my daughter squeal in the backyard and my father start to sing some song he created off the top of his head. "Pa Dan, Pa Dan, he's a marvelous man. He loves his Lucie June."

"I wish he wouldn't call her that," I said.

"Too bad. I think it's kind of stuck."

"I know. I find myself calling her that all the time."

"Your father won't know what to do with himself next year when she's in kindergarten. He looks forward to picking her up from preschool in the afternoons and spending this time with her."

I nodded. Dad was such a tremendous help to me with Lucie. He had suffered a back injury during the completion of work at the job site in Ohio and after that, he permanently returned home. For many years he sunk into a deep depression, watched "Saint Elsewhere" episodes on TV, drank Jack Daniels and played with his computer. One day he discovered an online auction site. He took a digital photo of a cookie jar he had stored in the garage and sold it to a buyer in Michigan. After that, he was hooked. He was overjoyed when he sold "The Best of Bread" on LP and 8-track to a buyer in Finland.

Mom was very comfortable being breadwinner. Now a full-time real estate agent, she routinely closed the deal on a house every month. I often saw her face on "for sale" signs outside prospective houses all over Hampton

Roads. "Ask for Eve," they said, and I always felt such pride for my Mom. Smart and sweet and such a good grandmother, though she asked never to be called "grandma." Little Lucie called her Ma Eve.

Mom and I walked to the back stoop together and the minute Lucie saw me, she clung to her Pa Dan.

"Aw, honey. Mommy's here," Dad said, kissing his granddaughter on her cheek as he carried her over to me, her legs swinging.

"Mommy, I don't want to go," my daughter said as she was passed into my hands.

"I know," I said. "Did you have a good time with Pa Dan and Ma Eve?"

She nodded.

"I'm glad. But we're late picking up Paul. You want to see Paul, don't you?"

The leg-swinging ceased. If there was any male she loved as much as Pa Dan, it was Paul.

"Say 'bye Pa Dan, bye Ma Eve," I told her.

At her reiteration, both my parents beamed at Lucie's preciousness.

As I was strapping Lucie down into her child seat, Mom was over my shoulder asking about dinner plans for the weekend. She wanted to know if Paul and I were free for a barbecue. I looked over at the barbecue pit and the benches pulled close to it under the branches of the oak tree, just now budding. There was no deck chair. It was gone now. Dad and I had burned it together right there in the barbecue pit. I never wanted to be tempted to relive the experience again and Dad didn't want to sell it.

"I don't know," I said, staring at the pit, the new grass and the branches. And then I saw eyes from a dreamed of past right there, staring up at me, wanting to know why I was suddenly so sad. "I'll have to ask Paul."

I connected the last buckle of Lucie's complicated restraints and then slid into the driver's seat.

Before we drove off, Dad ducked his head into my open window and waved to Lucie. I glanced at the Mustang and asked how it was doing.

"Running like a champ," Dad said.

"Maybe one day we could take it out and go antiquing together? On a Saturday, maybe?"

He clamped a hand over my forearm and gave a slight nod as though to say, "If it happens, it happens."

As I drove away that day, I remembered the time when I first headed out, my Buick loaded down with stuffed foot lockers and suitcases, pulling a U-Haul of yard sale furniture. I saw my parents in the rearview mirror, suppressing sobs, waving. They had given me the best childhood anyone could ask for. And I loved them both for it. But they needed to give me adulthood, too. We had all been on a beach together and I'd been squandering time, reaching for shell after shell, lifting each one and looking for clues on how I should go about the rest of my life. But with the two of them always in view, keeping me safe, there was no real urgency for me to focus on what I needed to do to make my life my own. I needed a life of my own. I needed to leave home.

And then came the day when I sat in the bathroom of the apartment that I decorated myself. I saw the plus sign on the pregnancy test. I took it as a positive that if I ever needed to get myself together and do something with myself the time had arrived, because it was no longer just about me; it was about a little being too.

Lucie was born on a cold Super Bowl Sunday. There were snow flurries, and Mom had taken me out to the beach to see the snow fall and dissolve into the rocking waves of the Atlantic, hoping that it would relax me because I had been so tense in the days leading up to the due date. By the time we got back to the house, I felt the first gyrations of labor and then I flooded a patch of the kitchen floor.

I don't remember who was playing that Super Bowl Sunday, but I do remember Dad was pissed that my water broke before kick-off. "Dan, it's your grandchild!" Mom bleated as she plied him from the sofa and all the chips and dips he had made for himself.

The labor lasted all evening and Dad watched the game on TV while I struggled in the birthing room. Mom fed me ice chips until my whole mouth was numb and I couldn't speak intelligibly. My words were so slurred the attending nurse thought I was having a stroke.

At 9 p.m. she was born, a healthy 7 pound, 8 ounces, all pink skin and inquisitive blue eyes. Her brown hair stood in whipped peaks on her tiny head. When I held her in my arms for the first time and she looked up at me, I kissed her on her forehead and told her, "Yes, you're alive." She was the most beautiful girl I had ever seen and I told her so her first few minutes of life because I knew that her father would have told her the same.

And here was an April again, another time when things were budding, blooming, coming back to life. Jack's birthday was yesterday. I didn't even realize it until I looked at my appointment book and saw teacher conferences coming up and made a mental note to buy wine and bathtub supplies for the aftermath. And there it was, April 11, and all the memories of that sweet boy and his limited life and the way he looked at me the last time we saw each other. It was as though by dancing we had kicked up some sort of fairy dust that clung to me still, enchanting me always.

In the middle of the night, I am wide awake. There is someone in the house who doesn't live here.

My heart is racing and I struggle to breathe. I reach for the phone, but my hands are clumsy and it drops to the floor. When I grope around for it, I hear noise, little zaps of sound. At first it sounds like the obnoxious beeping of a phone left too long off the hook. Then the beeps slow, form letters, become a signal.

• • •_____• • •

Over and over again I hear it. I finally manage to pick up the phone and I hear the operator.

The house is dark and silent when I walk down the hallway to my daughter's room. My feet are cold against the wood floors. My heart is still pounding. It's the only sound I hear.

Finally at the opened door of Lucie's room, I peer in anxiously. She is there, sound asleep, covers pulled up tight to her chin, her brown hair fanning out on the pillow around her pale, round face. Her Tinkerbelle nightlight supplies just enough light for me to see her. And to see him.

"She just wanted her snow globe," he tells me. And he looks up and smiles. "I see you finally made it."

I heard the pounding of my heart before I was made aware that I was awake. And then I heard myself gasp.

I looked at Paul's sleeping form and chose not to disturb him. But when the covers shifted, exposing some of him to the cold air, he asked what was wrong and I told him I had heard Lucie. He wanted to know if she was OK and I told him I had to check, just to see. He went back to sleep.

Everything seems very loud after 2 a.m. Passing traffic, ticking clocks and refrigerator motors take on added amplification when sleep is supposed to be taking place.

I heard my daughter's sleeping sounds just before I got to her room and my foot pressed against the warped plank that had been there since Paul and I moved in two years ago and Paul swore he would fix. The noise did not wake Lucie. She was quiet in her dreams and safe, her covers drawn up against her chin. The Tinkerbelle nightlight screwed into the outlet beside her bed gave her pale face a green and pink glow. Her brown hair was spread out on her pillow.

And in her hand was a snow globe.

For Thanksgiving we had gone to New York. I wanted Lucie to see the Macy's Parade as something that wasn't Thanksgiving Day TV programming. It was just the two of us, squealing in delight as the streets of Manhattan crawled with floats, marching bands and balloons of cartoon favorites. We both cheered and jumped up and down when Santa arrived at Herald Square. It was the first Macy's parade after Sept. 11, 2001, and it was good to be there and celebrate and know that New York is an ever resilient city that will always rise above even the darkest hours.

Lucie saw this snow globe at a shop and had to have it. She shook it in her small hands and saw the glitter falling on all of New York's landmarks and wanted to take it home with her. I thought it pricey for glass, glitter and a slightly off-tune rendition of "New York, New York." But I bought if for her and she shook it for the twenty blocks on our way back to our hotel, watching tiny gold flakes cover the financial district, Macy's, Tiffany's, the Statue of Liberty, the Empire State Building and the Chrysler Building.

She often asked to sleep with the snow globe and I always said no. I couldn't imagine her despair if she woke up one day to find the glass smashed on the floor with glittered water pooling on the floorboards should a sleepy hand lose its grasp. But sometimes late at night, someone else had other ideas.

She loved the snow globe because she said when she peered into it, she saw us, hand-in-hand, walking together, on the streets of New York.

I knew she was an adventurous child from birth when I saw her scanning the room with her bright, beautiful eyes, wondering where she could go. And some days when I was hoarse from saying, "Lucie, no!", a sweet voice was there to calm her to sleep. And when my arms weren't quick enough to catch her from running into a street choked with traffic and drivers distracted with cell phones and small soccer players in the back seats of their minivans, there were arms to halt her at the curb.

I liked to think she would always have someone looking after her, someone who knew something about helping out a lady in distress.

Edwards Brothers, Inc.
Thorofare, NJ USA
May 12, 2011